William Walker's First Year of Marriage: A Horror Story

MATT RUDD

WILLIAM WALKER'S FIRST YEAR OF MARRIAGE

A Horror Story

Harper
Press

Harper*Press*
An imprint of HarperCollins*Publishers*
77–85 Fulham Palace Road, Hammersmith, London W6 8JB

Visit our authors' blog at www.fifthestate.co.uk
Love this book? www.bookarmy.com

First published by Harper*Press* in 2009
4

A catalogue record for this book is available from the British Library

ISBN 978-0-00-730897-2

Set in Minion with Clarendon display by
G&M Designs Limited, Raunds, Northamptonshire

Printed and bound in Great Britain by Clays Ltd, St Ives plc

To Harriet

MAY

'Marriage is like life in this – that it is a field of battle, and not a bed of roses.'

ROBERT LOUIS STEVENSON,
Virginibus Puerisque (1881)

Sunday 1 May

I never had a threesome.

I never had an orgy.

I never slept with anyone from Sweden. Or Norway.

I never slept with a Scandinavian full stop.

I never slept with anyone with tattoos or pink hair or non-facial piercings or a career in pornography.

I never slept with Mrs Robinson.

I never slept with any married woman, and no, last night doesn't count because she was married to me.

Yesterday, I married Isabel, the girl of my dreams. Fantastic. I am married. Superb. I am a husband. Brilliant. I'll never sleep with another woman again so long as we both shall live.

'Hello, husband. I think I'm going to be sick.' These were the first words she said when she woke. Isabel. My beautiful wife.

'Morning, Mrs Walker.'

Despite the hangover, she starts trampolining around the four-poster, singing 'I've go-ot married yes-t'day morning' to the tune of 'I'm getting married in the morning', which doesn't fit. She sings like someone being stabbed in a shower: all commitment, no tonal control. This is not because she's singing and fighting back the urge to vomit. This is how she normally sings. It is one of her many endearing qualities.

'Mrs Walker. I like that. So much better than Miss Brackett.'

'This is why you married me? For my surname?'

'Yes, that's it. Couldn't go another year as a Brackett.'

'Well, now you're a Walker. Any second thoughts?'

'Yes. I wish I hadn't drunk so much.'

'No, about being, well, married.'

Until this morning, I've never had any second thoughts – well, not officially. Not so as to cause alarm. But from the moment I asked the woman I love to marry me, I've been expecting her to look dazed for a minute or two, blink a few times as if risen suddenly from a twelve-month coma, then look at me, look at the engagement ring and start screaming, 'Marry you?! Are you mad?' She could, I'm sure, even if I'm being objective, have had the pick of the field. A girl who looks even more beautiful in jeans and T-shirt than make-up and cocktail dress, an effortlessly glamorous head-turner, the sort of girl, honestly, you'd be quite chuffed to go on a date with. And I've got her to agree to spend the rest of her life with me. It's ridiculous.

'No, darling. No second thoughts. Even if you did knock the vicar out on my wedding day.'

If you ask Johnson, the world's most pessimistic usher, he'll tell you the wedding was a disaster. This is because he sees a friend getting married in the same way everyone else might see a friend being sent to prison. For life. He hasn't enjoyed his decade of matrimonial bliss.

If you ask me, the wedding had gone pretty well. Compared to what I'd imagined. It had taken several Bishop's Nipples the night before to convince the vicar I was not the infidel even though I only went to church once a year. After that, he'd been an absolute angel, until he'd fallen down the steps of his own church and come a cropper on the pew. I and a large part of the congregation had thought for several seconds that he had actually killed himself, but a glass of holy water brought him back from the brink. When he regained consciousness, he claimed I pushed him. I don't think I did ... I may have brushed past him as I helped Isabel and her dress turn, ready for the you-may-kiss-the-bride-and-get-out-of-here bit. Nothing he could do by then: we were already married.

And, despite Johnson's grave warnings beforehand and rolling eyes during, everything else went okay.

My tailored suit (posted from Hong Kong because do you know how much tailored tails cost in London?) had, miraculously, fitted. The Corsa (89,452 miles) had started. And Isabel, despite her 'best friend' Alex and his ridiculous equine chauffeur service, had got to the church on time.

I had been forbidden to look her in the eye 'emotionally' or 'with significance' at any stage during the service for fear of opening her floodgates. 'I don't want to do an Alison,' she had explained quite reasonably. Who could forget Alison's wedding? It had taken hours, maybe days, for her to sob, squeak and warble her way through the vows. By the time she reached 'till … sob … death … sob, sob, sob … do us … sniff … part', we all thought she was going to illustrate her point by collapsing on the spot. RIP Alison who died at her wedding from dehydration.

Despite the threats, I had felt an overwhelming urge to burst into tears myself from the moment Isabel rounded the corner and began the walk. Quite hard not to, what with all your friends and family going 'ooohh' and 'ahhh', and seeing the dress for the first time. An amazing Sixties number, not at all like the explosion in a meringue factory you get normally. Then there's the mysterious veil and the accompanying trumpet voluntary and your mum already blubbing away in her purple hat. Is this really not too much for any man to cope with? Did whoever invented weddings not add all this extra stuff to make it absolutely inevitable that the poor sap waiting up at the altar would weep deep tears of joy/run a thousand miles/pass out on the spot?

Isabel did what she always does when she's trying not to cry: she laughed, hysterically. She walked the entire length of the church laughing and blinking back tears, her dress and variable bridesmaids flowing behind her. Only in the last few feet did her eyes meet mine. She smiled; I smiled back with as little significance as I could muster – a sort of thin-lipped, cold-eyed, non-bothered smirk, the kind you'd throw a kid on a bike when he calls you a fecker. She burst into tears anyway.

Still, I passed the four tests …

THE FOUR TESTS OF A BRIDEGROOM

1. The vows. Don't shout them, don't whimper them, don't faint during them. Easy.

2. The speech. Thank everyone – but mainly in-laws, look happy, declare love for new wife and make bridesmaids cry. Had to follow Isabel's father, who did ten minutes on the traumas of her breech birth and made two members of the audience physically sick. Did fine, though, compared to Andy. I'd chosen him as best man over Johnson because he worked in the diplomatic corps and I'd remembered those Ferrero Rocher ads. As Isabel pointed out, he wasn't actually an ambassador but doesn't everyone in the diplomatic corps have tact? No, nerves destroyed his judgement and he never recovered from his choice of opener ('What's the difference between a bridegroom and a cucumber?'). His attempt to regain momentum involved raising all three topics he'd specifically been told not to (my scatological university tragedy, the vastly differing weights of the bridesmaids and my Hyde Park Corner fling with a floozy). It wasn't pretty.

3. The dance. Two lessons hadn't been enough to master the foxtrot. Isabel's toe crushed in the first verse of 'Fly Me to the Moon' and an elephantine triple-trampling in the second. I considered stopping in the third to summon a paramedic or podiatric specialist but she blinked away the tears, squeezed my shoulder very, very hard and whispered, 'Keep going.' I did, we finished with a twirl, great aunties sighed, friends said how beautiful we looked and I decided to take that at face value.

4. The consummation. Bridesmaids always ask the bride if you did or you didn't. If you didn't, they tell their boyfriends and husbands. Who tell all their friends. Who all snigger. So, despite fatigue and room spin and a frankly terrifying corset, we did.

Now it's Sunday and we can relax for the first time in six months.

Lunch was fun. No ribbons or corsages or speeches or Windsor knots or place mats or chauffeurs or confetti or wish-they-hadn't-come extended family. Just thirty of us at a pizza restaurant in Highgate going over the post-nuptial-mortem.

THE POST-MORTEM

One Boris Becker. Andy and a waitress – in a cloakroom, though, not a cupboard. He loves her. She loves him. He's moving to Sydney when her work visa runs out next Thursday. Already started Googling for flats on Manly Beach this morning. It won't happen.

One hospital admission. Not the vicar. He made a miraculous recovery. It was Johnson, emboldened by 'It's Raining Men', who needed medical attention after he stage-dived into an adoring crowd. There was no adoring crowd. There wasn't even a crowd. Witnesses say he scored a perfect belly flop, and in so doing broke his nose and his fifth metatarsal, and severely bruised his right testicle. Why not his left? Because it doesn't hang as low as the right one. I wished I hadn't asked.

One run-in with the law. My father showing love-sick Andy how to down a bottle of red wine, on the way back to the hotel at 2 a.m. 'Evening, gentlemen, everything all right?' 'Yes, officer.' 'On our way home are we, gentlemen?' 'Yes, officer.' 'A long way, is it?' 'Just over there, officer.' 'Best be on our way then, hadn't we, gentlemen?' 'Yes, officer.' 'Will you be taking the bollard with you?' 'No, sir.'

One storming out. Surprise, surprise, Watzerface who is the girlfriend of Alex who is the best friend of my wife who clearly isn't always a good judge of character.

Why did Watzerface storm out?

Official reason from Alex, while sadly not choking on his goat's-cheese pizza (amazing, he can even manage to find a pretentious flavour of pizza): 'She wanted marriage, but it felt too soon. You can't rush such an important decision, can you? Marriage should be for life, not a month or two. I'm so upset that she couldn't give me more time.' Misty-eyed nods from bridal group, eye-rolling from me, Andy and Johnson. He's confusing marriage with rescue dogs, and the girls lap it up.

Real reason: she'd had to find her own way to the church and reception because Alex, after much begging, had been given the job of chauffeuring. He'd been told 'nothing flash' then turned up with a white coach and six horses, none of which he could properly control. He had worn tailored tails and a waistcoat strikingly similar to mine except not from Hong Kong. He'd spent the whole service muttering gloomy imprecations, especially during the vows, which meant the vicar, sensing possibilities, had repeated the 'Can anyone see any lawful impediment?' question … twice.

Even before our first dance had finished, he'd tapped me on the shoulder, then refused to give Isabel to anyone else for the next three dances. And, once prised away, he'd marched up onto the stage, handed out sheet music to the band, declared how much he loved his best-friend-in-all-the-world Isabel, spat out how delighted he was she'd found the perfect man, then sang Whitney Houston's 'I Will Always Love You'. If I hadn't been so busy vomiting, I would have stormed out too.

* * *

Home late to the flat. More lugging over the threshold on Isabel's insistence, accompanied by what I took to be slightly sarcastic clapping from one of the idiots from the upstairs flat. India tomorrow. Tired, so tired.

Monday 2 May

'Someone's stolen my passport!' I was completely sure of it.

'No, they haven't.' But Isabel wasn't.

'Yes, they have.'

'No, they haven't.'

'Yes, they have.'

'No, they haven't.'

It doesn't take long for the matrimonial harmony to wear off, does it?

'Yes, they have, I had it on the Tube and that bloke opposite looked shifty.'

'So you were pickpocketed?'

'Yes, he must have followed us.'

'Thought you said you were like a coiled spring when you were travelling, a coiled anti-pickpocket spring.'

'Yes, well …'

'That if anyone tried it on with you, there'd be a blur, a flash and a whimper.'

'I —'

'That they'd be picking up their teeth with broken fingers.'

'Shut up and help me look in these bags!'

'Don't snap at your wife.'

'Yes, well, my wife is being incredibly unhelpful, the flight's about to leave and someone's run off with my passport.'

'Is it at home?'

'What?'

'Have you left your passport at home?'

'Of course I haven't.'

'You always leave something at home.'

'Don't.' 'Do.' 'Don't!' 'Do.' 'Don't!'

'What about Paris?'

'That wasn't a passport. That was the tickets.'

'Stop frowning. You always frown.'

'Hardly a surprise with you nagging all the time.'

'You'll get wrinkles if you scrunch your face like that. You were doing that right through the whole wedding.'

'I was nervous.'

'You looked like you were about to be tortured.'

'You told me not to look at you affectionately because you'd start blubbing.'

'Yes, but not for the whole day.'

'Well, I was nervous. It's much easier for a bride.'

'What?'

'It's easier. All you have to do is smile, look nice and walk up and down an aisle. I have four tests. I have to do the vows, I have to do a speech, I have to lead a dance, I have to have sex.'

'Have sex? That's difficult, is it?'

'It is when all your bridesmaids are placing bets on it.'

'Don't be stupid.'

'You don't be stupid.'

'You don't be stupid.'

'You don't be stupid.'

'You don't be stupid.'

'You don't be stupid.'

'Last call for flight BA One-seven-eight to Delhi.'

'You don't be stupid.'

Tuesday 3 May

The passport was on the mantelpiece.

Still, another night at home recovering from the wedding was a blessing in disguise. At least, that's what I suggested to Isabel, who didn't seem to see it that way. Will make it up to her in India …

'Darling, I'm sorry. I am an idiot. I will make it up to you in India.'

'It's okay, darling, I love that you forget things.'

'I love that you love that I forget things.'

Ahhhh.

Why I married Isabel

There was never really any question about it. Until Isabel, I had always assumed I would simply marry the girl I happened to be going out with when it was time to get married, i.e. thirty-two. That's how it worked for Johnson and every other bloke I knew. You spend your twenties trying to extricate yourself from any relationship that looks like it's getting too heavy (anything more than two years is dangerous), the first two years of your thirties bracing yourself, then the rest of your life as monogamous as possible.

Isabel changed that. I suddenly got it. Even though I was only twenty-nine, I knew immediately that she was someone I'd be glad to spend the rest of my life with. Mainly because she's different from all my other girlfriends.

In that she's beautiful rather than somewhere between pretty and elephantine. She has short dark hair with red bits in it. She is tall but not alarmingly so. She has freckles in the summer. She has a cute dimple where she used to have a nose ring. And she would have had a cute dimple where she used to have a nipple ring but she sobered up before it was her turn in the Mexican nipple-piercing shop.

[No, that's too shallow. It's not about looks.]

In that she's funny.

[Still no. Sounds like something you'd write in a personal ad (Must have GSOH).]

In that she does things impetuously. She isn't on the conveyor belt. She's lived in Paris and Buenos Aires; she's spent a year teaching in the Andes and three months as a beer wench in Munich; she quite fancies showing me her favourite bar in Quito one day; she wonders if the campervan we will one day drive to Bangkok should be a classic rust-bucket or one of the rather nifty new ones. Now, she works for a charity and she loves it. But next year she might decide to become a policewoman. Who knows? She's spontaneous.

[Still no. And I hope she doesn't become a policewoman.]

In that we were mates within five minutes of meeting, that it felt completely natural when we moved in together, that the thought of her and me getting hitched seemed like the most exciting idea in the world ever without any question, and that I can't wait to get on with married life. Johnson is wrong about women and I didn't completely understand that until I met Isabel.

Friday 20 May

Back from honeymoon, which I don't want to talk about. Ever. Except to say India wasn't my idea. Just so pleased to be home, even if home is a one-bedroom flat at the wrong end of the mean streets of Finsbury Park.

Marmite toast, tea, hot bath, bed, sleep, lovely sleep.

Wake to a message left on the answer machine from Alex. 'Great you're back, Izzy babes. Can't wait to hear all about India, babes.

Hope you loved it as much as I told you you would. Give us a call, babes. Bye babes.' Accidentally deleted.

Saturday 21 May

Slept for a whole day in lovely bed with lovely wife who still loves me despite honeymoon, then got dragged to John Lewis to rearrange wedding list. It's a shame they let you do this. Suspect Isabel knew all along. Lets me put lots of stuff on before the wedding, lets me get all excited when people buy them for us, then switches it all around as soon as I've signed the marriage certificate. Clever.

STUFF I WANTED AND DIDN'T GET

Gas barbecue: 'We don't have a garden.' 'We will one day.' 'We need something to eat off before then.'

Croquet set: same.

Black beanbag: 'We're not living in a bachelor pad any more.'

Rothko prints: same.

Chef's blowtorch: same. 'But what about crème brûlée?' 'You'll use it once and get bored.'

Juicer: 'Boy's toy. Pointless gadget. Kitchen clutter. No.'

Coffee machine: same.

STUFF SHE WANTED AND DID GET

Twelve dinner plates: I thought the seven we'd got would do.

Ditto side plates, bowls, spoons.

Towels: boring.

Toastie-maker: 'Isn't that a pointless gadget?' 'No, every kitchen needs one.'

Duvets: 'But darling, we've got two already.' 'Does that include the one with the candle burn from when you were trying to impress Saskia in your horrible Acton bedsit? When you lit a hundred tea lights and she thought you were terribly sophisticated and it was all perfect until the bed caught fire? I can't believe you told me that. I want that duvet thrown out. It's horrid.'

Yoga mat, hairdryer, pair of Birkenstocks: 'But darling, these aren't even on the original list.' 'I don't care, I'm still annoyed about the duvet.' The shop assistant gives her a go-girl look and types B-I-R-K-E-N-S-T-O-C-K-S into her annoying wedding-list computer with a triumphant flourish.

Saskia. The one crazy fling of my life. The only example of me behaving like a total cad. Ever. Pretty much. I still feel bad about it but that was a long time ago. And it's still coming back to haunt me, even now I'm married, even here at John Lewis, even though it had nothing to do with Isabel. Why did I ever tell Isabel about the bloody duvet?

Monday 23 May

I expected some sort of fanfare, going back to work. To be treated differently. I feel different. Very grown-up. Last time I saw everyone, I was Single Man, now I'm Married Man. I speak the language of Married Man. I'm part of the Holy Order of Married Men. I know the Code. I can do mother-in-law jokes.

Favourite mother-in-law joke

My father-in-law was pulled over by the police the other day. The policeman said, 'Sir, your wife fell out of the car five miles back.'

My father-in-law replied, 'Thank God for that, I thought I'd gone deaf.'

Second favourite mother-in-law joke

A guy brings his dog into the vet and says, 'Could you please cut my dog's tail off?'

The vet examines the tail and says, 'But look here, there's nothing wrong with his tail. Why do you want it off?'

The man replies, 'Because my mother-in-law is coming to visit, and I don't want anything in the house to make her think she's welcome.'

I deserve some sort of recognition. A plaque? But all Johnson and the other blokes want to know is if I managed to consummate the marriage on the night ('None of your business but yes'), and the girls only ask about the dress ('It was white'), the confetti ('Yes, there was some') and the honeymoon ('I don't want to talk about it').

Then they all see I'm not wearing a wedding ring.

'You're not wearing a wedding ring.'

'No.'

'Want to keep your options open, do you?'

'No.'

'Why aren't you wearing one then?'

'Because it's not traditional for men to wear jewellery. And I don't need to wear one to make sure I'm faithful. Our relationship is based on a bit more than a meaningless bit of platinum. And I looked stupid with a ring on.'

Can't wait to get home to my wife. Got home and she's out with bloody Alex. When she comes back, she says, 'Well, why aren't you wearing one?'

'We've already discussed this a thousand times. It's not traditional for men to wear jewellery.'

'Not traditional *in your family*.'

'I'll wear one if you want.'

'It's up to you but I think it would be nice. You know, I'm really, really proud to wear my wedding ring.'

This is something Isabel is good at: twisting an argument so that what a minute ago sounded fair and reasonable coming out of your mouth sounds like something about as acceptable as kitten-stamping. If you were cynical, you'd interpret this as manipulative. I know Isabel though: it's only 20 per cent manipulation, 25 per cent misguided reasonableness and 55 per cent being typically female.

Tuesday 24 May

Pub crisis meeting with Andy and Johnson. Johnson starts, as he always does, by sucking in his cheeks, crossing his elbows and rocking back on his bar stool authoritatively. He reminds me, as he also always does, that he's been married for ten difficult years; that if he can do it, married to the woman he is, then anyone can. What he doesn't know about patching up quarrels, dodging marital bullets and ducking domestic pincer movements isn't worth wasting good beer time discussing.

'Come on then,' Andy and I say in unison, ignoring, as we always do, the fact that Johnson's hard-working, sensible, intelligent, patient and long-suffering wife Ali has almost certainly had a harder time putting up with ten years of the infant Johnson than he has putting up with her.

'It's not traditional,' he offers at last.

'Said that.'

'How's a piece of jewellery going to make any difference whether you're faithful or not?'

'Said that too.'

'If you're going to shag someone, a ring won't stop you. You could just take it off.'

'Yep, didn't say that.'

'And besides, there's a certain type of woman who goes for men *because* they're wearing wedding rings. Predatory women who want sex. Terrible women, these. They come at you in a bar, you're sitting there having a drink, minding your own business, wearing your wedding ring, and they strike. These wanton, brazen, ravishing women with their short skirts and their stockings and their completely amoral attitude to fornication. The wedding ring is no defence. "Look, I'm married," you say. "I don't want a relationship, you sexy, sexy man," they purr, running their filthy-temptress fingers down your tie. "I want you. And I want you now."'

Johnson is running his fingers down my chest seductively.

'I've got the idea.'

'And before you know it, you're waking up in the wrong hotel room with some brazen harlot in some filthy negligée ordering postcoital *petit déjeûner*.'

Andy says a ring to him is like a symbolic chattel, a sign of ownership – a ring-cuff, if you will. Love, if it's true, doesn't need symbols of repression. I point out that Isabel has a wedding ring. Andy nods sagely and, not for the first time, I wonder why I ever bother asking my two best friends anything.

Nevertheless, it is worth one more try. I wait until Isabel is brushing her teeth before mentioning the brazen, harlotish, fornicating women in bars. She says she's prepared to take the risk, then spits for effect.

Getting a ring next week.

The trouble with asking Johnson or Andy anything about women

Johnson is an expert in the art of handling the opposite sex by virtue of the fact that he is older than me and Andy. He likes to use the standard line on this. 'Ten years, man, ten years – if I'd killed her instead of marrying her, I could have been out on parole by now.'

Before Johnson 'went soft' and came to work on *Life & Times* magazine with me, he was a hard-bitten crime reporter on the *Manchester Evening News*. Somewhere along the line, he has muddled his time working the sink estates, covering stories of social decay, organised crime and young lives wasted with marriage. He sees them as the same thing.

'I know what makes women tick,' he says. 'You can't trust them. Not ever. They will stab you in the back the moment you think they're your friend.'

'Are you talking about women or inner-city drug dealers?'

'Same thing, my son. Same thing.'

He thinks Isabel is the best thing that ever happened to me and can't understand why I had to ruin it all by marrying her.

Andy, meanwhile, is an expert in the art of handling the opposite sex by virtue of the fact that he has handled an awful lot of them. The only problem here is that he has never handled them for any length of time. He isn't a womaniser, he is an optimist. He travels the world falling in love when he should be representing Her Majesty's Government. Then, inevitably, visa issues, flight schedules, language barriers and, occasionally, husbands get in the way. He has now concluded that love transcends the boundaries of time and space. He thinks Isabel is the best thing that ever happened to me but that marriage is nothing more than several signatures on a meaningless piece of paper. 'True love transcends time, space and institution,' he says.

'So how is that waitress from the cupboard?' I reply.

'She will always have a place in my heart.'

'You're not moving to Manly?'

'And leave you two? All married and alone? I couldn't. I just couldn't.'

Wednesday 25 May

Isabel wants to know what Johnson, Andy and I always talk about at the pub, besides brazen, harlotish women in bars.

'Stuff,' I say.

'What stuff?' It's not the first time she has asked but this time she says she has a right to know.

'I am your wife. You shouldn't be going out with them any more. Not without telling me what you talk about.'

This is the sort of thing Johnson has been warning me about. I must nip it in the bud.

'Well ...' I begin with a sharp, scandalised intake of breath.

'I was joking,' she says. 'It's only that you never seem to come back from the pub with any news about the two of them. I was curious about how you pass the time.'

This could easily be a trick. If I was a better chess player, I'd be able to work out the various permutations before I opened my mouth. I don't think she's trying to trick me. She's simply making conversation. She likes talking to me when we get back from work. She likes it more than watching television. This is obviously a compliment but it does mean I am no longer up to speed with *The Bill*. It could also still be a trick.

'Well, you can come.'

'What?'

'Come to the pub.'

'Are you sure?'

'Er, yes.' Suddenly, I'm not. I should have just moved the pawn. That would have been fine.

'Okay, but you have to talk about the things you always talk about. No chatting about art and poetry and horse-riding just for my benefit.'

These are the things she really does like to talk about, which is sometimes a problem. I don't know very much about art but she does, on account of her highly arty family upbringing. The poetry of the Romantic Period was her special subject at university and, unlike everyone else who went to university, she still remembers it. And made me go to several poetry recitals when we first met just because she really, really wants to share the joy of it all. I almost got it. I almost did. I could see why she loved it and why I was a useless philistine for not loving it as much.

Horse-riding, though. That's where we really come unstuck. She loves horse-riding. When we're tired of London (about five years) and we've won the lottery, she wants to move to somewhere remote and horsey like North Wales. She wants to ride and muck out stables and give out carrots and blow in horses' nostrils because they love it. She likes smelling of horse.

We'll never see eye to eye on the joy of horses.

I phone Andy and Johnson, both of whom are suspicious, even when I tell them we don't have to talk about poetry. Reluctantly, they agree to meet me and Isabel in the pub on Friday – and pretend she's a bloke.

Thursday 26 May

Woke up with absolutely no idea of the eureka moment about to occur in the bathroom. Bath, teeth, flossed a little bit, nothing out of the ordinary. Attempt to shave, but last razor is on last legs. I'm busy hacking away like a tired peasant in a cornfield when, out of the corner of my eye, I spot another option lying provocatively on the shelf: Isabel's pink leg-razor. Isabel is still in bed and what she doesn't know won't hurt her. Amazing. It's all over in a flash, a clean shave, my skin all silky smooth. Pink girly razor: the best a man can get … I put it back, so no one will ever know. Skip to work, delighted that the years of hacking away and patching up cuts with bits of loo roll might be over.

Friday 27 May

Isabel found dark stubbly hair in her razor. Firmly told not to do it again or she'll tell Johnson.

'Evening, boys.'

'Evening, Isabel.'

The four of us are in the pub. Johnson is behaving like he's in an interrogation room. He squints suspiciously at Isabel.

'Well, since I'm the honorary bloke, I'll get the first round.'

While we sit in silence, she goes to the bar, returning minutes later with four pints of bitter, four whisky chasers and four packets of pork scratchings. Everyone starts to relax.

Three pints later, we are playing one of Isabel's traveller drinking games. A pint after that, Andy is explaining to us how breasts vary from one nation to the next. Then, Isabel tells everyone that I use a Ladyshave. Then Johnson tells us his post-pee dribble trick.

Johnson's post-pee dribble trick

You have to trick it. Finish the pee, shake as usual, put away, zip up, pretend you're leaving then retrieve when it thinks it's in the clear and have another shake. I tried it and it works. Andy did too. Can't believe I'm almost thirty and only now have I truly mastered the art of urinating.

Rest of evening spent discussing where to hold the door handle on the way out of the toilet. I always hold it at the top corner, where other people don't touch it. Johnson reckons that doesn't work because it's the bit least likely to be cleaned properly. Even though it's touched less, the germs have longer to prosper. Andy uses his shirtsleeve or waits for someone else to come in. Isabel thinks we should get out more.

Saturday 28 May

Andy is unconscious, perhaps dead, on our sofa. Johnson called to say he fell asleep on the night bus and woke up in a depot near Hounslow. I feel as sick as I did on the third day of our honeymoon after eating the warm lamb rogan josh.

Isabel, on the other hand, is eating toast and contemplating a fry-up.

'I think I'll skip the next few pub outings. You three are light-weights.'

'Fine by me.'

'And it really is true, isn't it? Blokes can spend a whole night in a pub talking about absolutely nothing whatsoever. No "how was the honeymoon?" or "how's work?" or "sorry things didn't work out with the waitress" or "terrible what's going on in Bangladesh".'

'Blokes don't need to natter on the whole time.'

'Oh, I see. Okay. Still, at least I know how to shake my willy.'

Johnson was right – women should not be allowed to gatecrash bloke-nights.

WHY BRITISH MEN DON'T NATTER ON THE WHOLE TIME

It's exhausting.

We're not Italian.

Life is too short.

We spend our (too short) lives being nattered at by women. It is therefore only sensible to think of male company as a pause between bouts of nattering. Isabel can't see this because she is a woman. While she made a good honorary bloke last night, she has reverted to type this morning by nattering. Even if she did make an excellent fry-up.

Monday 30 May

Met Isabel four years ago today. Seems like much, much longer. Not in a bad way.

Dinner at Andrew Edmunds (note for next time, refuse downstairs table if upstairs full and go somewhere else instead because left smelling like lamb chops), then a tour of all the bars we'd got drunk in back when we were all excited and unfamiliar with each other. Isabel gets super-nostalgic: 'We sat on this sofa, you ordered those drinks, you tripped on that step and ruined the dress of a girl sitting at that table. And you were wearing that horrible off-centre skintight jumper.'

I explain, as I did at the time, that it was bias-cut, very fashionable, chosen by a fashion PR who'd felt sorry for me. She explains, as she did at the time, that I will never be fashionable with my sticky-out ears and my sticky-out nose and my pointy little head. And I remember why I fell in love with her. And how we met on a speed-dating evening neither of us had planned to go to.

What if she hadn't gone along to support her recently dumped friend? What if my mate Tom hadn't forced me to go along with him because he wasn't going to turn up on his own 'like some creepy pervert'?

The speed-date girls I could have ended up with

'Hello, I'm William.'

'Hello, William. I'm Alison. Isn't it hard to meet people these days? Just so busy at the firm … working all the hours. Not a min, simply not a min to meet a man. Wouldn't be here otherwise, course. If I had some sensible job, you know. Not going to meet someone between my flat and the office, am I?, which is the only time I ever get out these days. I'm not going to fall in love with the fat middle-aged guy who looks up my skirt on the Tube every morning, am I? That's why I'm here. Not because I'm desperate.'

'Hi, my name is William.'

'Right, William. I'll be straight with you. I've been mucked about by men far too much and I'm sick of you lying bastards. Yes, I'm blonde and yes, I have very large breasts but that doesn't mean I'm a tart. I want to know, right now, before we go a single second further, if you're seriously looking for love, if you want to have a relationship. You know, with actual dating and cinemas and walks in the country. I'm not interested in wasting any more time with no-hopers. Capiche?'

'Good evening, I'm William.'

'William. Charlotte. Do you ride? Horses, that is. Hahahahaha. I love riding. I'm still talking about horses. Hahahahahahahaha-haha-snort. I ride three. Still horses, William, you filthy-minded man. Hahahahaha. Another glass of ssshampypampy? Oh go on. Oops. Spilt it. Bit squiffy, which is odd because I've only had two glasses. We should go riding sometime. Not talking about horses any more, William, hahahahahaha.'

JUNE

'Marriage is a wonderful invention;
But, then again, so is a bicycle repair kit.'

BILLY CONNOLLY

Wednesday 1 June

REASONS TO BE HAPPY

Married for a month, only one proper argument and that was under immense airport-related stress. Don't know what Johnson was worried about. If anything, life with a wife is even more exciting than life with a fiancée. Apart from the John Lewis thing, the Honeymoon That Dare Not Speak Its Name and the new, tougher line in bathroom politics, my first thirty-one days hitched have been nothing short of blissful. Everything is the same but everything is different. In a good way.

And I like my job. It doesn't matter that I am never going to get a half-mill bonus to blow on a gin palace called *That's My Buoy*. Or that I will never be able to splash ten grand on a corked bottle of wine in a snooty restaurant. Or that I won't have a penthouse serviced by an elevator that has a retractable floor which, if required, drops enemies into a shark-infested swimming pool. Well, it matters a bit but the main thing is I no longer work for *Cat World*. I have a great boss. I get paid enough to enjoy the simple things in married life: the occasional dinner out, the odd weekend away, a subscription to *Money Can't Buy Happiness Monthly*.

REASONS TO BE UNHAPPY

None.

Thursday 2 June

REASONS TO BE UNHAPPY (REVISED)

One.

A new marital rule has been snuck in before I'm even properly awake. It was Isabel's turn to make the tea, which she did and brought back to bed, looking like butter wouldn't melt. But the tea tasted bitter and strange. Gave her a 'this-tea-tastes-strange' look; she pretended not to notice, went on reading her magazine. Had another taste, looked at her again.

'Darling, there's something wrong with the tea.'

THE THREE DIFFERENT USES OF 'DARLING'

1. Darling. Traditional term of endearment between two partners. As in 'I love you, darling' or 'I'm home, darling.'

2. Darling. Irritating term of endearment between two posh friends. As in, 'Darling, you look simply super.' 'Thank you, darling. And you look simply radiant.' Very irritating but not as irritating as 'babes', which Alex calls Isabel at every opportunity. 'Hi babes, bye babes, love you, babes.'

3. Darling. Traditional start to an argument between two married persons. As in 'Darling, there's something wrong with the tea.'

'It's got goat's milk in it. You can't taste the difference.'

'I can taste the difference.'

'You can't. It tastes exactly the same.'

'If it tastes exactly the same, why would we be having this conversation?'

'We're not having cow's milk any more. It's hard to digest.'

'What?'

'Cow's milk is designed for calves.'

'We're not goats either.'

'What?'

'We're not goats. We're humans.'

'Look, goat's milk is much better for you.'

'But goat's milk tastes like cat spray.'

'You should try drinking tea without sugar as well. It's bad for you.'

'What?'

In our wedding vows, we had both promised to honour, love and obey each other. At the time, it seemed like a good idea. We're a modern couple. We were both up for a bit of obeying. Rather sexist if it was only Isabel who said it. The vicar, in one of his compulsory marriage classes, had explained that obeying in a marital context didn't mean doing what someone said anyway. Oh no, no, no, no. It followed its original Latin meaning, 'to listen', as in 'to empathise', as in 'to be lovely to each other all the time'. Which seemed to have slipped Isabel's mind this morning.

'But I like sugar in my tea.'

'You'll get used to it without. It's only because I love you, and care about your health, darling.'

And with a gentle pat of the bed linen, she signified that this discussion was over. *Henceforth, tea shall be taken with goat's milk but without sugar*. So speaketh the wife.

Feeling quite put upon, I ordered a double espresso at Moorgate. Then drank sugary cow's-milky tea all morning. Then ate a whole packet of nuts to reduce sugar- and caffeine-poisoning effects before lunch. Then had no appetite for lunch and had to eat a sandwich at 5 p.m. so then had no appetite for dinner.

NOTE TO SELF: now that you are married, you must capitulate more often. Resistance is inadvisable. At best, it will throw a day's eating patterns out of kilter. At worst, it will make you wonder what on earth you let yourself in for when you said 'I do.' And it's far too soon to start thinking like that.

Friday 3 June

Not only am I not working on *Cat World* any more; not only have I joined a reputable magazine that does proper grown-up stuff about proper grown-up things like politics and economics and how to look good in a cheap suit, but I am getting a pay rise. Thank you, editor, for recognising my hard work and dedication over the last twelve months.

REASONS TO BE UNHAPPY (RE-REVISED)

None.

'Congratulations. I'm really pleased for you,' says Johnson on our way to the Tube. 'Obviously, bum-licking is seen as a more useful skill on this magazine than the ability to string a sentence together.'

'You mean bum-licking is a more useful skill than hosting and winning the World Throw the Paper Aeroplane Out the Window and See if You Can Hit a Traffic Warden Championships?'

'Teacher's gerbil.'

'Low-income earner.'

'Bottom-dweller.'

'Tramp.'

I know Johnson is secretly pleased for me – even if he is a miserable old bastard. He's always been my mentor – it was him who saved me from *Cat World*. If he hadn't lied about how good I was, I wouldn't have got tea-maker on *Life & Times*. I'd still be tasting new Whiskas flavours every month in my famous 'Good enough for your dinner plate?' cat-food column.

Isabel is much more excited. She's popped the champagne before I've stepped through the door, even before I can point out that the champagne almost certainly cost more than my pay rise is worth.

'Do you want to go out and celebrate?' she says.

'No, let's have a night in. Just the two of us.'

'Why, I'd love to, Grandpa.'

This is another great thing about being hitched. We can have a quiet Friday night in. We can even watch *Gardener's World*. And *Have I Got News For You*. And the news. With a cup of hot cocoa. Because we're incredibly old and incredibly boring and we don't have the willpower to go out at the weekends and stand in loud bars communicating by sign language any more.

Bliss.

Except upstairs is having a party. I know this because two hours after the DJ starts, one of them (the actor, claims to have been in *EastEnders*, has a nose ring) comes down to warn us they're having a party.

Until that point, I'd been planning his and his two flatmates' execution intricately. It would involve a pitchfork, a corkscrew, two bicycle pumps, a pair of size-eleven ice skates and one of those old-fashioned elevators with the iron concertina sliding doors. Isabel tells me to stop being so aggressive, they're only young, they're allowed to have a party. Then the doorbell goes, the guy who says he's from *EastEnders* says he's having a party and, instead of ripping his head off or even saying something dry like 'no kidding', I say, 'Oh right, a party. Good-o,' and gyrate my hips a bit. 'No problem at all, thanks awfully for letting me know.'

Now it's 3 a.m.

Would forgo ice skates and corkscrew for simple but effective baseball bat. Isabel ear-plugged and valerianed, dead to the world. Really thought she was actually, prodded her to check, got a tut. How can she sleep through this?

And why, at the age of twenty-nine and almost a year, am I still living in a middle-floor flat, trapped like a noise-sensitive piece of ham in a sandwich of irritation? A sandwich on a platter of other rundown sandwiches full of people who spend all day mugging each other. So tired.

Now it's 4 a.m.

Scratch previous comments on being happy with lack of half-million bonus/yacht/shark-lift. Am putting the flat up for sale tomorrow morning. I don't care how far the housing market has crashed. And when I sell, I'm moving to the Isle of Skye.

Saturday 4 June

Surprise, surprise, Isabel's not sure about the Isle of Skye idea. She says she likes living in Finsbury Park. It's colourful and multicultural and vibrant and alive. She likes our flat, she likes being near her friends. She's hardly going to commute to work from Skye, is she?

'Two months ago, you wanted us to move to a flat around the corner from your favourite bar in Quito. The Isle of Skye is a lot closer than Quito.'

'Two months ago, I was stressed about the wedding. Now, I'm blissfully married and very happy here, thank you very much.'

But I play my trump card …

'Think of the space, the trees, the nature, the organic farm we could start. With yaks and llamas and our own biltong shop.'

She really loves biltong, enough to hesitate for a split second.

But only a split second.

'We can move to the outer reaches of civilisation when we're in our thirties.'

When I suggest I am in my thirties, practically speaking, she says we're married now and that it's not 'I' but 'we', 'I' might be practically middle-aged, but 'we' are still almost two years off.

By the time I have had my morning coffee (I am allowed cow's milk and sugar because I'm grumpy), I am recovered. I like living in Finsbury Park too. I like being near my friends. I like our first marital home.

Things continue to improve.

Although I was dreading today's chore – getting the wedding ring I thought I'd managed to dodge – it couldn't have been easier: turned up, put my finger through a spaghetti measure, gave the man with the monocle £300 and it was all done. Easy. Unlike the first ring I ever bought.

The engagement ring

Unless he's a surfer or a scoundrel who tries to stall for time with a 'friendship' ring, the engagement ring is the first ring a man buys.

Two months' salary is the rule: it's fun watching flashy bankers with a penchant for ordering champagne in pubs work that one out. They go pale.

I am obviously not a banker but I didn't have two months' salary tucked under the mattress either the day I decided I would marry Isabel. I ransacked everything, from my Post Office account to my piggy bank, scrabbled for coins in the sofa, my old suit trousers and the hard-to-reach bit around the handbrake of my car. I had a princely £1,426.32.

'How much would you like to spend?' asked the man with the monocle.

'Oh, two thousand. Maybe two thousand five hundred,' I replied without hesitation. I think it was because I'd had to ring a doorbell to get into the shop. And then been shown in by a security guard. It intimidated me into making wildly inaccurate summations of wealth. The man with the monocle still looked unimpressed, scrabbled around in the dusty bit of the display and found some itty-bitty diamond rings.

There is a cruel diamond ratio you only learn when you have to buy one. A small high-quality one costs the same as a large low-quality one. Girls know the difference, which means you must ignore the size-is-everything rule, and go for quality. That was Johnson's advice. (Andy suggested I write a poem and engrave it on the side of a silver tankard instead.)

So I brushed away the big sparkler that would have impressed my ignorant mates and went for the near-perfect, near-invisible solitaire.

'It's beautiful,' she had lied when I'd got down on my knee, done my speech and opened the velvet box. Still, she'd already burst into tears and said yes by that point, which is what she was supposed to do.

Sunday 5 June

Lunch at Alex's to meet his new girlfriend (who he seems to have rustled up despite his alleged grief at being dumped by Watszerface) and to go through wedding photos (which, apparently, he can't wait to see). Consider knifing myself to get out of going but it is made clear that this is not an option. I must stop behaving like a child. It's very unattractive. Alex, bless him, has made a Moroccan tagine to go with his new Moroccan-themed terrace and his new conveniently Moroccan girlfriend. Don't know what's wrong with roast chicken. It is a *Sunday* lunch after all. He says Sunday lunch is the new Saturday night and threatens to make this the first of several 'day dos' through summer.

Despite my silent, desperate prayers, it doesn't rain, the tagine isn't burnt beyond recognition, he doesn't suffer anaphylactic shock from the couscous and the afternoon is simply splendid.

Although I'm left exchanging pleasantries with the Moroccan girlfriend while Alex calls Isabel babes a lot, says all the right things about how wonderful the dress/flowers/father's speech was, and touches her on the arm repeatedly.

THREE INTERESTING THINGS I LEARNT ABOUT MOROCCO WHILE SOMEONE HIT ON MY WIFE

1. The average temperature in the desert in July is 38°C, which is hot enough to fry an egg in. Not that that's a priority.

2. Most souks close for lunch and on Fridays.

3. In the city of Oudja, a large number of deaf men use sign language. It is hard to determine how many women are capable of sign language because they do not speak it in the streets.

The only other way to kill time is to go to the toilet a lot. Alex's flat, sorry, maisonette, sorry split-level garden apartment, is so minimalist that you can't even find the doors without feeling your way around like a blind person. So it wasn't my fault that on the nth pretend toilet stop, I accidentally found myself in his office/spare room/mirrored gym absent-mindedly wondering how to sabotage the chest-press.

Or that I accidentally spotted a torn photograph of me poking out from under a sheet in the corner.

Or that I accidentally lifted the sheet to discover bundles of photos from the wedding, all chopped up.

'Can I help you?' Alex, all smiles.

'No, just looking for the loo,' I replied, dropping the sheet. 'Didn't know you had copies of the wedding photos.'

'They're my own. They're not ready for you to look at yet. The loo is where it's been all afternoon.'

Isabel isn't talking to me on the way home, despite my immense efforts at being nice all day, and despite me revealing the shock news that her 'best friend' has a chopped-up pile of photos from our wedding in his spare room.

Apparently, I was moody and I am ridiculous to even suggest that Alex might have spent the last few weeks chopping up the wedding photos of the girl he loves and the man he despises.

So unfair.

Monday 6 June

Two blocks down from our flat, a new one of those yellow incident boards had been put up. We get a lot of them round our way, but this one was different.

Incident. Saturday 4 June. A man and his dog were stabbed. Did you see anything? If so, please call.

I can't believe they stabbed the dog. What had the dog done?

Tuesday 7 June

'Let's just get an agent or two around to value the place. We don't have to move or anything but it would be nice to know what sort of move we could make if we decided we wanted to … move, that is.'

'OKAY, I suppose it would be nice to have a little garden. And if we don't go too far, I quite like the idea of commuting.'

'Excellent, darling … Hello, I'd like to arrange an evaluation … Tomorrow? That's rather sudden … No, no, that would be lovely.'

Good night's sleep ruined by a horrible nightmare. I was having a drink outside a pub with my childhood pet dog Fluffy, miraculously reincarnated twice as large and twice as fluffy, with the ability to drink beer. Across the road, a woman screams as a terrifying bloke with a baseball cap and face tattoos grapples with her handbag. Fluffy barks, the terrifying bloke stops mugging the woman and turns to confront us. He's laughing maniacally and being all sarcastic about how fluffy Fluffy is.

As he advances, a huge knife glinting in his hand, I reach for my pocket penknife. For what seems like ages, I can't get it open. When I do, it's only the nail file. He's getting closer and closer as I find the corkscrew, then the letter-opener, then the tiny little nail scissors.

As the terrifying bloke raises his knife, which is now a very efficient giant pink razor, above his head, I am cornered with nothing but the hole punch. Like a fluffy blur, Fluffy is there, flying through the air like Lassie. Except Lassie wouldn't have been razored clean in two. The last thing I see is a look of total astonishment on Fluffy's fluffy little face. Then I wake up clutching one end of a pillow.

Thursday 9 June

Three estate agents come round to do flat valuation. Needed a shower afterwards. However much I scrubbed, I still felt dirty.

'Mr Walker. Hi, Arthur Arthurs from Arthurs' Arseholes.'

'I'm sorry?'

'Arthur Arthurs from Arthurs & Sons. For the valuation. Pleasure. May I? Lovely, lovely hallway. Mmm, yes, oh, lovely carpets. Neutral. Perfect.'

'This is the only bedroom.'

'Oh gorgeous, the space, the light, the scope, the movement.' He's a stamp collector who's discovered a penny black, an art collector who's tripped over a Rembrandt in the attic, the first archaeologist at Sutton bloody Hoo.

'Look at this kitchen, will you? Just look at it. Look at this well-appointed, well-equipped, well-planned little minx of a kitchen.'

It's a tiny kitchen in a tiny flat on the wrong side of Finsbury Park that he may have to sell at the height of a property-market crash but he's excited.

'Oh yes, the walls. Oh yes, the marble surfaces. Oh yes, the hood, the hood, the hood. Mmmm, lovely. The toilet! Aarrrrhhhh. Ooooooh. Bidet. Smooth. Simple. Soft. You cheeky bidet. You halogen lighting. You naughty, naughty power shower.'

He was the least repellent of the three. And suggested the highest selling price.

Saturday 11 June

This was always going to be a difficult day: both sets of parents coming up for an afternoon stroll, then wedding photos, then dinner. Seemed so simple – we have nice, non-problematic, hang-up-free parents. No messy divorces, no excessive corporal punishment, no strange method-parenting guaranteed to instil some deeply hidden psychological bomb set to go off any time in early adulthood. But then you have to consider the conflicting requirements: it's like doing the catering at an allergy-sufferers' convention.

My mum: South African interior designer, impatient; loves short walks, dogs, home improvements; hates cats, overcooked vegetables, old art-house movies from Japan.

Her mum: Polish doctor, impatient; likes cats, home improvements, cleanliness; hates dogs, undercooked vegetables and walking anywhere that isn't strictly necessary. 'I escaped through the Iron Curtain, my darlinks, with only forty zloty, some silver spoons and my university certificate hidden in my tights. I walked through Europe to be here. I have done enough walking.'

My dad: English; traditional; slowing down a bit. Likes not saying very much, except when he tells a story, which can take hours. Leaves rest of liking and hating of cats, dogs, vegetables and home improvements to Mum.

Her dad: ditto, but more so; doesn't suffer fools, gladly or otherwise. In fact doesn't really suffer anyone or anything. Especially short walks. Short walks are stuff and nonsense. In his day, he walked 100 miles just to buy the milk.

Even before the lunch began, I knew it would be difficult. Isabel in big mood because her razor is blunt and her legs, consequently, look like streaky bacon. I obviously know nothing, which only makes her more grumpy. Then, the family arrives.

The walk

'I will stay here. I don't want to go for a walk,' says her mum.

'A short walk never killed anyone. It is a short walk, isn't it?' says mine.

'Come on, let's get on with it,' say the dads in unison.

We all leave the flat, and set a course for Hampstead Heath.

'Are these plantains?' Three hundred yards in, my dad, like a moth to an ultraviolet insect zapper, has been drawn to a Caribbean vegetable store on the Holloway Road.

'I think so, Dad. Leave them.'

'Excuse me, young man, how long does one cook plantains?'

We wait outside a wig shop for ten minutes while Dad gets the lowdown on plantains from the Rastafarian vegetable stallholder. During the delay, her mum keeps breaking for the flat, mine looks at the wigs. Her dad tuts at people with shirts hanging out. Sheep-dogs have an easier job.

'What is that man doing? He's almost naked.' We have inadvertently wandered into the heath's nudge-nudge, wink-wink meeting place for lonely hearts. Her dad has stopped and is pointing at a man in a red G-string reading the *Guardian*.

'He's reading the *Guardian*, Dad. Don't worry about it.'

'There's another one. Reading the *Guardian*,' says my dad.

'Lot of *Guardian*-readers round here,' says her dad. He's a *Times* man.

'Why are they all sitting in this field, separately?' says mine. 'It's suspicious to say the least.'

'In knickers.'

'G-strings, I believe they're called.'

'Please, let's go,' Isabel and I say together.

'Are these men after a bit of nookie, with strangers?' asks her dad, loudly. Just because he's hard of hearing, he thinks everyone else is.

'Like that MP, you mean?' asks mine.

'Yes, it's what they call dogging, isn't it?' says hers.

'No, I think dogging is when you watch other people having sex in cars,' says mine.

'Kinky stuff they're into these days, don't you think? Mind you, we weren't much better back in the Sixties, were we, darling?'

'Now is not the time to talk about our era of free love, darlink. I have a blister,' says her mum.

Isabel is looking like you'd expect her to look after finding out her parents really swung in the Swinging Sixties.

'This is turning into a long walk,' says my mum.

The wedding photos

'You look wonderful. I look dreadful,' says her mum to my mum.

'You look wonderful. I look dreadful,' says my mum to her mum.

'Not put them in an album yet, William?' enquires her dad. 'Just going to have them out in any order like that, are you?'

'That Alex made for a rather dashing horseman, wouldn't you say?' says my mum. 'Look at him looking splendid in his tails.'

'Yes, tailored especially on Savile Row,' says her mum. 'And hasn't he got a lovely voice? That song he sang for you both was so beautiful.'

The lunch

'Red snapper? Not in our day. Sounds like a fancy fish. Cod, hake, John Dory – whatever happened to them?'

'Yes, good honest fish, they were.'

'Halibut.'

'Tuna.'

Then her mum changes the subject to sphincters. Her colleague had a patient in the other day with a bleeding bottom. His wife had attempted to pleasure him with her Prada stiletto but the point had been worn down into something too sharp for the sphincter wall to tolerate.

Why does she tell us these things? Why is it always when we're eating? What is it with doctors, anal adventures and clinical story-telling?

My dad changes the subject.

'Are you still working for that charity?'

'Yes, she is. And they're still not paying her properly,' says her dad, because children are never allowed to answer for themselves. 'I keep telling her, just because they're saving the whole of Africa doesn't mean they can't pay you a living wage.'

Isabel regresses into a teenager: short-tempered, impatient, tutting, crossing arms aggressively. I do the same when they move on to my time at *Cat World*, even though it's in the past and I shouldn't care.

Minutes before they are all strangled, they all head off together, making jokes about getting stabbed on the way to the Tube and going off to the fish 'n' chip shop for a nice bit of marlin.

'I've changed my mind. We should move,' says Isabel as we stand exhausted in the doorway. 'The rent boys and plantain-sellers of north London shouldn't have to put up with our parents.'

Monday 13 June

Alex has delivered a handmade wedding album he claims to have been working on night and day for the last six weeks. The accompanying note said he was sorry I had slightly spoilt the surprise while 'looking for the toilet in my study' but that he hoped this handcrafted work would be a lasting memento of what he was sure would prove to be a long and happy marriage.

'Ahhh,' goes Isabel, thumbing through the infinitely detailed photo montages. Yes, he's made mosaics of our faces, thousands of intricate combinations of heads and hands and more heads, all touching and overlapping and linking up.

'It's incredible. Like a beautiful stained-glass window,' opines Isabel.

'It looks like a Hieronymus Bosch version of Hell. Hasn't the guy got anything better to do?' opine I.

Isabel looks genuinely upset. She says I really should stop being so difficult about Alex. He clearly wants us to be happy. He's gone out of his way to make our wedding special. It's important that I don't stop her having friends. I have to promise to behave like a grown-up. So I do, with my fingers crossed behind my back.

Wednesday 15 June

Alex is not a psycho. Alex is not a psycho. Alex is not a psycho. If I say it enough times, I might believe it.

Isabel, home late and glowing, has found a new yoga class in Holborn. Says she received new energy from the ground or something. Astrid, the yoga teacher, uses crystals to help centre her pupils. Argument ensues when I look sceptical.

Thursday 16 June

A banker and his girlfriend came to look at the flat today. We hid up the road, behind the *Man and His Dog Were Knifed* incident board. Someone has graffitied 'A cat person?' underneath the can-you-help? bit. Arthur Arsehole calls afterwards to say they loved it, loved the space, the light, the angles, the dynamic, the touch. But they wanted a garden.

Friday 17 June

It's been a long week. I get home late from work, am grumpy, am hot and bothered, am looking forward to a nice bath.

'Don't have a bath, have a shower.'

Here we go again.

It is only because Isabel is hugging me when she says this that there is no immediate bloodshed.

I consider a bath with a whisky after a long week at work to be one of man's inalienable rights – a period of quiet reflection, contemplation and the making of amusing bubble-bath hats. But I considered sugar in goat's-milk-free tea with a similar reverence until only a few days ago and look what happened to that.

'Why not?'

'It's a waste of water.'

'I want a bath though.'

'One bath is the same as four showers.'

'I'm having a bath.'

But as I sat in the bath, trying to enjoy my inalienable right, I knew its days were numbered. From the speed-date to the wedding, Isabel had never attempted to change me: it's one of the reasons I love her. But now we're married, we both sense a change.

She is my wife, she has the power, she just doesn't know quite how much power yet. Like a young Jedi knight, she will learn.

Saturday 18 June

What a brilliant day: went to what may be the worst wedding ever. Jess, horrible property developer, marrying poor Tony – creative, sensitive, artistic, in-touch-with-his-feminine-side Tony. In short, he's gay, she knows it, but she wants kids and he's the best she can find. And he just needs a wife so he can pretend he's straight forever. It was the wedding you always dream about, one that unravels before your very eyes.

The service

They had written their own vows. Tony said, 'With my arms, I will cradle you.' Jess said, 'With my arms, I will encircle you.'

For what has to be a virtually sexless marriage, they really were laying it on a bit thick.

Best man composed and performed an electric piano piece for their exit. Almost entirely atonal, it was quite upsetting and made three babies cry. Brilliant. 3/10.

The meal

Some sort of mutton offcut, cooked for 10,000 years in the hellish furnaces of Gomorrah. Served on a bed of what might have been risotto but was in actual fact mashed potato. Isabel has Banker Man on her right, all pink shirt and big hair. I have Acronym Man on my left. He's in IT, setting up his own ISP, depending on the FAP of the NRT in QPE, or something. 1/10.

The speeches

Father-of-the-bride walked out on mother-of-the-bride six months ago for glamorous and youthful secretary. Mother mutters and scoffs through all fatherly marital advice. Father finishes with '... and in short, Tony, I would advise you to ignore all my advice. I married her, after all, which shows how little I know. So please, can you all be upstanding ...?' Chaos and stormings-out from then on. Brilliant. 1/10.

The first dance

They just clung to each other, revolving slowly like chickens on a supermarket rotisserie to the tune of bloody 'Angels' by bloody Robbie Williams. Nasty. 4/10.
TOTAL 9/40. A new last place, but for all the right reasons.

Sunday 19 June

Phoned Johnson about the inalienable rights thing. He says men lose all inalienable rights such as having a hot bath on a Friday the moment they say 'I do.' That's the unwritten law, it's just that women are too smart to point it out explicitly in case men notice and rebel. So they sneak in all the restrictions over the first year of marriage. Before you know it, you're a house-trained husband, unable to recall whether the things you do, such as having a cold shower on a Friday, are your own idea or part of the new regime.

I suggest that I quite like having someone caring enough to challenge my inalienable rights. Goat's milk is, after all, better for you than cow's milk.

It won't stop at goat's milk, warns Johnson.

Went to bed with the papers, a cup of tea (goat's milk, no sugar) and my wife at 10 p.m. Used to go clubbing on a Sunday. Well, once or twice. Now, I'm only a few notches off slippers at seven. Very happy.

Until I had another nightmare.

Isabel and I have somehow agreed to go to Saskia's wedding reception (we weren't invited to the service). Only we've been seated on different tables. I'm on the top table, in between Saskia, who is wearing nothing but stockings and suspenders, and her groom. Isabel is crammed onto a small table at the back with seven octogenarians: she's the only one without an ear trumpet or a Zimmer frame. I try to move her cutlery onto our table, but the food starts to arrive: everywhere I step, I block whole squads of waitresses with their huge platters of lobster and inexplicable jelly towers.

The chaos is unimaginable; they fall over like dominoes and it's all my fault. I just stand in the middle holding a knife, a fork and Isabel's place name. The head chef, who is Gordon Ramsay, effs and blinds his way out of the kitchen, and starts bludgeoning me with one of the ruined crustaceans. Isabel is being held down by the octogenarians and only Saskia, standing dominatrix-style over everything, can help.

I wake up to find Isabel looking straight at me, an expression of utter disbelief on her face. Someone is shouting 'Saskia, Saskia, Saskia' and it only takes a few bleary seconds to realise that it's me.

Monday 20 June

In the cold light of day, it wasn't an easy dream to explain.

'No, darling, I wasn't shouting Saskia, Saskia, Saskia in a sexual way. I wanted Saskia to save you, darling, from the octogenarians that were pinning you down.'

Even without mentioning the stockings and suspenders, it sounded like a sex dream, only an incredibly perverted one involving ear trumpets. By the time we both left for work, I think I'd succeeded in convincing Isabel that I wasn't still obsessed with Saskia; unfortunately, I think I'd made her believe I was on the verge of a nervous breakdown instead.

How Saskia destroyed my last-but-one relationship

The relationship was in terminal decline anyway. It was that last three-year one, the one where you know it's your final practice run before you meet the woman you're going to marry. It's as much about timing as anything. You're slightly too young to propose like you have to when you're in your late twenties, slightly too old to walk away easily like you could when you were younger, so you just carry on going out aimlessly, waiting for something dreadful to happen.

Saskia was the dreadful thing that happened. I was at a party; she was also at the party; Elizabeth wasn't because she was at another party with other friends doing other things. And it's not every day that the sexiest girl at a party asks me if I'd like to go somewhere – pause for double meaning to become lip-quiveringly obvious – quieter. I knew the right and honourable answer was no, but Elizabeth and I were in the doldrums. We were sick of each other. And Saskia was beautiful. So I said something cool but contradictory like, 'Sure, this place is dead anyway,' and before I could catch my breath we were having sex in Hyde Park.

It was a seedy, torrid affair, and one conducted largely outdoors because we had nowhere indoors to go. My flat was usually out of the question because of Elizabeth. Saskia's flat was always out of the question because it was owned by a forty-year-old stockbroker she had been having an affair with but who, in an effort to avoid hefty alimony, was now trying to rebuild his marriage. I thought this was all incredibly exciting but entirely unsustainable. Apart from all the obvious reasons why being a philandering, cheating, good-for-nothing two-timer is inadvisable, there's the sheer stress of it all. Lying and cheating is exhausting. Besides, Saskia and I had nothing in common and we both knew it. A month after we met, I told her we had to stop meeting in public parks like this; she said fine, kissed me goodbye and went to live in New York. But not before she phoned Elizabeth and told her I was a cheating bastard.

I suppose I should have been grateful. I was too pathetic to be honest and tell Elizabeth it was over. Saskia saved me the trouble. Without Saskia, I might never have met Isabel. In many ways, Isabel should be grateful.

Tuesday 21 June

Another flat viewing but the husband said he wouldn't feel happy letting his wife walk home on her own at night. What an idiot. Arthur Arsehole said he'd explained about how the area was colourful rather than dangerous but they were going to look at smaller properties in Chiswick instead.

Wednesday 22 June

I was right. Isabel does think I'm having a nervous breakdown. She says she's spoken to Astrid, her yoga teacher, and Astrid says men benefit from her type of yoga even more than women and that I should come to the next class. Which is tonight.

I'm just trying to choose the most appropriate form of dismissive laugh when Isabel says, 'Please come, it would make me happy,' which is blackmail.

* * *

In a small, sweaty room above a holistic healing shop in Holborn, nine women and one man, all in Lycra, spread their mats as Astrid spreads her crystals, while I bite my nails.

I don't have a mat so I have to borrow one from a cupboard. The only place left to unroll my mat – which is pink and smells of sweat – is right behind the man in Lycra. The next hour seems like four or five. There are the boring positions ('Put your arms in the air … stretch a bit … hold it … hold it … feel the energy …'), the impossible positions ('Put your leg over your arm … put the other leg round the other arm … spread all your toes … hold it … hold it … keep breathing, William …'), and the disgusting positions – which are all of them when you have a man in Lycra blocking your view. A man who laughs happily every time he lets one off. I don't think I'll ever be able to blot out the downward-facing dog.

'Thanks, guys. Great session. And remember, don't walk on the Earth, walk with the Earth. See you all next week.'

No.

It gets worse. Message from Alex when we get back to the flat.

'Hi, guys. Almost two months married. Hope it's all sweetness and light over there.'

[Wanker.]

'Look, I know this is a bit out of the blue but I've got a friend who does marketing for Ferrari. You know, the racing team.'

[Wanker.]

'Anyway, he's hosting a race day down at Brands Hatch on Saturday. You're probably too blissfully married to spend a day apart but I wondered if William might be free? And perhaps Andy? For a bit of a race. Be good to hang out with my best mate's new hubby.'

[Wanker – but it is Ferrari.]

Saturday 25 June

So let me just explain how it happened.

We arrived at Brands Hatch and it turned out they wouldn't let us into the actual Formula One cars. We were in buggies, which was still cool. Andy had fallen for Alex's pretend friendliness, hook, line and sinker. As we watched the safety demonstration, they were all jokey and matey and laughey.

But I was onto him. I could tell from his feigned interest in my week, from his relentlessly inquisitive chattiness, from his horrible chiselled jaw line, that today was all about humiliation. I got the girl so he had to show he was a better racing driver. Well, life doesn't work like that, buster.

We had a few practice laps. Alex was being all encouraging and non-competitive when Andy was within earshot, but asked me if I always drive like a kerb crawler when he wasn't. Divide and rule. Clever.

We did some quick laps individually. I was faster than Alex. He pretended to be pleased for me in an I'm-letting-you-win-at-the-moment kind of way.

Then, it was time to race. As we got ready, Alex came over to me and said, 'Good luck, old boy,' which he would later claim he said to everyone, just to get us in the spirit.

Six of us lined up, me and some marketing joker at the front, Alex and Andy in the second row, two other marketing jokers behind them.

I was ahead for the whole of the first lap, but on the second lap Andy and Alex overtook the marketing joker and began to challenge me for the lead. Then Andy, mistiming a corner, spun out, taking the marketing joker with him. At that point, Alex changed. When everyone was watching, he was the consummate gentleman driver. Now, out on our own, he was driving like a maniac. As we began the final lap, he drove up my inside and, rather than take the first corner, just sort of steered us wider and wider. I missed a head-on collision with three hundred tyres only by braking and going around the back of them.

Alex should have been well gone. But he wasn't. He was waiting for me to catch up again. As we went through the back of the course I tried to overtake but he charged me again. I ended up ahead but he started ramming me from behind.

I looked back and saw only the dead eyes of a psychotic maniac.

Into the final corner, I had the edge. I can't remember exactly what happened, except that I crossed the line first.

Andy, on his way back to the pits, saw it all. He claimed I rammed Alex off the road. I remember Alex trying to ram me but losing control. Either way, I only noticed he had rolled his buggy once I'd crossed the line.

Sunday 26 June

Back so soon at Alex's horrible maisonette, dropping off some grapes.

'Sorry about the arm, Alex,' I offer warmly.

'Don't worry, William. It was an accident. And it's only a fracture,' he replies. You would think he might apologise himself for trying to kill me, but then everyone else in the room might actually believe me.

'William is like a toddler, Alex. He can't just play nicely,' says Isabel unhelpfully.

'Great day though, mate. Thanks again,' says Andy, traitorously.

Andy thinks Alex is great. Isabel thinks Alex is brave. I know Alex is a psycho. I know he probably has a rocking chair and a wig hidden somewhere around the flat.

At least tomorrow is the start of another day.

Monday 27 June

Start of another day already ruined by half eight in the morning when Arthur Arsehole calls. A lot of interest in the flat. Sixteen hits on the website alone. But it's a bad time for the market. Tells me to keep my pecker up, Willy. I tell him I'll smash his face in if he ever calls me Willy ever again ever or makes any reference to my pecker whatsoever. But only after he's hung up.

Tuesday 28 June

Andy has been around to Alex's again to help make him dinner. 'What's the point in arguing? Alex is a nice guy,' he tells me. 'You're a ridiculous hippy,' I reply. Of course, he always has been a ridiculous hippy. The first time we met, in Freshers' Week at university, his hair was down to his shoulders, his trousers were stripy and he smelt. Since then, he has learned to wash, bought new clothes and cut his hair, but the hippy still lurks within.

And you can never rely on a hippy to understand that an evil maniac is trying to ruin your marriage.

Wednesday 29 June

The only reason I went back to Astrid's sweaty room in Holborn is because of the whole Alex buggy-crash debacle. I suspect Alex, with his broken arm, is winning the charm offensive. I need to be seen in Lycra again, just so Isabel will stop giving me that look every time anyone mentions the race.

It is just as sweaty as last week but I make sure we get there early and that I bagsy a place right at the front. This means I get told off by Astrid for yawning but sweaty Lycra guy has to spend the whole lesson staring at my clenched buttocks and not vice versa.

I think he likes it.

Thursday 30 June

Shit, shit, shit, shit, shit, shit, shit. Isabel sent straight from doctor's appointment to hospital. Something gynaecological. Something about an operation …

She called me from the hospital, sounded very shaky. Couldn't talk because mobiles are banned and she'd run out of coins. Just starting to explain what was wrong when the beeps started. Cut off saying, 'Hopefully the doctor will …' beep, beep, beep.

Took ages to get from work to the hospital because of the sodding Northern Line. Absolutely the worst hour of my life. I love her so much. Realised by King's Cross that if I lost her I would never recover. Wouldn't want to. Realised by Camden Town that I even loved her for her goat's milk and her ridiculous yoga. Promised by Archway I would never argue with her again.

Three a.m. now. She has a Bartholin's cyst, which means her bits, or more specifically one bit, has swollen like an orang-utan's bottom. They wheeled her away an hour ago just like they do in *Casualty*, which was dreadful. Wanted to follow her through the flappy doors but the big, scary nurse-bitch wouldn't let me. Nice little nurse has let me stay in the ward with the groaning old ladies. One is on morphine, in and out of consciousness, muttering wildly.

Will buy Isabel an enormous bunch of flowers tomorrow.

Assuming I can get to the flower shop, what with the dead leg that won't go away. Apparently, I was asleep for a whole two hours in the metal chair by Isabel's bed. Couldn't feel my leg at all when I woke up. Actually thought I might have permanently paralysed myself, it took so long to recover. Is that possible? Will check on Wikipedia.

Isabel was very worried. 'Poor you,' she said when I woke. 'You look so tired.'

She's amazing. Not even Florence Nightingale would have been worrying about my dead leg if her private parts looked like a monkey's arse.

JULY

'The chains of marriage are so heavy that it takes two to bear them, and sometimes three.'

ALEXANDRE DUMAS

Friday 1 July

She's alive! Operation was a success. Important stuff intact. Not counting the dead-leg chair-nap, I haven't slept a wink. Went home for a couple of hours to change pants and so forth. Tried to rest but had nightmares about being attacked by a gang of inflamed orang-utans. Whoever said all men's dreams were about sex was lying.

Isabel releases herself mid-afternoon (like in soaps when the patient ill-advisedly tears out her own tubes and storms out of the ward), and we get home just in time for one of the idiots upstairs to start practising his new set of drums.

I am in no mood for drums.

As I ring the upstairs doorbell, I am a creature of crimson terror, a brooding, fearsome primeval ape-man from the dawn of time: hideous, malevolent, aggressive, coiled. I am the Incredible Hulk in shirt-splitting mid-transition. I am King Kong with hunger anger.

The door is opened by one of the idiots.

'My wife has just had a major operation on her labia,' I roar-whisper, the way an unpredictable serial killer would. 'She has just spent a whole night being operated on and then a whole day in an NHS ward full of moaning grannies and superbugs. She could well have MBNA. She has survived an ordeal and I. Am. Her. HUSBAND.'

Pause for effect. I exude boiling, molten rage.

'Do you mean MRSA?'

The idiot shifts his cool, slouchy weight from one foot to the other.

'It doesn't matter what I mean. What are you going to do about it?'

More boiling moltenness but he doesn't look as threatened or apologetic as I had hoped. He looks a little sleepy.

'Do about what?'

'THE DRUMS. THE BLOODY DRUMS. Would you mind not playing your drums today?'

Another pause. More boiling.

'Or for the rest of the week? … Or, in fact, for-fucking-ever?'

He looks at me nonchalantly. I look at him as if I'm a stick of dynamite.

'I don't have any drums,' he says with a cool, calm shrug. 'That's why you can still hear drumming even though I'm here talking to you. It's the flat next door.'

* * *

For the rest of the day, I'm in full hand-and-foot waiting mode.

Initially, this is an immense pleasure. My poor recovering wife needs me. I have a role. I am a man with a role. I am protecting the womenfolk. I will silence drummers and top up hot-water bottles. It is the north London equivalent of forming a defensive ring of prairie wagons, then fending off Red Indians with Smith & Wessons.

'Can I have some Marmite toast?' Of course, darling, coming right up.

'Oh, can you cut it into soldiers?' No problem, sweetie.

'Can I have another cup of tea?' That's fine, sugar.

'Oh, you've just sat down but I need another cushion from the bedroom. Are you sure you don't mind?' Your wish is my command, buttercup.

Gradually, the novelty of being needed wears off. Yes, I'll get your magazine, your book, your bed socks, your smelly candle. But do you really want chicken soup, dearest? We've got vegetable soup. Nice organic vegetable soup. It's your favourite. No? Okay, I'll go back to the shops where I've just been to buy your Purdey's and get some chicken soup.

By eight, it is clear that I am being exploited.

'Darling, I'm sorry. Can you get my face cream, my lip balm, my hair band and some Shreddies with double cream?' For someone who is allegedly unwell, she rattles off the list with surprising sprightliness. And she's got a lot more colour in her cheeks. I sigh like an overworked, underpaid NHS nurse at the end of another grinding shift and go about my duties.

Then, the TV premiere of *The Bourne Identity* clashes with a two-hour documentary about Rudolf Nureyev.

'Aren't you tired, darling?' I ask hopefully.

No.

'The doctor did say you should rest as much as possible in the first forty-eight hours.'

No.

'Wouldn't you rather watch something less taxing than a documentary? *The Bourne Identity*, for example, is on at exactly the same time as *Nureyev: the Man, the Ballerina*, and it's supposed to be great fun. Very light.'

No.

SOME OF THE THINGS I NOW KNOW ABOUT RUDOLF NUREYEV

He was born on a train going to Vladivostok, where his father served in the army.

At ballet school, he was incredibly stroppy, perhaps because of an internal conflict over his sexuality.

He didn't like non-celebrities.

He might have slept with Anthony Perkins.

Saturday 2 July

Alex came around early and unannounced, gushing concern like he would gush blood out of a deep arterial wound if I took an axe to him: 'I didn't know, I hadn't heard, oh my God, babes, are you okay? You poor, poor thing.'

Despite his allegedly broken arm, he has carted a bunch of flowers the size of a small tree with him, which he picked and arranged himself. And some organic chicken soup.

'I know how you love chicken soup when you're under the weather, babes. We'll have you right as rain in no time.'

After an interminable chat about how wonderful last night's Nureyev documentary was, he leaves, wincing a bit to remind us of his injury as he goes. He has bought last-minute tickets to the matinee at Sadler's Wells, a surprise for his Moroccan girlfriend, who also loved the Nureyev documentary. What a guy.

Monday 4 July

Quite relieved to get out of the flat. I offered to stay at home and continue being Florence Nightingale, but Isabel is almost back to normal now. Or else she's quite keen to get me out of the flat.

The usual frustrations of the day seem harder to deal with today, possibly because I am suffering from post-traumatic stress syndrome by proxy. No one ever looks after the carer.

Frustration one

It's the start of the week and I still appear to be no closer to ever escaping Finsbury Park. I manage to get a seat on the Tube. A fellow citizen of my 'hood, a gangsta rappa with headphones the size of grapefruit, manages to get the seat next to me. The music is so loud I can hear the vocals: *'I don't know what you heard about me; But a bitch can't get a dollar out of me; No Cadillac, no perms, you can't see; That I'm a motherfucking P-I-M-P.'* I ask him to turn it down. He says: 'Interrupt my train of thought again, bitch, and I'll cut you.' Then the Tube stops mid-tunnel: someone in another train in another tunnel has pulled the emergency cord. I have to spend the next thirty-five stationary minutes sitting with a man who just threatened to knife me.

Frustration two

A woman with a loud voice has just got a job in the book department of *Life & Times*, which involves her sitting two desks away from me. After an alarmingly short I'm-in-a-new-job-so-must-be-on-best-behaviour honeymoon period (five days), she has settled in and revealed her true colours: she is a phoner of friends and a sorter-outer of home administration at work. This is dreadful news.

Last week (her first in the office), she booked a holiday to the Maldives ('I just need to get away from it all for a while'), arranged for a quote on a garden spa bath ('how much more are those underwater speakers? It wouldn't be proper without a bit of Courtney Pine bubbling away,' snort, guffaw, snort) and had a two-hour argument with her daughter about the pros and cons of Gordon Brown.

This morning, I arrive late because of my one-to-one face time with the knife-man and she's already mid-conversation with an unspecified friend.

Johnson is making slit-throat mimes but I don't know why he's complaining – he sits seven desks away and, because he likes rock and roll, he can't hear properly anyway.

'My BUPA insurance has always reimbursed me. Mmm, mmm, mmm, so why's she taken him off the diet if the stools are only grey? Mmm, mmm. I suppose all I would say is that there is probably a psychological aspect to it, in that she's a bit of a hypochondriac. Mmm, mmm, mmm. But if they were green … mmm, mmm.'

My appetite for a morning croissant is ruined.

Frustration three

When I call Isabel, mid-afternoon, Alex is there. He has taken the afternoon off work because his arm is too painful and he thought they could convalesce together. Isn't that sweet?

Tuesday 5 July

'Barry? Barry? *Barry?*'

I haven't even switched my computer on yet.

'This is a bad line, Barry. Can you hear me, Barry? I wondered whether you were free on Sunday? … *Free* … On *Sunday*! No, *Sunday* … I've bought a lamb … Not a lamp.

'A *lamb*. From the nice place in Wales where we went last summer … No, a lamb. It's cut up and in the fridge … No, I'm fine, Barry. I said the lamb's cut up and in the fridge. I'm going to do the shoulder on Sunday. Wondered whether you'd like to come? No, a lamb. I'll call you back.

'Not a lamp. It's Sandra. No, I'll call you back. *I'll call you back.*'

This conversation is repeated throughout the day. The woman is organising a Sunday roast with a group of deaf or stupid people.

I wish a piano would crash through the ceiling and kill either her or me, I no longer care which.

When I tell Isabel I wish a piano would crush either me or Sandra, she says I should be more tolerant.

Wednesday 6 July

'… and I walked in and he was just lying there, in the hallway …'

This sounds better than the lamb.

'… I thought he might have just been resting, but when I touched him, he was cold. His body was stiff. He was gone. Gone forever. I should have done something. I should have noticed his suffering sooner. He didn't deserve to go out like this. I should have put an end to it all. But I let him go on. I let him fight on bravely. To suffer. All for my own selfish motives. And now this. *Now this … Dying alone … Alone … On the floor … In the hall.*'

Hacking, racking, sloppy sobs. I'm guessing a husband. A lucky husband who's taken the easy option: slow, painful death in a hallway rather than slow, painful life with Sandra.

'I picked him up, wrapped him in kitchen towel and flushed him down the loo. He meant so much to me.'

A goldfish? A bloody goldfish? I have to listen to all that for a bloody flipping goldfish. Surprised it wasn't her husband. I'd have killed myself long ago if I'd been married to this. Or just killed her.

The managing editor ushered me into his office later in the day and pointed out that since Sandra had been recently widowed, it was somewhat tactless to go on about it. I said I had no idea about the widowing and that I hadn't been going on about it. He said I had. I said I hadn't. He said I'd been overheard ranting about how I'd have killed myself if I'd been married to Sandra. Or at the very least killed her. I said I'd only thought that, I hadn't actually said it. He said I had. I said I hadn't. Unless of course I had been thinking out loud, which sometimes happens. This didn't seem to make him any happier. He said he'd have to put it in my record. I said fine but that Sandra was really annoying.

Thursday 7 July

Isabel's magical dissolving stitches aren't dissolving. By the time I get home, Isabel is lying spread-eagled on the kitchen table, clutching a pair of sterilised eyebrow pluckers.

'Darling, we must get them out now. They're itching.'

'But shouldn't we go to hospital?'

'No, Mummy said it was easy. It's not worth the schlep back there.'

'What about the GP?'

'It can't wait.'

'Okay.'

'Now call Mummy.'

'Sorry?'

'Call her. She's going to instruct you.'

'Your mother is going to instruct me to remove your stitches? ... From your —'

'Come on. I'm getting cold.'

Clutching the pluckers, I call her.

'Right, William. Are the pluckers sterilised? Good. Are your hands washed? Good. Are Isabel's legs open? William? William? No time to be squeamish now, William. None of us was born yesterday. Now, you see the labia majora?'

Oh God.

Friday 8 July

Isabel is staying with her parents for the weekend to recuperate further. I don't have to stay with her parents for the weekend because Arthur Arsehole has lined up some 'very keen' prospective buyers. I am charged with being present but not present. I must vacuum. I must plump cushions. I must keep the flat spotless, keep our drummer/party animal neighbours silen-t/-ced, and have the bread machine wafting suitable aromas at prescient moments. But whenever Arsehole opens the door, I must be gone.

This is the first time I have been alone since we got married. Isabel says this is probably a good thing: what with wishing a poor widow at work dead, I could do with some time on my own to relax and recuperate from what is clearly a stressful time of my life.

Hahaha, I say.

The overwhelming sense of freedom is intoxicating, as is the whisky I down naughtily the moment I get in from work. I don't know why I was so excited … I'm very happy being married. I love Isabel. Isabel loves me. Sure, the honeymoon is over (the honeymoon that dare not speak its name, complete with its constant diarrhoea and its inescapable taxi drivers and its long-haul economy class syndrome, and I thought honeymoons were supposed to be relaxing and, yes, it's still too raw to talk about). But even in this post-honeymoon phase, where it's all got a bit trouble and strife and ball and chain, I don't know what I'd do without her.

Well, actually I do.

FIVE QUICK AND EASY STEPS BACK TO BACHELORHOOD

Step one: find note from Isabel. 'Will miss you, darling. Vegetables in fridge need to be used. And there's still some quiche left. Love you. Call later.'

Step two: feel quite tired. Can't face cooking or eating of vegetables. Have a Scotch and dry. And another. Decide to have a curry. Fortunately, the curry house number is still on speed-dial seven, right between the video shop and the laundrette. I am asked if I've been on holiday when I give my name and ask for the usual. 'No, no, just married,' I reply. 'Ahh,' comes the reply. 'Extra poppadums for you, sir.'

Step three: leave the flat and walk down the street to the curry house. It is the walk of a free man. Nelson Mandela had his Long Walk to Freedom. I have my Short Walk to Memories of Bengal. Put vegetables and leftover quiche (evidence) in bin between flat and curry house.

Step four: video store adjacent to curry house. To kill time while waiting for chicken madras ('hot like in the olden days, sir?'), nip in. Plan is to rent one film with explosions and car chases, but they have a Rent Two, Get One Free offer and it's only 7.45 p.m. So I rent two films with explosions and car chases and a PlayStation zombie shoot 'em up.

Step five: I have absolutely no idea how it got to 4 a.m. Still playing zombie shoot 'em up. Still haven't switched the light on. Have escaped the underworld prison and am in the zoo, fighting zombie elephants. Have finished all the beers and almost all the whisky. Definitely don't want any more to drink but because I am free, free as a bird, I have another one anyway.

Step six: room spin. I love Isabel so much. I love her. I love her. I love her. I don't want to be alone any more. This sofa is comfortable. I might just lie down for a minute before going to bed.

Saturday 9 July

Doorbell. Then, a second later, a key in the door. Then, another second later, Arthur Arsehole and two blond people (in trouser suits even though it's Saturday) standing in my living room. I am still lying in my living room in my clothes from yesterday. Shoes and everything. As I struggle to sit upright, I follow the trouser-suited gaze over beer cans, curry trays and other squalid bachelor detritus. From the look on their executively blond faces, it could have been tin foil, teaspoons and encrusted heroin resin. Or a leper colony.

I smile nervously.

They smile nervously.

I apologise.

They mutter no, no, noes.

Arthur Arsehole looks as furious as an estate agent can look.

The aroma of leftover madras and stale beer is not as effective a sales tool as freshly baked bread. Still, the blonds go through the motions: they point at our stainless-steel cooker hood, caress our heated towel rail and tape-measure our bedroom. Meanwhile, I struggle to tidy myself and my living room up.

It is as the church bells across the road ring a painful 10 a.m. that the shock of unexpected expected guests subsides enough for me to notice that I have a dreadful, dreadful hangover. Beer then wine, fine. Beer then whisky then beer then whisky then whisky, then beer, whisky, whisky, whisky, Drambuie, Pernod – not a chance.

The sudden onset of pain and nausea is almost unprecedented. My head throbs so alarmingly that I have to check to see if the throbbing is visible in a mirror. If I lie back on the sofa, it subsides slightly, but then comes the urge to vomit so I must sit up again. By the time the blonds return from their tour, I am considering gouging my own eyes out with the coffee spoon. As they mutter goodbyes, I stand up and try to apologise to them again. This sudden movement coincides with a full-frontal waft of Arsehole's aftershave, and I have no option but to retch. I throw up mostly in my mouth, a tiny bit on one of the trouser suits. They leave. I throw up again.

It takes three hours to recover enough to become mobile. During this time, I develop a surprisingly ferocious self-loathing. Without Isabel, I am a sad, lonely man who gets drunk pointlessly and still plays computer games at the age of twenty-nine and thirteen-fourteenths. I eat junk food and fail to ablute properly. If I was American, I would live in an Appalachian trailer park, shout 'Jerry, Jerry, Jerry' at the television and cultivate maggots in the folds of my stomach.

As I lie in a foetal position, clinging desperately to the base of the toilet, I hatch an extensive plan to restore my self-respect. The minute, the very minute, that I feel better, I shall shower and change and clean the flat and go for a run and write a letter to my godmother and start reading Dickens and go out and buy a present for my sister and change the Hoover bag and stick the bit that's fallen off my backgammon board back on.

Sadly, the very minute comes at the same time I remember I haven't watched the second movie. And a small voice says, 'Why don't you just watch the film, my precious? Isabel won't know. There's still time to tidy.' And then it says, 'Bloody Mary will help, my precious. Drinking in the daytime is good. Write letter to godmother another day, my precious. Play more computer. Play more. Play more.'

It's 4 p.m. and the doorbell goes again, and it's Arthur Arsehole, amazed that I'm still loitering, gobsmacked that the flat is still looking like a Glaswegian squat. He has in tow a nice couple who smile and introduce themselves. I stand and stumble on legs shot through with pins and needles. I offer a gnarled and clammy gamer's claw. They umm and aahh their way around the mess: 'Umm, you've reached level forty-seven. Aahh, we're not buying a flat from someone who drinks vodka in the daytime.'

Andy calls. He's back in the country. Am I free for a couple of beers? No, I explain through tears of anguish. I must stay in and tidy.

I stay in and play the zombie game. I am horrendous.

Sunday 10 July

Isabel returned today. We had a lovely evening watching her programmes and eating vegetables. I didn't even flinch when she mentioned that her mother had found a suitable house for us in her village. And that we could have a look at it on the way to Francesca's wedding next Saturday.

All I said was, 'But I thought you weren't sure about moving out of London just yet.'

And all she said was, 'I know, but it does look very spacious. And you're right about growing vegetables. It would be marvellous.'

And all I then said was, 'Okay, not a hundred per cent on your mum's village but worth having a look.'

And all she said, 'So how did the viewings go?'

And all I said was, 'Fine.'

THINGS I DON'T WANT TO BE DOING WHEN I'M 50

Playing PlayStation

Behaving like a bachelor in any way whatsoever

Wearing jeans

Waking up on a sofa at 3 a.m. in a dark room lit by a flickering TV

Wearing the same underpants two days running

Only ever eating anything green when someone forces me to.

Monday 11 July

Another bad start to another week. It was Isabel's turn to make breakfast, which means soggy cereal. What she does is go into the kitchen, get the bowls out, pour the cereal in, pour the milk in, then put the kettle on, wait for it to boil and make the tea. The proper way to do it is to go into the kitchen, put the kettle on, do whatever you like while you wait for it to boil *except pour the milk in*, and then, right at the end, pour the milk in.

I hate soggy cereal. She loves it.

When I complain, she gets angry: 'I've got up and made breakfast and brought it to you in bed and all you can do is complain.' When I say I'm only saying so for next time and that I hardly think it's worth enduring a lifetime of soggy cereal just to avoid a minor altercation, she says there isn't going to be a next time and that I can get my own damn breakfast.

Then, like a stupid wildebeest that climbs into the river right next to that big crocodile-shaped log, I say, 'You don't do toast right either.'

A flash of powerful jaws, a crunching death roll, a last desperate antelopian gasp for air and I'm dragged to my death in the Zambezi that is my marriage.

This seems unfair. I have, after all, been bent to Isabel's will on tea (goat's milk, no sugar) and baths (none, especially hot ones, except if she's in a good mood on a Friday). Surely I can lay down some rules on breakfast?

RECIPE FOR MARMITE TOAST

2 x slice of white bread, one day past sell-by date

Butter, must be pre-softened

Marmite

Place the bread in the toaster. Start the toaster. Get butter ready. Get Marmite ready. Get ready. The split second the toaster pops, *Go! Go! Go!* Semi-spread butter for both pieces on first piece, then place second piece on top of first piece to create bread furnace. Count to four. Remove second piece. Spread melted butter on both pieces. Then the Marmite: not too much, not too little. Race to bedroom and eat.

This whole process should take no more than twenty seconds. Your butter-knife movements must be Zorro-like. If there is any delay once the toast has popped, discard cold, hard, useless, horrible toast and repeat as above.

No sign of Sandra at work. Her desk is empty; her phone is in its cradle. I'm hoping the lamb was off.

Pub with Johnson and Andy for advice on toast stand-off.

Johnson understands the toast thing. He says Ali used to add fish sauce at the last minute to stir-fries so the whole thing tasted of the floor of a shabby fishmonger. When he finally plucked up the courage to complain, she came right back at him with overcooked poached eggs. In his defence, he said he couldn't stand any clear bits in an egg, not since Edwina Currie. She said a yolk had to be runny and she'd risk clear bits.

Then things began to snowball.

He said he liked the skin left on cucumber. She said she'd prefer her Sunday omelette with less cheese. He said capers don't go with chicken. She said oranges don't go with beef. He said that only happened because the butcher didn't have any duck. She said she didn't like pepperoni on her pizza. He said fine, we'll just have different pizzas. So she got a pen and a piece of paper.

By the end of the argument, Johnson and Ali had drawn up an extensive agreement to disagree and now prepared most meals separately. 'That's the secret to a happy marriage, mate. Negotiate hard, never give anything away for nothing in return, and don't whatever you do let them cross the line. My line was fish sauce. Yours is cold Marmite toast.'

Andy doesn't understand the toast thing. He is now in love and therefore spending the rest of his life with an ambassador's daughter who lives in Kenya. She is a vegetarian so he is a vegetarian too. Actually, the diet is very healthy. Actually, tofu isn't that bad at all. Actually, Andy feels a lot better since he became a vegetarian, yesterday. And no, he won't have any pork scratchings, thanks very much. '*That's* the secret to happy marriage. No red lines. Total harmony. Who cares if your Marmite toast is cold?'

Isabel is asleep when I get home. A note reads: 'Hi darling. Exhausted after yoga session. Arsehole left message: no luck with weekend viewings because of curry. What curry? Don't wake me. X'

It's the first time she's ever written me a 'Don't Wake Me' note.

Tuesday 12 July

Still no Sandra. Just the dull hum of computer radiation, the occasional squawk of the sandwich woman and the hammering and drilling of workmen in the office above. Thank the lord for the killer lamb.

Wednesday 13 July

Sandra has been found dead at home with a man called Barry. She had been poisoned. Police are treating the circumstances as suspicious. I know this because the police are waiting to interview me when I arrive at work. The managing editor summons me to his office where two men from CID eye me suspiciously.

'Routine inquiries at the moment, sir. You're not under caution. Apparently, you had a problem with this poor widow?'

'No, not really. She just rabbited on a lot.'

The one who isn't asking the questions writes something down in his notebook.

'And you were overheard making threats?'

'No, no, no, no, no, no, it was just because she was making such a meal out of the death of her goldfish.'

'Her goldfish?'

'Yes, she went on and on about it so much, I thought she was talking about her husband who I didn't know at the time was already dead and when it turned out all the fuss was about the goldfish, I just muttered something about how I was surprised it wasn't her husband. If I'd been her husband, I'd have killed myself by now. Or her. It was just a joke.'

Neither of them is laughing.

'Right, sir. That will be all for now. Not planning on leaving the country, are we, sir?'

Still not laughing. Isabel finds it funny though. CCs me in on a group email to all her friends headed, 'I married an axe-murderer.'

Thursday 14 July

'We've had a tip-off that you repeatedly expressed the desire to crush Sandra with furniture, sir.'

'I just said I wished a piano would fall on her head. It's different.'

'How is it different, sir?'

'Well, crushing someone with furniture is quite, well, serious, whereas wishing a piano would fall on someone's head is just, well, like a cartoon. And anyway, who told you that?'

'I'm not at liberty to divulge sources, sir. Can you tell me where you were at around 8.30 p.m. on Saturday night?'

'I was at home.'

'Alone, I suppose, sir?'

'Unusually, yes.'

'That's all for now, sir.'

Isabel says she might have told a few friends about the piano but only because she thought it was quite funny. And not when she knew Sandra was dead and that I was a suspect. Which she also found funny. But together, perhaps, she realises they might not be that funny. She is adamant that none of her friends would snitch. It's much more likely to be someone at the office: maybe the managing editor had a report about the piano death wish too? I'm not so adamant. Although no one sees it but me, Isabel does have one friend who has something to gain from getting me locked up for the rest of my life.

Friday 15 July

Toxicology results show it was the lamb that killed Sandra. A freak build-up of mercury. Total accident. No apology from the police who still can't accept that wishing someone might be squashed by a piano doesn't count.

Back from work, Isabel late at hers so, if I'm lucky, I have time for an illicit but well-earned hot bath and whisky. The least I deserve after being ruled out of a murder inquiry. I'm not lucky. The car has been stolen. The bath is obviously out of the question. Who would steal an M-reg Vauxhall Corsa with 89,892 miles on the clock? Why didn't they steal the BMW parked next to it? I call the police and it turns out Islington council has stolen it. I phone the number they give me.

'Car pound.'

'I think you have stolen my car.'

'Registration?'

'M-seven-three-nine DGH.'

'M?'

'M-seven-three-nine D —'

'M-seven …'

Ten minutes later …

'Yeah, mate, towed at half four.'

'On what grounds?'

Tap, tap, tap.

'Got a ticket at half three, dinnit.'

'On what grounds?'

Tap, tap, tap … I can tell he's typing with one finger.

'Yellar line, wunnit.'

'No, it was in a residential bay.'

'Sorry, mate, sez ere it was on a yella. Three inches on a yella to be precise.'

'But why did you tow it? You could have left it with a ticket.'

'Can't say no more than that, mate. If you have a problem wivit, you can appeal, but you'll have to pay double the charge.'

'What's the charge?'

Tap, tap, tap.

'Forty quid …'

Tap, tap, tap.

'… plus two-eighty for the tow.'

'Where is my car?'

Tap, tap, tap.

'Clifton Street, EC-one.'

'But that's miles away. That's in the city. Why'd you tow it all the way over there?'

'Wouldn't worry about it now, mate, it's closed till tomora.'

'But I'm going to a wedding tomorrow.'

'Shouldavethordabatthatwhenyaparkedonayellashouldnya?'

Saturday 16 July

I arrive at eight on the dot to collect the stolen car. I still have to wait for forty minutes in a waiting room full of people who all look as furious as me. Then, I pay a man behind a sensibly bullet-proofed glass partition surrounded by signs saying, 'We will not tolerate abuse of our staff.' He only accepts cash which means I get to see the huge amount of money I'm losing in the flesh. As I leave the building, I swear that from now on I will never be nice to traffic wardens ever again.

Went to look at the house in Isabel's parents' village on route to Francesca's wedding. We have all of five minutes because of the towing.

Pros: it is the same price as our tiny box but is a house, yes, a house, with three bedrooms, two bathrooms and, saints alive, a garden. We will be able to sit outside in real sunshine surrounded by real plants and real grass, breathing real air. It is also not in Finsbury Park: the biggest threat to personal safety will be a twisted ankle on the cobbled pavements. And you can park wherever you damn well like.

Cons: it is an hour's train from work but three minutes from the in-laws.

Probably best to wait till someone shows some interest in our flat before we decide to make an offer.

The wedding

This is the wedding of people we didn't invite to ours so I don't know why we have to go to theirs. Isabel's university friend Francesca, whom I've only met twice, is marrying Archie, a banker I've never met at all but who is friends with Alex so he must be an arse. Even if he isn't, I hate going to weddings where I don't know anyone. Worse still, both have recently rediscovered Jesus. Properly. They're not even just putting it on so they can get married in a church.

The service

Most weddings I've been to, mine included, are presided over by vicars harbouring resentment at the transient congregation. There is no such resentment from Reverend Adams. He knows Francesca and Archie: indeed, he was instrumental in their return to the flock. So he glows with pride and waxes lyrical: his vocation isn't pointless, there is a God. Two hours later, we escape. 1/10.

The meal

In an enormous marquee in the grounds of a castle. Clearly Christians don't have to renounce all worldly wealth. Food posh but horrible: overcooked lobster for starters; grey beans, grey beef, grey carrots, cold, all cold, for mains. Then profiteroles. I hate profiteroles.

Because we're C-list friends, we get the table with the vicar, his wife and four more of the vicar's flock. The wife is a pneumatic blonde who, as she explained even before we'd picked through the lobster, had been a porn star before meeting Roger. 'I was in a dark, dark place back then, but Roger and the Lord Jesus Christ found me and saved me, praise them both. Have you found the Lord, William?' There's nothing more unappetising at dinner than an ex-porn star trying to convert you. 4/10.

The speeches

A confessional approach taken by Archie, who regretted his time as a banker, regretted his wild ways at university, regretted turning away from God as a teenager, regretted pretty much anything and everything. Clearly someone had got to the best man: not a single inappropriate joke. 2/10.

The first dance

Robbie Williams again, courtesy of the chamber orchestra. Shoot me. 2/10.

TOTAL 9/40. Plus one for the fireworks.

Sunday 17 July

Alex sits next to me rather than Isabel at the wedding breakfast, no doubt to demonstrate how hard he is trying to get on with me despite my continued unreasonableness and his broken arm.

'How's the arm?'

'Much better.'

'Pretty quick, wasn't it?'

'What?'

'Well, the mending.'

'I took arnica – and it's still very sore.'

'Right.'

'So sorry about all that nastiness with the police.'

'It wasn't nastiness. It was just routine inquiries.'

'Listen, as soon as my arm's fully better, do you fancy playing squash?'

'Err, sure.'

'Is it safe, you two trying another sport?' asks Isabel.

'No chicanes in a squash court,' replies Alex, and we all laugh.

What a cock.

Tuesday 19 July

Guilt plus disgust today. Guilt because everyone in the office except me has been invited to Sandra's funeral. I have to stay and answer the phones. Disgust because a new survey has revealed that toilet seats in offices are twenty times cleaner than keyboards. Apparently, it would be more hygienic to eat your sandwich off the bog than off your desk. While I decided not to take this advice literally, I decided to eat my lunch in the park, assuming perhaps wrongly that a park is cleaner than a toilet. I don't know where this leaves the debate about which part of the toilet door handle is best to use.

Wednesday 20 July

This really is turning into another bad week.

'Hi, Will. Long time no speak. Can't believe you're not at *Cat World* any more. Who will taste the new rabbit flavour now you've gone? Anyway, New York is great but I'm coming back for a week in August. It gets so damned hot here. Even when I'm completely naked, I can't sleep. Wondered if you wanted to catch up on old times?'

How did Saskia, the Destroyer of Relationships, get my email address? Johnson just stares at the screen for about twenty minutes. Then he says don't reply. Then he says reply. Then he says, no don't reply. He keeps doing this for another twenty minutes. Because it is the perfect email dilemma. If I reply, I am communicating with the Destroyer of Relationships, which we both agree is a bad thing. If I don't reply, and shut it down, she might try to make further contact when she comes back to London.

I decide not to reply.

Thursday 21 July

No further emails from DofR so potentially in clear.

Might turn out to be a good week after all.

Except then Isabel calls to say Alex has finished with his Moroccan girlfriend. He needs a shoulder to cry on. Obviously it has to be Isabel's shoulder. Do I mind if she cancels our dinner?

'No, darling. I hope he's okay,' I hear myself lying.

Johnson has already left so I call Andy and endure a whole hour of pub time listening to how amazing his new life in Kenya will be before I can tell him about Saskia.

'Ignore it,' he advises before continuing on about Kenya for another hour until I can mention Alex.

'Listen, he's a nice guy. I like him.'

'What?'

'He's a nice guy, man.'

'You know you actually said "man" then?'

'Well, I think you should give him a break. You're obsessing about nothing. He's done all that stuff for your wedding, he invites us racing, you drive him off the road.'

'He was trying to kill me.'

'Of course he wasn't. You're the husband of his best friend. He loves you, man.'

'You said it again.'

'And now he's going through a difficult time. I know what heartbreak feels like, believe me. This life is a rollercoaster: there are highs as well as lows.'

'There are loop-the-loops?'

'There are loop-the-loops.'

'Jesus.'

This is how the conversation goes when she gets back (late) from the cocktail bar he chose to do his shoulder-crying in.

'Hi, darling.'

'You're late.'

'He was in a bad way, poor lamb. She meant a lot to him.'

Three things are incredibly irritating in just these two sentences. One: if he was in a bad way, why did he choose a romantic cocktail bar to be in a bad way in? Two: poor lamb? Why is she saying 'poor lamb'? It's only one step away from 'sweetheart'. Three: if the Moroccan girlfriend meant a lot to Alex, why did he dump her?

I go with the last point.

'If she meant a lot to him, why did he dump her?'

'Because he knew he wasn't right for her.'

'I'm sorry?'

'Because he knew he wasn't right for her.'

'You mean he knew she wasn't right for him?'

'No. She was right for him. He loved her but he knew she could find greater happiness with someone else. He released her.'

'That's one of the most ridiculous things I have ever heard. Are you drunk?'

'We did have quite a few cocktails. Great bar. I'm going to take you there.'

'I don't believe this.'

'Don't believe what?'

'This is ridiculous.'

'What's your problem?'

'My problem is Alex. He is a slimy sleaze-bag. He's got slimy hair and a slimy job and a slimy flat in a slimy street. He lives in Slimeville, County Slime, the United Kingdom of Slime. He dumped her because he's a philandering slime-bag, and he grassed me up to the police for a crime I didn't commit. He's a bastard.'

'Blimey. Is that all?'

'No, I don't trust him. I don't want you seeing him any more.'

It just came out like that and immediately I knew that I had crossed the line. I had issued a diktat. I should have stopped at slimy sleaze-bag. Or a bit before that. But I'd let it all build up for so long … and it had all come out in one misjudged rant. And ordering my wife not to see another man? That was proper Victorian stuff. I had pressed the red button, released the irreversible long-range missiles, dropped the hand grenade in the wrong hole. Why do arguments have a habit of doing that?

EXPLOSION. 'You don't trust him? What about trusting me?' Door slam. Silence except for the sound of a small voice in my head saying, 'You idiot, this isn't a soap opera. Why didn't you keep your mouth shut?'

Then the door opens again.

SPEECH. Along the lines of: 'William, I love you very much. You are the man of my dreams, the first person I can call my soul mate. But you are also a dickhead. Alex and I have been friends since we were kids. He has been generous and loving and supportive all my life. I know he has a habit of irritating anyone I'm having a relationship with, but he's also been there when I've been badly treated. And I've been there for him when he's been in trouble. He is a friend and I'm not going to get rid of him because of your paranoia. You need to stop trying to control me.'

To which I say something along the lines of, 'But you're trying to control me. You won't even let me have sugar in my tea.'

To which she shouts, 'Me controlling your tea is not the same as you controlling who I'm friends with.'

Another door slam.

The Marmite Argument was nothing. The Lost Passport Argument was a mere bagatelle. As a hairline crack cuts its way from the top of the door to the ceiling, I am left in the smoking aftermath of what I now realise was the First Really Proper Argument of My Marriage. And surprise, surprise, it was entirely Alex's fault. And maybe mine a bit as well.

Friday 22 July

Never go to sleep on an argument, said some blue-stockinged spinster who's obviously never had a proper late-night argument before. It is perfectly good advice if you have all your arguments in the morning. With a 10 a.m. argument, there's plenty of time to huff about, cool off, apologise a thousand times, buy flowers (no carnations, no roses), make a self-deprecating joke, then apologise another thousand times and be back in the good books before bedtime.

With an 11 p.m. argument, there simply isn't time. Isabel and I just lay there in moonlit silence, me wishing I hadn't said the bit about the not trusting, her probably plotting divorce and elopement. The only ice-breaking option I had was the pretend half-asleep roll to leave one of my arms draping over one of her arms. When I tried it, it was parried with the classic half-asleep cold shoulder. In the same manoeuvre, I lost any hope of same-day reconciliation and the duvet.

This morning, she left without speaking to me, which is a first. So I decide I would have left without speaking to her if I'd had the chance and storm off to work, collecting a really sugary latte on the way in.

Johnson still thinks Alex is evil, even if Andy has fallen for his lies. 'You did the right thing.'

'Yeah.'

'He's a smarmy bastard.'

'Yeah.'

'He's the sort of person that gives men a bad name.'

'Yeah.'

'I told you marriage was a nightmare.'

Hang on.

So then there's another email from Saskia.

'Hi, sweetie. Have I got the right email address or is this some other big Willy? Would be great to hear from you, even if you're the wrong William. I need an Englishman again, after all these Yanks. Only joking. Can't wait to catch up.'

And I'm all upset and confused and irrational so, without thinking, I type, 'Sorry, been away. How are ya?'

And without thinking, I hit send.

And with thinking, I try to stop it by closing my email, switching my computer off, throwing the keyboard in the bin, hiding the bin under the desk, closing my eyes tightly, praying a bit. But it is too late: I have made contact with the Destroyer.

'Ahhh, there you are! Missed you. What are you wearing? Guess what I'm wearing?'

I email Isabel, wanting everything to be all right again. No answer. I call her on her mobile. No answer. I get home and my cheery greeting goes unanswered. She's cooking angrily. I feel sorry for the shitake mushrooms which are being diced to smithereens.

The situation is grave. I have expressly forbidden her to talk to her best friend who at least one of my two best friends thinks is a really nice guy. I have also struck up an online relationship with the floozy from New York who never wears knickers, and always insists on telling me that.

I must regain control of things before some irreparable damage is done. I have no option but to employ the fake injury trick.

The fake injury trick

Origin: Tibet. Twelfth century. A closely guarded secret passed down through the ages to those chosen few ready for the knowledge. The process is simple: pretend to injure yourself, lie there in agony and wait for the angry woman to abandon the stony silence and come to your rescue. But it only works if used sparingly and performed convincingly. If you are not a good actor, it may be safer to do yourself real harm. Injuries, fake or otherwise, must be eye-watering. E.g. bad toe-stubbing, banging of head on a kitchen cupboard corner, standing barefoot on a drawing pin, falling down stairs (then, if argument is serious enough, lying motionless).

I fall down the stairs between the living room and the kitchen. Isabel stops castrating the courgettes and runs to my aid, helps me to the sofa, makes me a cup of tea and, as soon as I'm focused enough to speak again, listens to my pained, gasping apology. I trust her, I say. She's the most special person in the world, I say. I know Alex is just a good friend, I say. And I hope his Moroccan ex-girlfriend sets her Moroccan older brothers on him, I think.

I am forgiven. More than that, Isabel apologises back. She knows I don't like Alex but he's been a friend of hers for years. Still, she probably overreacted.

Have actually injured myself. Very sore neck. Possible break?

Monday 25 July

Ignore another email from Saskia even though the cocktail bar Alex took Isabel to has come top in the *Evening Standard*'s poll of London's sexiest bars. 'Want to guarantee your hot date becomes a hot night of passion?' says the review. 'Then go to Alto with its seductive sofas, its smoochy lighting and its naughty, naughty cocktails. It'll be "coming in for a coffee?" guaranteed.' Won't mention to Isabel but can't believe she can't see what Mr Super-Transparent Slime-bag Shithead is up to.

Neck is not getting better. Think it would have been better to still be in Isabel's bad books.

Tuesday 26 July

Called into managing editor's office: pay rise is being revoked due to budget cuts and the recent poor staff relations. I tell the managing editor to stick his job and stick his pay rise and stick his staff relations. But only in my head. Can't believe how rubbish work is at the moment. At least on *Cat World* we didn't have people dropping dead and other people blaming me.

Not only that, I'm a month shy of thirty and I'm an old man with a twisted neck. I have a small pot-belly, like an anaconda that's just swallowed a quail. My hair, famously thick throughout my twenties, is starting to thin a little, I'm sure of it, around my temples. I still don't have hair on my back but it can only be a matter of time.

Not only that, Saskia has sent another email and I stupidly respond.

'Great to hear from you. Life after *Cat World* is great. I'm married. I'm very, very happy. I'm moving to the country to grow vegetables and maybe keep a Vietnamese pot-bellied pig.'

She replies immediately. 'That doesn't sound like the naughty William I knew. Sounds like I need to come back and get the party started again. Before suburban married life destroys you.'

'Hahahahahaha,' I reply. 'Unfortunately, I'm away that week.'

'Where?'

'On assignment.'

'Where?'

'East Timor.'

'Why?'

'Orchids.'

'What?'

'They've found some orchids that eat snakes in the jungles of East Timor. I'm going to investigate them.'

'How marvellous. Can't wait to read all about it.'

My editor says I can't go to East Timor to make up a story about snake-eating orchids. Why did I ever reply in the first place? Idiot.

Wednesday 27 July

Neck worse, if that's possible. The pain has spread down my spine so I can no longer bend at all. Getting dressed is agony, can hardly brush teeth, and Isabel leaves before I put my shoes on so I have to force my feet in without undoing the shoelaces so the backs are all rucked and uncomfortable all the way to work. No one stands up to give me their seat on the Tube.

Thoroughly regret throwing myself down the stairs. It's all Alex's fault, and I don't care what Isabel says. Everything is shit.

Thursday 28 July

On the advice of Johnson, I have been lying on various frozen vegetables all night. We have everything except peas. I'm eating Nurofen by the pound and I've applied so much Deep Heat that I glow in the dark.

Last night, Astrid, Isabel's yoga teacher, recommended an osteopath. Apparently, they are better than physiotherapists because they've been to a proper osteopathy school for four years. And Astrid's one is part-osteopath, part-faith healer. Astrid has told Isabel to tell me to pay attention to his hands – they will become incredibly hot when he's treating me. Oh good.

I book an emergency appointment. His name is Serge and he speaks so softly I can hardly hear anything he's saying.

After noting down my history ('I sit in front of a computer for nine hours a day and I don't go to the gym'), sage-like nods and tuts throughout, he whispers: 'Can you take your shirt and trousers off?' Before I know it, I'm standing in my underpants being held from behind by a man called Serge. Serge is still whispering in my ear: 'Turn your neck to the right, move forward from the waist, touch your toes, gyrate your hips. Does it hurt when I do this?' I wish he would stop whispering.

After a long hold of my hips, he tells me to lie down on his bed. I lie down and he just holds me for what seems like ages because it is ages, his hands around my back, rocking me back and forth gently, whispering sweet nothings in my ear. His hands are very warm. I feel as if I should be wearing a nappy.

The prognosis isn't good: according to Serge, falling down the stairs was my body's way of telling me that my head is too large for my weakened neck muscles. Serge says I have to go to the gym and do lots of neck-strengthening exercises or by the time I'm forty, my head will just flap around like a throttled chicken's. Before I go to the gym, though, I have to see Serge a couple more times. He needs to do some more semi-naked holding. I hand over my £40, borrow a neck brace and waddle away.

'How was Serge?' asks Isabel when she gets back from yoga. 'Did his hands get warm?'

'I don't want to talk about it,' I reply. Some things are best kept bottled up.

Friday 29 July

No one at work can understand why I had to take my trousers off for Serge. At least I seem to have been forgiven for the whole Sandra debacle.

Saturday 30 July

Lunch at the in-laws' so Isabel and I can have another sneak look at the house we might buy. I like her parents, I really do, but the stiff-upper-lipped-English-medical-Polish combo makes lunches a minefield.

'How's married life, dear boy? Busy working on getting me some grandchildren?'

'Now, darlink, don't pressure them. Isabel is still recovering from her swollen labium majus. How is everything down there, darlink?'

'Stuff and nonsense, dear. There are just two reasons people get married these days: first, to get a nice new set of saucepans, and second, to have kids. It's not so they can have sex and move in together. They're already doing all that long before they get married. Jumping into bed before they've even been properly introduced. Isn't that true, William?'

This incredibly inappropriate and largely unanswerable line of questioning stretches across the equally unpalatable main course: cabbage stuffed with cabbage on a bed of cabbage. To not clean your plate is not an option ('My boy, we wouldn't have won the war if we were a nation of fussy eaters, would we?'), and to not have seconds is downright heretical ('My darlink, you are skin and bones with a big head and no neck muscles. You must have more, my darlink, so you have strength like a good Polish farmer').

But it is only when the strudel arrives that things really take a turn for the worse.

'So Alex is alone again, my darlink. Such a lovely boy. So polite. And with such a good appetite. Of all your friends, he was the best eater.'

'Yes, good chap, Alex. Doing very well, isn't he? Architecture, now that's a proper, respectable job. He's just done Sting's Moroccan garden, you know? Big job that. And he knows how to shake your hand and look you in the eye.'

'And he adored you, didn't he, my darlink? One little kiss and he was around here with flowers and chocolates every day for a week.'

I look at Isabel. Isabel looks at me.

This is something of a revelation.

Pretty Woman. Julia Roberts won't kiss Richard Gere. She'll have sex with him repeatedly but she won't kiss him. Why? Because kissing is more intimate. Now it's hardly sensible to take a view based on a slushy Hollywood movie, but what does one little kiss mean exactly? Isabel might have explained it as one little kiss to her parents, but that probably means you have to add on a couple of bases to get to the murky truth.

Did they use tongues?

Did he squeeze her bottom?

Did he touch her breasts?

How could she have let him touch her breasts?

How could I have married someone who let him touch her breasts?

Why didn't she tell me?

Why hadn't I guessed?

How much longer do I have to sit here looking through my father-in-law's Japanese theatre programme collection before I can get some answers?

On the way home, Isabel answers my questions without me having to ask them. 'It was during a summer vacation. We snogged. He was keen to make something of it. I was going out with Chris. And that was it. I didn't tell you because you already behave like a child whenever he's around and this was so long ago, it's irrelevant.'

No, no, no, no, no, no, no, no.

Sunday 31 July

Back to Serge for a special Sunday appointment. He dims the lights seductively as I step into his office. 'I've missed you. It's been so long. Take off your clothes off and hop into bed.'

After another £40 and another thirty minutes being held semi-naked by a man called Serge, it emerges that my neck is on the mend but I now have new stress in my shoulders. That'll be because the woman I love has kissed the man I hate. I don't bloody care how bloody long a-bloody-go it bloody was.

Isabel can't understand why an osteopath would have a dimmer switch in his surgery or why he'd see one patient specially on a Sunday. I haven't mentioned Alex since yesterday's revelation and nor has she. At the pub, Andy suggests calm, caution and perspective. Johnson suggests a campaign of violence and intimidation. 'Let's warn him off. If he doesn't get the message, we'll kneecap him.'

AUGUST

'Husbands ought to love their wives as their own bodies. He who loves his wife loves himself. After all, no one ever hated his own body, but he feeds and cares for it … For this reason a man will leave his father and mother and be united to his wife, and the two will become one flesh.'

The Holy Bible, New International Version, *Epistle to the Ephesians 5:25–33*

Monday 1 August

REASONS TO BE HAPPY

I've been married for three months. What I've lost in hot baths and tea with sugar, I've gained in Isabel being a permanent part of my life. I have someone living in the same flat as me who cares about everything I do.

A girl who finds my jokes funny is now sitting where the sadly deceased Sandra sat.

Assaults on traffic wardens in London have risen by 17 per cent in the last year. According to council statistics, every traffic warden can expect to be attacked an average of 2.2 times per twelve-month period.

REASONS TO BE UNHAPPY

I have a pot-belly and I'm not even thirty.

Either I've become a jealous and overprotective husband with an irrational suspicion of my wife's male friends, or I've been right all along and one of her male friends – who snogged her – is trying to steal her off me.

And he still hasn't forgotten about the game of bloody squash.

And Saskia, the Destroyer of Relationships, is going to be in London for a whole week because, even when she's naked, New York is too hot for her. There are only ten million people in London to hide behind when she arrives because I told her I'm in East Timor.

Serge says we're going to have to see each other more regularly.

Arthur the Total Arsehole calls Isabel (he doesn't call me any more – I have succeeded in the impossible; I have pissed off an estate agent) to explain that August is a particularly slow month for selling flats, even if the flats have cooker hoods. We may grow old or die trying in Finsbury Park.

Pinch, punch, join a gym. Only by building up my neck muscles can I end my relationship with Serge. Only by becoming fit can I beat Alex at squash, since he is a squash player and I am a tennis player. Except I'm not even a tennis player, that's just what non-squash players tell squash players to make themselves feel better.

The gym nearest us is called Iron Man and was the scene of a drive-by shooting in January, so I jog to the next nearest which is called Avocado but is almost two miles away. I arrive exhausted and consider turning around and going home again. Then I think of Serge and step inside. There is a fruit basket in reception, TV screens in front of the treadmills and a woman called Denise dressed head to toe in Lycra. Her arms are crossed, her back is rigid, her legs are apart: if she was wearing a tiara, she would be Wonder Woman. I haven't even got fully through the door and she is explaining her determination to revolutionise the way my body works for me.

As she measures my vitals, she asks a few lifestyle questions. Despite being about nineteen, she is, with the annoying use of first-person plural, patronising in a way only people who work in gyms can be.

'Now, Will. How much do we drink?'

'Not as much as we used to. Say, a couple of glasses of wine a night, more at the weekend.'

'… Mmm, right … we're a heavy drinker. Let's bend forward and breathe into this, there's a good boy. And what about our diet, William? Do we eat a lot of dairy?'

'Well, I have goat's milk in my tea.'

'Hardly going to keep our arteries unblocked now, is it, Will? But it's a start, I suppose. Hold out our right arm. Good. What about exercise?'

'Well, I'm joining a gym, aren't I?'

While she fills in my induction form, she mutters and shakes her head gravely. While she makes me run for ten minutes on the treadmill, she looks off into the mid-distance as if pondering the recent expected but nonetheless tragic death of a close relative. While she takes my final pulse readings, she adopts the resigned expression of someone who knows they are fighting for the greater good, but that the fight is futile in a world full of people who just don't know what is best for them.

It appears that if I don't radically alter the way I'm going with my life, I will be dead within the year, obese in two and impotent before I hit thirty-five. I sign up for a month – 'No, I don't want to waive the joining fee by signing up for a year. I don't expect to be here in a year.' 'Oh, it's not quite that bad, William.' 'No, I mean here in Finsbury Park' – and start the long jog home.

Denise wants 'us' back on Thursday to begin to take action to stop the rot to turn 'our' clock back to a new beginning.

Wednesday 3 August

I'm not sure we're having enough sex. Think it might be a blip – my sore back hasn't helped. Nor has the stupid arguing about Alex. But this is all the stuff of blips rather than trends. But what if it's a trend rather than a blip?

Thursday 4 August

It's just a blip. I'm sure it's a blip.

Gym. I could feel my muscles actually doing some work. On Denise's advice, I only did a low-impact workout. We need to build a foundation, she says. We need to reset our body, undo the damage, then launch into a hyperbolic curve of fitness and win the battle against self-loathing. Which sounds positive.

Shall go to the gym at least three times a week.

Friday 5 August

It's not a blip. It's a trend. Oh God. We have definitely gone down a notch. It's not a big notch but it's a notch. We have gone from having sex once every two days to having it twice every week and once during the weekend, which means we've dropped from a 50 per cent probability of copulation each night to 42.86 per cent. If the weekend sex is skipped, as it was last weekend, then the percentage drops to just 28.57 per cent.

When we started going out, the probability was in the high nineties. On one particular night, it was 200 per cent, if you count the next morning. Two hundred per cent to 28.57 per cent in a few short months. If this is a trend and not a blip, then we will be sleeping in separate beds before the year is out.

Will go to the gym tomorrow.

Monday 8 August

It's a blip.

Gym quite tiring. Couldn't stop yawning on the rowing machine. Denise says it's our body's way of getting extra oxygen but we think it's because we're knackered from all the rampant sex. Hoorah.

Tuesday 9 August

A date has been set for my squash match with Alex. On the plus side, Isabel is delighted that we're 'getting on'. On the minus side, we aren't. This is just another one of his schemes to make me look stupid.

Johnson says I have to beat him – my reputation as a man depends on it. Andy says I should take a chill pill. This is the perfect chance to let bygones be bygones.

Wednesday 10 August

Serge says that although my neck doesn't hurt any more, I should keep seeing him just a couple more times to ensure that everything has settled down. The subtle movements Isabel says Astrid says he'll be making to realign my spine have become so subtle, I'm not sure there are any. He may just be holding me now.

Had a terrible nightmare. Serge isn't an osteopath at all. He went to osteopathy school but was thrown out after a late-night experiment pushing the boundaries of osteopathy to the limit went very wrong. In the intervening years, his grudge against the world of osteopathy has developed into full-blown hatred. He has become a serial killer who only kills men whose spines are perfectly aligned. The plastic skeleton in his office that he uses to show new 'patients' how vertebrae work is not plastic at all. It's the skeleton of his last victim, replaced each time he kills again. In my nightmare, I work all this out while he's holding me – that this isn't a surgery, it's a cellar, that the skeleton in the corner has hair, that the diploma on the wall has another man's name crossed out with the word Serge scrawled angrily above it in blood. I try to get up and escape, but my legs don't work. So I try to grapple him off, but he just presses something in my neck and my arms fall useless to my sides. Whispering calm osteopathic clichés – 'keep your back straight, don't arch it', 'there's no quick fix when it comes to bones', 'breathe in, and hold, and breathe out' – he produces a surgeon's scalpel and starts his serial killer's work at my feet.

Saturday 13 August

That's it. It's all over. It's definitely a trend. This morning, I passed up a perfectly decent opportunity to have sex. I hopped out of bed at an ungodly 8 a.m., said something terribly middle-aged like, 'Come on, darling, it's the best part of the day', and bounced off to the kitchen to do the washing up. Last night, I couldn't be bothered to do it – sex, that is, not the washing up, although that as well – because it was too hot. Eight days until I'm thirty and I'm now regularly passing up opportunities to have sex. And I'm the man. Men are supposed to want it all the time. The average red-blooded heterosexual male thinks about sex every two or three milliseconds. Isabel hasn't started coming up with excuses.

It's me.

Maybe I'm not red-blooded? Maybe I'm yellow-belly-blooded? My libido is in free fall.

When I confess to Isabel, she doesn't bat an eyelid. She says it's a cliché that men always want sex and women never do. It's just something people write in sitcoms.

'But we used to have sex every day.'

'Only for about a week.'

'Well, we used to have sex every other day then.'

'It's probably only a blip.'

'I think it's a trend.'

In her experience, men never want sex as much as women, particularly when they get older. This is, on the one hand, disgusting because I don't want to have to think about Isabel's experience with other men ever, particularly older ones. On the other hand, it is reassuring. Why else would they have invented Viagra? The older we get, the more support we need.

Monday 15 August

Saskia's flight landed this morning. I'm in Finsbury Park, not East Timor. Knowing my luck, I will bump into her, so when Isabel and I walk to the Tube, I suggest we take an alternative route through the park. Just because I fancy a nice stroll with her.

I refuse to have lunch outside the office.

I refuse to go to the pub with Johnson, even though he's having an argument with Ali about which day they should have fish and chips, and which day they should have curry.

I sneak home via the park again. Tomorrow, definitely wearing sunglasses and a beanie.

Tuesday 16 August

I've told Serge it's all over, this has to stop, we can't go on like this. It's not him, it's me. We're just not right for each other. We both need to move on. And besides, £40 half-hours really start to add up. He takes it well. I am allowed to leave his cellar without being skinned alive and turned into an osteopath's dummy.

Can't be bothered to go to the gym. My neck feels fine, I need to keep my energy up for sex and tomorrow's squash match and I'm depressed anyway because of the sixteen people invited to my birthday dinner party on Saturday, only four can come. And the more I'm out on the streets, the more I risk running into the Destroyer of Relationships. And I am, to all intents and purposes, thirty. I am unpopular, I live in an unsellable flat, I have a low sex drive.

Wednesday 17 August

Phone rings. Unlisted phone number. Don't answer it. Isabel asks why I'm ignoring my phone. I say it's a work thing. I'm lying to my wife about another woman calling me.

It wasn't Saskia, it was Denise from the gym. 'Is William being a naughty boy?'

She is as annoying as Saskia.

'Six days, William, six days. We've got off to such a good start. We need to keep it up, William. Self-loathing might be winning the battle, but let's not let it win the war.'

I obviously forgot to tick the box on my joining form to say I didn't want to be contacted by carefully selected associate companies or patronising fitness instructors.

Alex is already on the court when I arrive. He gives me one of his nine racquets and we start rallying. He's all chatty and matey, but also quite I've-hardly-played-at-all-this-year-what-with-the-broken-arm, and I'm all I-haven't-played-for-three-years, so he's all yes-but-my-arm-still-really-hurts.

The stupid ball doesn't bounce and it's really hot so he wins the first game to love. Except, as he points out patronisingly, you don't say love in squash.

He wins the next game to love as well, despite complaining about his stupid arm. Then he suggests we rally a bit. I feel like I'm going to be sick, mainly because my tall, gangly physique is clearly not suited to this squitty little game. So I agree.

We rally.

Then he says, can I offer you a few suggestions?

And I say no, piss off, in my head, but yes, that would be great, I am a tennis player, to his face.

He says I need to take the racquet up and back much earlier, I need to face the side not the front, I must never step in that triangle or that triangle and I must watch him as well as the ball.

After that, I can't even rally any more. He laughs encouragingly so I suggest we play one more game. While I'm trying to remember all the patronising things he has told me in his pretence of being friendly, I lose the first six points quite quickly. Then he sniggers. Then I take a mad, exhausted swipe at another horrible ball from him, lose control of the racquet and hit him square on the jaw.

He yelps, falls to the floor and spits out half a tooth.

'Sorry about that.'

It takes the rest of the evening to convince Isabel that it was an accident.

Thursday 18 August

Wearing a mac and a trilby hat, I take the circuitous route to the gym. Denise gives another stirring speech to her troop. Come on now, we really must put the time in, mustn't we? A little effort now will save a lot of pain later. It's the posh London gym equivalent of the sergeant major's, 'Right, you horrible little piece of filth on the bottom of my boot. Drop and give me twenty.'

More yawning on the rowing machine and on the treadmill. When Denise isn't looking, I hop onto the edges and let the bloody thing run itself. I'm grateful and everything but I don't see why she has to bully 'us' and only 'us'. Why can't she bully the fat bloke, the horrible sweaty fat bloke who is always one machine ahead of me on the circuit? The fat bloke who doesn't wipe away his sweat properly because there's so much of it. He's hardly trying at all and I can hardly grip anything he's been on because it's all moist.

Friday 19 August

Isabel meets me at work unexpectedly and behaves quite erratically. She wants to take me out for a pre-birthday drink. I say we have to go home and clean the flat, ready for the four people who were bothering to turn up to the world's least-attended thirtieth. She says to hell with it, we're going for a drink.

We have to go to a bar in Soho. One where we used to go when we couldn't stop snogging each other. One where Saskia and I used to go because it had a hidden downstairs bit. It is the last place I want to be. Saskia is bound to strut in any minute. I contemplate coming clean to Isabel, given the fact that I haven't actually done anything wrong, but she's in such a good mood, and she's obviously more excited about my wretched birthday than I am. So I don't. I continue to live the lie.

Then, halfway through the drink in the bar I don't want to be in, Isabel receives a mysterious mobile call, won't say who it is, then says we have to go home, she's not feeling well. No, we can't finish our drink. We have to go now. Right now. Then she takes another call as we're on the way to the Tube, mutters something to whoever it is, tells me it's her mum, then says she's feeling better, let's go for another drink.

As soon as I've battled to the bar of some horribly busy it's-a-Friday-night pub, established it is Saskia-free, got drinks and settled down, Isabel says she's feeling unwell again.

Period pain.

Before I can protest, we are on the Tube; then we're run-walking through Finsbury Park. If I slow down, Isabel says hurry up. When I say I'm not going any faster and that if she's feeling unwell, shouldn't we take it a bit easier, she says she's got diarrhoea, which makes me have Vietnam-style flashbacks to the honeymoon. So now we're sprinting down our road, making a big scene, and I'm carrying all the bags so Isabel can get the key ready. I don't know why she couldn't have gone to the toilet in the pub and I don't know why I have to run as well. When we reach the flat, Isabel opens the outside door and stops.

'You go first,' she says. 'I've got a stone in my shoe.'

'But I thought you were about to explode,' I reply, hot and bothered, as I push past her and climb up the stairs. While I fumble for the key to the door of the flat in the pitch darkness of the upstairs landing, Isabel is standing in the hall not looking very unwell at all. I'm weighed down by her ridiculously heavy work bag and she's just standing by the light switch that quite clearly needs flicking on while I scratch away at the paintwork on the door with a key that I can't be sure is the right one because it's so dark. And that's when I snap.

'Turn the light on, you stupid cow,' I shout in a flash of fury brought on by a freak combination of alcohol, exhaustion, Saskia-related stress and eve-of-thirtieth depression. This is easily the worst thing I've ever shouted at Isabel. I'm not the sort of person that calls people stupid cows, not to their faces anyway. And never Isabel, woman of my dreams, etc, etc. It was just a sudden, uncharacteristic verbal splurge, never to be repeated.

So it's a shame that, in the same second the blasphemy comes out, the key finds the keyhole, the door swings open and I step into a room full of friends standing motionless, clutching party poppers.

'Happy birthday!' they all shout, their faces etched with My God We Didn't Know He Was a Wife-Beater horror. Half-heartedly, someone blows a party whistle. Hoorah, I am popular after all. Or at least I was.

Saturday 20 August

Thirty, thirty, thirty. Sod it.

Mum called, as she does every year, at 7.04 a.m. and tells me her birth story.

'This time thirty years ago, I was lying prostrate … thirty-eight hours of agony … a student doctor … epidural headache … forceps weren't big enough for your head … came out sideways … your father thought he had a brain-damaged wife and a mongrel for a son …'

Isabel wakes while I'm on the phone and scrawls on a piece of paper, 'I want you packed and ready to leave in one hour.' So I stop Mum mid-sentence and follow Isabel through to the kitchen, the full impact of my 'stupid cow' faux pas sinking in only now. But it turns out she's coming with me … on my surprise weekend away. The 'stupid cow' thing is long forgotten, silly me. She is so great.

Two hours later we're in a traffic jam crawling south but it's okay because this is all part of the surprise weekend and at least we're out of London and away from Saskia and I'm determined not to spoil it.

It's a furnace-hot August day and, now that we're in the country, the overpopulated stinking metropolis well behind us, even the fact that I am thirty isn't bothering me. Thirty is nothing. Barely even started. Decades and decades to go.

Now we're in Sussex, driving up a drive so long and well-weeded, I thank my stars I did go for chinos rather than jeans, even though that's something someone in their thirties not their twenties would do. Isabel parks us between a Jaguar and a Bentley in the car park of the very beautiful Bailiffscourt, country house hotel, spa and highly suitable venue for the start of my new decade. This is perfect, I think, as a man unloads the boot of our Corsa without the slightest hint of disapproval.

Champagne waiting in the room – nice. Open fireplace – unnecessary but nice. Peacocks outside the window – also unnecessary but nice. Four-poster bed – marvellous. What could possibly spoil the perfect birthday?

'My God, this is a coincidence.'

And there it was, the only thing worse than Saskia, the only thing that could ruin the perfect birthday. Alex, sitting alone in the corner of the restaurant, about to tuck into his *amuse-bouche*.

'What are you doing here?' spluttered Isabel. Even she was shocked.

Yes, what are you doing here, alone, in a romantic country house hotel on exactly the same night we're here?

'I read about the place in the *Guardian* a few weeks ago. Thought it sounded romantic. Booked it as a treat for Monica, then' – pause for effect – 'everything, as you know, went' – sniff for effect – 'wrong. Seemed a shame to let the weekend go to waste so

I came down on my own.' He looks even more pathetic with his bruised cheek and his missing bit of tooth.

'Couldn't you have cancelled and got a refund?' I asked, and for a moment, I saw a flicker of confusion in his eyes. Like he hadn't thought through every plot hole in his premeditated tale of woe.

'I've been in such a mess over this whole break-up, I clean forgot to call until Thursday, by which time I could only get a fifty per cent refund.'

Damn he was good. So good he actually gives me a smirking grin while Isabel is stepping out of the way of a waiter.

'Anyway, why are you here, guys?' The smirk vanishes as quickly as it appeared.

'Because it's William's birthday. Surely I must have mentioned it?'

Yes, you maniac, because it's my birthday, as you very well knew. And Isabel is taking me away for a quiet, romantic weekend, which you also very well knew, you evil psycho-stalker.

'Happy birthday, William. Now look, your table's ready. Don't let me get in the way of your evening. You might attack me with my own squash racquet again.'

'Hahahahahaha. Fine, see you later.'

And it all would have been fine, extremely weird but fine, if we'd left it there. Except, as we make our way across the restaurant, Isabel whispers to me about getting Alex to join us at our table. I whisper no way and she says she knows, she really does, but this has happened, it's a bad coincidence and now we can't really sit at tables on opposite sides of a room ignoring each other, can we? Even if it does mean ruining our romantic meal.

[Yes we can yes we can yes we can yes we can yes we can yes we can yes we can yes we can can can can can can can can.]

'No, I suppose not.' And then I have to get up and ask Alex if he'll join us.

'Oh, I couldn't.'

'You must.'

'I couldn't.'

Well, don't then. Just fuck off back to London.

'You must.'

'Oh, all right then. But I'm ordering champagne.'

Two's company, three is a complete and utter disaster. And guess who coincidentally had the same slot booked in the spa the next morning.

'I couldn't.'

'You must.'

'I couldn't.'

Well, you're bloody going to anyway, aren't you?

I decide the journey back to the stinking, overpopulated metropolis is the right time to mention what's been on my mind for the last week.

'What exactly does "a kiss" mean in relation to Alex?'

'A kiss,' she replies after a lot of theatrical eye-rolling.

'Oh, come on. That's what you told your mum. No one ever tells their mum the truth.'

'This is ridiculous,' she says, stalling. 'Can we not talk about Alex any more this weekend? I've had enough of him.'

'Believe me, you're not the only one. But tell me, I won't mind,' I say, lying.

'It was ten years ago. You really don't need to go on about this,' she says, still stalling.

'Look, I want to know what happened. I'm not going to go on about it.'

'It was a kiss.'

'With tongues?'

'I can't remember.'

'Did he touch your breasts?'

'The traffic light's green.'

'Did he touch your breasts?'

'I can't remember. Go, it's green.'

'Bra or no bra?'

'No bra.'

Monday 22 August

'How was East Timor?'

'Hot.'

'Not as hot as New York. I've found that if I cover myself in baby oil and stand right next to the fan, I stop getting all steamed up. But only for a minute. It's just sizzling over here.'

'I thought you were back in London.'

'Had to cancel. Work. Men. Thinking of moving back at some point though.'

'Great.'

'Really?'

You see, that's why she's the Destroyer of Relationships. She twists everything into innuendo. And always turns perfectly innocent expressions such as 'great' into something more … intimate.

Wednesday 24 August

The tension in the Walker household has been palpable since our return. She doesn't find it funny when, every time I open a cupboard, I shout, 'Ohmygod Alex, what a marvellous surprise. Why don't you join us for dinner or breakfast or how about full sex? Why don't we just all get married and spend the rest of our lives together?' I don't find it funny when she keeps reminding me

I called her a stupid cow, which I thought we'd agreed we'd forgotten.

In other crises, I have four missed calls from Denise at Avocado, but I don't care – I'm allowed a week off for my birthday. And the strange couple who live below us have put their flat on the market as well. It's bigger than ours and they're asking less. And they're with Foxtons, all branded Mini Coopers, virtual tours online and ten viewings a minute. We're still stuck with Arthur Arsehole. We don't stand a chance.

Sunday 28 August

The phone rang off when I answered it this morning. Either a wrong number who couldn't be bothered to apologise or a stalker who once fondled my wife.

Tuesday 30 August

Force myself to go to the gym but my heart's not in it. The sweaty fat guy is pushing himself so preposterously hard that he's leaving whole bits of himself on the machines. I tell Denise that I think he's pushing himself too hard and she tells me to stop transferring my own inadequacies onto others. 'Now get back on that running machine and do twenty minutes at four per cent incline and seven miles per hour.'

I feel really inadequate for the rest of the evening.

Wednesday 31 August

Emergency pub session. Johnson helpfully explains that a first-base kiss to parents is a second-base breast-fondling to the husband which is a third-base groping in reality. Andy says I should stop asking questions and behave like a grown-up. Isabel loves me, not Alex, but the more I behave like I don't trust her, the more likely she is to run off with Alex.

Until then, I hadn't actually considered the running-off possibility. Andy says, 'Well, he's a nice guy. He's not neurotic like you, my friend. And you've broken his arm and his tooth in the last two months alone. Isn't that enough hostility for now?'

Then he tells me to take a leaf out of his own highly researched book on the opposite sex and trust them. He's now planning to move to Geneva with a girl he met last week in Liberia. She's the one, although he doesn't speak French and she doesn't speak English and they've only communicated their undying love through sign language. Trust, he says, is the fertiliser upon which love grows.

I tell Andy to go stuff himself. I've never done that before.

SEPTEMBER

'My advice for any newlyweds is stick at it, you will always have the snags but use a bit of sense!'

Gladys Mott, 81
on celebrating her diamond wedding anniversary
with husband Percy, 90, as reported in the
Lancashire Evening Telegraph, 12 August 1999

Thursday 1 September

Denise was right: I am transferring inadequacies. I am the sort of man who would lose a woman to another man. I used to be mildly adventurous. I used to take the occasional risk. Now, I worry about forgetting not to put the rubbish out and feel threatened by my wife's male friends.

I need to do something exciting with my life.

Isabel gets in from the first in the new term's yoga classes and, when I tell her I'm bored, I'm having a midlife crisis and I need some new challenge in my life, she suggests I give yoga another go. I wait for at least ten seconds for her to show she was joking but she wasn't. I phone Andy, apologise profusely for telling him to get stuffed and ask him if he can help me find myself again.

He suggests hang-gliding. Googling 'hang-gliding' and 'killed' brings up 40,928 results. I decide that it's all very well wanting a fresh adventure in life but that there are limits. Abseiling will do fine. I book onto a course in the Peak District after Andy promises to come too.

THINGS I CAN'T DO NOW BUT COULD HAVE DONE WHEN I WAS YOUNGER

Abseil

Learn French

Remain calm during take-off and landing

Toboggan the really steep slope where my parents live

Enjoy queuing and paying to get into a trendy bar, then queuing to get to the bar to get a drink, then having to stand holding my drink inches from my face because the bar is so packed, then not being able to have a conversation with anyone because the music is so loud.

THINGS I CAN DO NOW BUT COULDN'T WHEN I WAS YOUNGER

Drive without terrifying my passengers

Intimidate an intimidating waiter

Get up early and make the most of the best part of the day (and, in so doing, pathetically avoid having sex)

Prefer a nice, quiet evening with friends in a country pub.

Friday 2 September

Barely two weeks have passed and the strange reclusive gnomes in the flat downstairs, the ones with the dingy subterranean living room but without the new kitchen, have now got an Under Offer sticker emblazoned across their For Bloody Sale sign. Their bedroom is painted in swirly blood red and purple. They have no stainless-steel cooker hood. Their kitchen smells of urinary infection, not freshly baked bread like ours. Arthur the Absolute A1 Arsehole is unreachable but could I please leave a message?

'Oi, Arsehole. The flat downstairs is already under offer. The one with the dingy basement and the much higher risk of being broken into by heroin addicts if you go on holiday. Whatrugonnadoaboudit?'

… or words to that effect.

Saturday 3 September

Another look at the house in Isabel's mum's village and one a few miles away and one a few more miles away. I like the one quite a few more miles away but it's been on the market for months.

'Why does no one else want to buy it?' I ask Isabel, hopefully. 'It's lovely.'

'Maybe it's because its bedrooms are downstairs and its kitchen is upstairs, because it's on the hard shoulder of the M25 and because no one's quite sure if that mobile phone mast at the end of the garden will mean we have deformed children,' replies Isabel. 'I think we should make an offer on the first one.'

So I say, 'The one near your mum's?'

So she says, 'Yes.'

So I say, 'I'm not sure I like the kitchen.'

So she says, 'I know, we'll have to start saving for a new one.'

So I say, 'But, but, but, but, but …'

So she bats her eyelashes and flutters her eyelids and squeezes my arm.

So now it looks like we're moving into the house near her mum. If Arsehole can ever shift the flat.

Monday 5 September

An even worse start to the week than I've come to expect over the past few months. First because the world's dumbest criminal tried to steal our car last night. Dumb because, of all the cars in the street, ours is the oldest and slowest. If he was a joy rider, he wasn't ever going to get much joy from a 0.997-litre Vauxhall Corsa Breeze (Breeze, I think, because it has a sunroof). Dumb also because he didn't manage to steal it, or the radio. All he did was bend the whole door open, jemmy the radio just enough so it doesn't work and steal only one of my favourite shoes, so neither he nor I can enjoy them.

I go to work in my second favourite pair of shoes and find I have been awarded a work-experience girl for the next two weeks. She's starting tomorrow because today she's interviewing Bill Clinton for a magazine she was doing work experience with last week. Oh God.

Tuesday 6 September

By 10.15 a.m., I have run out of things to make the work-experience girl do. She has filed everything, made an Excel spreadsheet to denote her new filing system and everyone in the office is having a caffeine overdose because she's made so much tea. Her name is Anastasia, she speaks five languages, got a quadruple first from Oxford and a Master's from Columbia, has 58 A-levels, 3,276 GCSEs, worked as a peace envoy for the UN in Sierra Leone last summer, plays hockey, rugby, tennis and mahjong, and, at the age of sixteen, won silver for England in the under-21s three-day-eventing world championship.

She is proficient in everything computery, can type 900 words per minute and knows shorthand. In her spare time, she organises charity balls, fights Third World debt and enjoys listening to music. Why on earth she wants to do work experience here when she should really be running for prime minister, I don't know. Perhaps it's just to make the rest of us ageing mortals feel even more inadequate.

Saw Alex walking past my office at lunch but managed to avoid him. Strange because he works in Victoria. Can't mention it to Isabel because, since the breast revelation, the topic is entirely taboo.

Wednesday 7 September

'If you wannit perfickt, it's gonna cost ya, mate,' says the mechanic, scratching his chin as he surveys our bent door.

'Yes, obviously. How much?'

'Ohffffffff,' he says, as if I've just asked him to estimate how long it will take to climb the Eiger via the west ridge without ropes. 'Pffffffff,' like he's trying to calculate how many matchboxes it would take to stretch to the moon. 'You're looking at, oooooooh, seven hundred quid for a new door. Maybe, tssssssssskkk, another two hundred parts and labour.'

'Isn't the door the parts?'

'Yeah, right. But there's 'inges 'n' panelling 'n' stuff.'

I phone my insurance company and a woman who sounds like she's trying to stifle a giggle says I have to pay the first £500 of a claim tap tap tap and that if I make a claim, my premium will go up by approximately tap tap tap tap £420 next year. In my head, I go around to the insurance company and machine-gun the woman and all her colleagues to death for being such evil, tricksy bastards. In reality, I thank her, decline her offer to initiate a claim, hang up and tell the mechanic just to bend the door back as best he can.

Thursday 8 September

Horrible dream last night. It was the day before my finals or A-levels or GCSEs. I couldn't tell which because no one had told me, and I hadn't even started to revise. I was in a library, hemmed in by giant stacks of books and folders but I wasn't a student, I was me: the thirty-year-old magazine journalist. Worse, I had the mind of a thirty-year-old magazine journalist. I started leafing through some of the textbooks, and it was all complicated political theory and graphs and timelines. There were long essays full of long words in my handwriting but I couldn't understand any of it because I had the useless brain of a thirty-year-old. I started reading frantically, conscious I had only twelve hours until the first exam, entitled British Political History 1747 to 1979, began. Every time I reached a point where I almost understood something, my mind was invaded by thoughts of Isabel. Not sexy thoughts. No dreamy fantasy with stockings and university tutor outfits. Only panicky thoughts about losing her, about letting her get away, about driving her away with my own blockheaded stubbornness and/or her stupid loyalty to Alex. With all that going on, I hadn't even reached the Industrial Revolution and its Impact on the Political Structure of Eighteenth-Century Britain before it was time to wake up and go to the exam. Except when I woke up, exhausted, there wasn't any exam at all.

On the bright side, it rained for the first time in weeks and our garden-free flat in sweltering Finsbury Park became slightly more bearable and slightly less like the perfect venue for humidity-induced wife-killing.

On the less bright side, our car is no longer waterproof and Isabel is blaming me for not insisting the garage did a proper job and not getting a proper insurance policy and just generally being me.

I asked Anastasia to research an article on Russian billionaires and their role in London society. I had hoped it would take her a week but she finished it in an hour and a half, then just sat opposite me looking bored while I tried to work the fax machine. (Try putting a 'nine' in front, she says. As if that would work. Oh, thanks.) After lunch, I told her to update a spreadsheet of contact details for every celebrity on our database. Fifty-four minutes. I told her to stick some front covers on the wall. Fourteen minutes. And make coffee. Three minutes. And fact-check my article. Seven minutes, during which she found four typos, a split infinitive and two sentences that could have been expressed better.

I tell her I'm going to the gym tonight.

She tells me she's going to kick-boxing class.

I tell her I'm going abseiling in the Peak District at the weekend.

She tells me she's going base-jumping in the Massif Central.

I tell her to go and make another cup of coffee.

Friday 9 September

'Would I like to increase my sperm volume by five hundred per cent?' ask the first seven emails I open this morning. The sex thing that I hoped was a blip and was in actual fact a trend has now bottomed out at twice a week. Isabel says that as our love grows and our marriage strengthens, physical love becomes less relevant. Advertising tells us we should be having sex all the time but life is richer than that. It sounds like something Astrid, her yoga teacher, would say, which means she has been talking to Astrid, which means it is an issue she has to talk about, which means I may have to increase my sperm volume by five hundred per cent.

Anastasia wants to leave early today so she can catch her flight to France to do her base-jump. I don't have to leave early because I'm only going to the bloody Peak District to do stupid abseiling tomorrow.

Saturday 10 September

Even though it's not base-jumping, there really wasn't enough safety training for my liking. Our instructor was called Barney and he had long hair, round glasses and a pair of tie-dye poo-catchers. He wouldn't have looked out of place on a beach in Bali in the Seventies. He did look out of place explaining how the ropes we were entrusting our lives to worked. 'The green one feeds through … errr … this loop, and this one goes … errr … no, it's the yellow one that goes through that loop and the green one goes here. Hahahahahaha, always getting those muddled. Hahahahahaha. Right, off you go.'

I let Andy go first, straight off a sixty-metre-high viaduct. I waited for a scream, a crunch and a splatter, but Andy just seemed to be enjoying himself. Finally, he emerged ant-like and whooping at the bottom of the bridge and yelled an echoey 'Your turn' back up. As he did so, a minibus pulled up next to me and Barney, disgorging a dozen skinheads from a borstal in Stockport. 'Part of the new day-release programme,' muttered their hounded instructor to Barney. 'See if we can't lose a few today, ey?'

The skinheads were so excited to be out of their detention centre that they were trying to set each other on fire with cigarette lighters and deodorants. Only the sight of me climbing up onto the ledge distracted them long enough to save the skinniest one from incineration.

'Go on, mate, see if you can fucking fly, you fucking cock,' they said encouragingly. But I couldn't move. I just stood up on the rail, rooted to the spot. Then I got disco leg: I wobbled involuntarily to a non-existent disco beat. The cruel laughter swam around me, the soft encouragement of Barney doing little to help. I thought of my life back in London, of the leaking car, the unsellable flat, the wife. And then I thought of the bloody infinitely bloody talented work experience who right now was jumping off a two-mile-high cliff without any ropes. And then I jumped.

You're not supposed to jump.

You're supposed to walk over the edge. I swung back into the side of the viaduct; there was a loud snapping sound. 'I think I broke my foot,' I shouted up to twelve hysterical skinheads and a hippy. None of them believed me.

When I did eventually get to the bottom, I sat waiting despondently for Andy to have another go – naturally he had taken to it like Spiderman – before we went to hospital. The humiliation was complete when the nurse told me it was only a broken toe and there was no need for a cast – and no, I wouldn't need crutches. I couldn't even injure myself properly.

Monday 12 September

Anastasia wasn't killed base-jumping. In fact, nothing is going right until Isabel makes a surprise visit to my office to meet me for lunch. That goes right only briefly, until she picks a fight with a total stranger. We go to a place claiming to be a French deli and she orders a ham and cheese croissant. It isn't fresh, despite claiming to be and costing £3.49, so she starts remonstrating with a teenage manager about how this place shouldn't be allowed to claim that it's French because no one in France would serve a £3.49 croissant that isn't fresh. Almost immediately, a very aggressive security guard comes over to help the discussion along and things start to get heated. Just when she's telling him to mind his own business, he actually prods Isabel in the chest. I grab Isabel and we leave. Isabel says I should have grabbed the security guard, not her, and says I should have defended her.

I spend the rest of the afternoon throwing security guards through windows and down stairs and off viaducts in my mind, while the work experience gets on with my job.

The sweaty fat bloke is sweating less and his fat is looking less fatty. I think he may be getting muscles. I tell Denise I can't do much today because I broke my little toe.

'We can focus on our upper body, don't we think?' she replies. 'If we think we're up to it.'

Tuesday 13 September

Day six of ten and Anastasia is now having meetings with important people around the office. It's only a matter of time before she starts telling me to do the photocopying.

Back home before Isabel and, for the second time this week, the phone rang, only for the caller to ring off again when I answered it. Tried 1471-ing it but the caller had withheld their number.

My toe hurts.

Wednesday 14 September

I saw Alex today, I'm sure I did, standing motionless outside my office, then disappearing into the crowd when he saw me. Just staring, a cold, cruel look in his eyes.

I break the Alex embargo and tell Isabel when she gets home and she just sighs, shakes her head sadly and goes into the kitchen. She doesn't believe me. He's so clever, dividing and ruling. Driving us apart so he can strike. I'm about to follow her into the kitchen when the phone rings, then goes dead when I answer it.

When the phone rings again, I answer by screaming, 'STOP BOTHERING US, YOU SICK MANIAC, AND LET US GET ON WITH OUR MARRIAGE IN PEACE,' to which Isabel's mother replies, 'That's no way to talk to your mother-in-law. Please put Isabel on, darlink.'

Johnson suggests we go around to Alex's maisonette-cum-psycho-control-centre and mess him up a bit.

Andy suggests I move to Papua New Guinea. Take Isabel with me. Spend the rest of our days on a Robinson Crusoe island, just the two of us, far away from the tedium and misery of modern Western culture. Like Gauguin without the paedophilia.

I go with option C, to skip last orders, go home and continue brooding.

Thursday 15 September

Woken in the middle of the night by a scraping sound, then a banging sound in the street below. In my half-sleep, I imagine it is Alex, finally flipped, here to take Isabel by force. But as I reach the window I see right below us, under the full glare of the streetlamp, a tattooed hoodie mounting a frenzied attack on our car, bending back the bent door and banging his fists in fury against the window. He is clearly drug-crazed, clearly has a knife and clearly would stop at nothing to get into our car. Like lightning, I make an assessment that it is too dangerous to get involved. Life on the mean streets of London is cheap and, while we had a lot to lose – a wonderful marriage, a perfectly decent though strangely unsellable flat, more crockery than any normal person could ever make use of – this chap had nothing. All he cared about was where his next shot of crystal meth was coming from. So I sprinted into the kitchen, quickly dialled 999 and, without hesitation, asked to be put through to the police.

While I was put on hold, a low roar erupted from the bedroom, growing suddenly and terrifyingly into a shriek of jaw-dropping, foul-mouthed profanity. It was Isabel.

'What are you doing?' I shout, running back to the bedroom just in time to see the drug-crazed maniac shake his fist up at us threateningly before leaping over a fence and disappearing.

'I'm stopping that idiot from pulling our car to pieces. What were you doing?'

'Calling the police.'

'How's that going to help? Why didn't you run down there and stop him?'

I explain about my lightning assessment and the mean streets of London.

'Don't be ridiculous.'

'Hardly a day goes by when you don't see the headline "City Worker Killed After Battling Drug-Crazed Robber".'

'He was about twelve.'

'He was not. And now, thanks to your screaming fit, he knows where we live and how posh we are.'

'What do you mean, posh?'

'You sound posh when you swear.'

The policeman who arrived to take down our particulars didn't help.

'Yes, sir,' he said in the most patronising, disapproving, accusing tone he could muster. 'You did the right thing. Just do nothing – that's the spirit. This child —'

'Youth …'

'Sorry, yes, youth. This youth could have had a weapon. A gun, a machete, a peashooter, anything.'

'Did you say peashooter?'

'No, I said machete. Don't you worry now. I'll check your premises are all nice and secure and safe and tucked up, look at the vehicle and give you a big girly number.'

'Did you say big girly?'

'No, I said crime report number.'

Friday 16 September

I've thrown a cup of tea over the work experience. Thank goodness it was a cold one. I don't know what happened. I just snapped. She was banging on about how she'd met the European editor of *Newsweek* at a cocktail bloody party last night and he was into base-jumping too. Then she asked me if I'd get *her* a tea. So I just stood up and threw a cup over her and shouted, 'Here, have mine.' Apparently, I ranted at her for about ten minutes as well, using phrases like 'in my day' and 'no respect' and 'think you can just waltz in here'. I have a meeting with the managing editor on Monday to discuss my behaviour. Unless he's forgotten about the whole Sandra affair, I will inevitably be sacked.

Saturday 17 September

The weirdos downstairs are moving out today with their smug little faces and crappy little furniture. They say they don't know who's moving in. It was all done through some sort of offshore trust fund. Which probably means it's going to be a buy-to-let. Probably going to get some more party animal cretins like the ones upstairs. We will be trapped in a residential nightclub. Until, of course, we get repossessed because I can't afford the mortgage because I got sacked because I threw (cold) tea over a work experience.

Arthur Arsehole finally returned my ninth call. He says the market is really down at the moment. He says he can't understand how the flat below us shifted so quickly. He says he thinks it will pick up when everyone gets back from their summer holiday. I point out that that happened three weeks ago. He says October will be a strong month. I say we will have to reconsider our position, and hang up.

Monday 19 September

I am not sacked! The managing editor started the meeting by asking if everything was okay. It was just a cursory question requiring a 'Yes, fine thanks' answer but I chose to let it all come out. This was my Oprah moment. With tears in my eyes, I told him all about the horror of turning thirty, the ruined birthday weekend, Alex the stalker, the botched attempt to jump off a viaduct, the failure to defend my wife against security guards and seven-year-old car thieves. I told him I was becoming emasculated, that I was ruining my life with my own neuroses. I even told him about the trend that had been just a blip. It was more than he'd bargained for but it meant I kept my job. He told me not to throw tea over workies again, that I should take the rest of the week off and that I would be required to spend a day next month on an anger-management course.

Tuesday 20 September

With my time at home, I shall build some shelves in the living room. The reason the flat isn't shifting is that my two structurally unsound, bright-blue, bought-when-I-was-living-in-a-bedsit bookcases teeter towards each other from their respective alcoves. It makes the whole room look as though we have subsidence. Some nice white built-in shelves will change the whole mood of the place.

Progress is slower than I'd hoped. It takes all day to do the measuring, partly because the walls aren't straight either and partly because I get sucked into the vortex that is daytime TV. By the time Isabel gets home, I have seen a pregnant fourteen-year-old mother-of-three from Derby tell her fifteen-year-old boyfriend that he probably isn't the father of any of them, it's his thirteen-year old brother; a housewife from Baltimore explain to her husband, a cable-TV evangelist, that for the last eight years she's been working as a stripper, stage name Flaming Lily; and a Minnesotan transsexual tell his/her partner of five years that she/he used to have a penis, only for the partner to reveal that he's running off with a trucker called Leonard.

I have watched four rip-offs of *Tomorrow's World*, back to back.

I am also convinced of the essential benefits of a walk-in bath, the need to make provisions for my funeral so as not to burden loved ones when I die, and that I am entitled to compensation for breaking my little toe in a workplace, at home or anywhere else.

Wednesday 21 September

Much better progress today after unplugging television. Have had MDF cut, have painted two coats, have done sawing and sanding and prepping. If a job's worth doing, it's worth doing well. Alex is meeting Isabel for a drink tonight but I don't care because if there's one thing that women hate, it's paranoia, jealousy and lack of trust. Three things, then.

Well, she had dinner with him, which is slightly more annoying than I'd bargained for. The swanky bastard knew the chef at this new place in Shoreditch. Sure, it was candlelit and romantic and totally inappropriate for two friends who were supposed to be having a quick drink, but he wanted to drop in to lend his support to the chef. It just happened to coincide with the night he was meeting Isabel for a drink.

Thursday 22 September

Fucking hell. Have ruined the flat. Stupid bloody fucking drill recommended by spotty DIY teenager … on the hammer setting, it just rips out a hole the size of a football in half a second. On the normal setting, it doesn't do anything. Unless of course I hit a soft bit in the brickwork, in which case it goes in so deep, so fast and at such an uncontrollable angle, I've drilled a bloody 'W' shape before I can switch the damn thing off.

I manage to get three holes for the first shelf in perfect alignment, but the fourth one slips down a bit and the wall plug gets jammed so I have to leave it and drill a new hole. It's too high but I carry on anyway so the shelf is crooked. The next shelf I had to abandon altogether and the third wobbles thanks to some strange cavity in the wall whose existence I could in no way have predicted.

I call Dad for advice and he puts Mum on who suggests matchsticks to try to fill the cavity but we don't have any matches in the flat – that would be far too easy – so the excess hole for the fourth shelf is now plugged by three toothpicks and a shard of picnic fork.

By lunchtime, I have created a home-made Beirut. I have reduced the value of the flat by several thousand pounds, got red brick dust all over the carpet because, as Isabel will say, I never cover the floors properly when I'm working, and ruined my new pair of jeans because, as Isabel will also say, I always wear my best clothes for DIY. Disconsolate, sweaty and apprehensive, I decide to take a break, plug in the PlayStation and shoot some zombies. Before I know it, it's 8 p.m., I haven't got dinner ready as I'd promised and Isabel is saying all the stuff I knew she would.

Friday 23 September

I have agreed with Isabel to get rid of the PlayStation because I am thirty and I am pathetic and I spent the whole of my last day of enforced leave playing Speed Rally IV. I have given up on the shelf plan ... we now have one alcove of partially built-in shelves at random heights and one still with the old blue monstrosity. I think it looks fine and even quite artful now we've filled most of the surplus holes.

Saturday 24 September

Miraculously, Arthur Arsehole brought two couples around to the flat today. I'm pretty sure the first were just two other estate agents from his office pretending to be prospective buyers. The second were a knock-through couple. They spent the whole viewing tapping walls knowingly and saying to each other, 'We could knock this through' and, 'We could knock that through.' I don't know why they don't just buy a barn or a field and live in that. As he left, Arsehole said he would add the built-in shelves to the property details. I can't work out whether he was being sarcastic or not … so hard to tell with estate agents.

Monday 26 September

Everyone at work thinks it's funny to cower when I walk past. Even Johnson keeps shouting, 'Don't hit me, don't hit me,' every time I wander over. At least Anastasia has left, probably to run for president of UNICEF or to become the first work experience in space.

Having followed IT geek at work's advice and put the PlayStation on eBay with no reserve to attract attention, it has sold for £12.17. The buyer wants to know if they can collect in person to save the postage. I will now have to kill the IT geek.

First time to the gym in a week. Not only is sweaty fat guy looking thin and muscle-bound, he seems to have brought his glands under control. He leaves the machines dry. He is also, rather brilliantly, occupying most of Denise's attention. I am left to my own devices and spend most of the session sitting on the rowing machine reading a year-old copy of *Hello.*

Tuesday 27 September

Surprise, surprise: the last two couples have declined to make an offer on the flat. At least it means I can get Isabel to agree to wait a bit before making an offer on the house three seconds from her mum's house.

Thursday 29 September

Great news: my built-in shelves are now part of the selling details for our flat. It says 'Spacious living room with bay window, fitted curtains, original features and designer shelving.'

Friday 30 September

Our five-month anniversary today. Breakfast in bed for Isabel, then conclusive proof that it was just a blip and not a trend. Twice in two days and not just because I felt I had to keep the numbers up.

To mark our anniversary, I decide to cook a splendid five-course feast for my beautiful wife. Got home then went all the way to Waitrose especially and was minding my own business in the partridge aisle when I heard that voice.

'William, you naughty boy. Fancy seeing you here.'

And there she was. Saskia. Eighteen feet tall, seventeen of them legs, a trademark six inches covered by skirt. Bottle-blonde hair, hypnotic blue eyes, come-hither lashes, life-raft lips and a smile that makes men tremble and women spit with rage. Saskia: the Destroyer of Relationships.

'Saskia. What a surprise.'

[Keep calm. Keep calm. Keep calm. Don't panic. Don't panic. Don't panic.]

'Good heavens. How wonderful to see you.'

[Good heavens? Who says good heavens? And stop being so friendly. Keep calm.]

'If it isn't the man who molested me on Hyde Park Corner and then sent me off to America in disgrace.'

'Hahahahahahahahahahahahahahahahahahahahahahahahahahahahahahahahahahahahahahahahahahaha. Aren't you supposed to be in New York?'

[Don't go red. Don't go red. Don't go red.]

'New York's over. The men are wimps. So I'm back. Want to show me the sights of London again? Or are you jetting off after snake-eating orchids again?'

'Yes, no, marvellous. I'm married now.'

[Well done. Very cool.]

'Yes, you said that. To Elizabeth?'

'No, to Isabel. As it happens, today's our five-month anniversary.'

'Ahhh, how sweet. I'd like to meet her.'

[That won't work. That will never work. It might have done if I hadn't bragged like a big fat idiot about the Hyde Park thing to Isabel when I was trying to impress her with my wild and thrilling past. Or lied about East Timor. Or never mentioned any email contact. Idiot.]

'Okay, I'll give you a call.'

[That's better. Take the number, buy the partridge, get the hell out.]

'Here's my card, it's got my mobile on it. I'm having a flat-warming tomorrow. You should come over. Bring Isabel if you like.'

'Can't, I'm afraid. I'm doing partridge.' I hold up the partridge as proof.

'Oh well. Give me a call. Or I'll start to think you're avoiding me. Which would be silly, wouldn't it? We're both grown-ups.'

'Yes, of course. Bye then.'

[Well done. Walk away. Keep smiling. Walk away. Bye-bye, Relationship Destroyer.]

Back at the flat, I'm calmer. No one needs to know anything. Everything is fine. I haven't done anything wrong.

'Is that lipstick on your lips?' asks Isabel, peering at the lipstick Saskia obviously sneaked onto my lips because she's one of those people that thinks kissing on lips is a perfectly acceptable way to greet friends.

'No, I just bit my lip,' I reply brilliantly.

No one needs to know anything. Everything is fine.

While I'm preparing the partridge, the doorbell goes. 'Come and meet our new neighbour, darling,' calls Isabel.

'Sorry, can't. Partridge is almost ready.' I don't want to meet the new head-banging neighbours and Isabel knows it.

'Come on, darling, don't be antisocial.' There's an edge to her voice so I trudge up the stairs, bracing myself for the skinhead death-thrash metal rock band that's bound to be standing at the door.

'I thought you were doing partridge tomorrow night, you naughty man,' rasps the pneumatic blonde in the inch-long skirt.

Saskia. The Destroyer of Relationships. My new neighbour.

OCTOBER

'The deep, deep peace of the double bed after the hurly-burly of the chaise longue.'

Mrs Patrick Campbell
on marriage (1865–1940)

Saturday 1 October

Last night, on my five-month wedding anniversary, I slept under the same roof as two women I have copulated with. Of all the flats in all the world, why did she have to move into the one below ours? What are the chances? I've slept with eight people properly in my entire life, five if I'm being honest. Four if I'm being really honest. There are six billion people on the planet. So that's one in more than a billion. Why couldn't something else improbable like winning the lottery have happened instead?

On the plus side, she's only there for a couple of months, house-sitting for some friend of a friend of a friend who's bought the place as an investment. On the minus side, she's there for a couple of months, with her legs and her lips and her massively inappropriate innuendos.

Isabel has reacted quite frighteningly, in that she has hardly reacted at all. 'She looks like a bit of a tart. Can't believe I married someone with such trashy taste in women.' That's all she has said, although there will inevitably be more.

After running out of every excuse but the obvious one ('Sorry, we can't come because we only know each other because we used to have illicit sex together and I'm now happily married thank you very much and my wife knows about Hyde Park and the burnt duvet and doesn't want us to have anything to do with you and good riddance'), we drop into Saskia's flat-warming. Half an hour later, we drop out again because everyone is five years younger than us, they're all snogging each other and, while Isabel is being chatted up by a Frenchman wearing a mesh T-shirt, Saskia asks if I remember every detail of our first night together because she does.

She appears to have forgotten about my time in East Timor.

Sunday 2 October

It is a beautiful autumn day so I suggest we drive down to Kent and have another snoop at the house in Isabel's mum's village. Isabel asks if this is because I'm trying to get on her good side because I slept with the trollop downstairs who is now in the process of turning our address into a notorious brothel. I say it isn't, which is a lie: I don't care if we end up living in the same bedroom as Isabel's mum, I have to get away from Saskia.

We snoop. I say I love it. Isabel looks at me suspiciously. I say no really. I want to grow vegetables and eat locally farmed sheep and get a train to work and go sailing and mountain-biking and orienteering at the weekend and she says great, we'll put an offer in on Monday if it's still available. Then we walk the six yards or so to her parents' for a cup of tea, during which the following conversation takes place:

'We've decided to make an offer on the house,' says Isabel.

'But I thought William wasn't sure he wanted to live here,' says her mum.

'He is now that an ex-girlfriend – sorry, a girl he was seeing when he was going out with Elizabeth – has moved into the flat downstairs.'

'That's not the reason, darl—' I interject.

'The one he met on Hyde Park Corner,' she interjects.

'Hyde Park Corner? But that's a roundabout,' her mum interjects.

'Anyway, I really like this vill—' I interject.

'What's this about Hyde Park Corner?' Her father has come in from the potting shed, mid-re-itemisation of his Japanese theatre programme collection.

'Nothing,' I say.

'Bloody treacherous, if you ask me,' he offers.

'It is if your boyfriend goes there with a trollop called Saskia.'

I step outside for some fresh air, marvelling at the timing. Why couldn't we have had the inevitable argument on our own? Why do it in front of the parents? Isabel's grandfather, a fit but almost entirely deaf ninety-year-old, is sitting on a bench minding his own business. He beckons me over and we sit watching the small part of the world we can see go by. I know he's ninety and not long for this world, but at least he doesn't have much to worry about any more. As if to exemplify this, he reaches out for his afternoon cucumber sandwich, upon which an enormous grasshopper is perched.

'Mr Jeffreys, there's an enormous grasshopper perched on your cucumber sandwich,' I say.

'Ey, duck?' he enquires, crunching through the doomed critter.

'Nothing,' I reply, because he's already swallowed it and, as with a lot of things in life, what you don't know won't hurt you. Then I spend the whole drive home wondering whether grasshoppers are poisonous.

Wednesday 5 October

Good news: haven't seen Saskia since Saturday – she appears to be keeping herself to herself (although it may be because I have been creeping in and out of our flat like a burglar). And our offer on the house near Isabel's mum's house has been accepted, after we assured the seller that we would be in a position to move quickly because flats in Finsbury Park were selling like hot cakes. I phone Arsehole, who is now so overfamiliar with me that he calls me 'Big W'. I tell him we want to drop the price for a quick sale. Then, Isabel and I go out to celebrate with Andy and Johnson and … Alex. Her idea. But the mere fact that I'm still married and that there's a light at the end of Saskia's tunnel, so to speak, means I don't care.

'How's it going, babes?'

He is still a cock, though.

'Fine, looks like we've found somewhere to move away from William's floozy.'

Oh no, not again.

'What floozy?' He looks, for the briefest moment, like all his Christmases have come stacked high on top of each other in an enormous pyramid of festive joy. But he hides it before Isabel notices and then, having revelled in the telling of the whole unfortunate coincidence, takes his usual Machiavellian tack.

'Come on, babes. It's not William's fault that a girl he was unfaithful with has moved into your house. You should be more trusting. He's hardly going to be unfaithful again, is he? Are you, William? Of course you aren't. Once bitten and all that. Now, drinkies, anyone? It sounds like we have something to celebrate. The imminent move to the country, I mean. Not this terrible situation with the floozy. Hahahahahahaha.'

I hit him so hard in the face that his body flies clean across the room, crumpling over a rather angular chair in the corner. Then, as he staggers to his feet, I knee him four or five times in the crotch before round-housing him over the bar and into the display of drinks beyond. Then he asks what drink I want, I stop fantasising and ask for a double Scotch on the rocks.

In the toilet, even though we both know men aren't supposed to chat there, Andy says that he's sorry he ever thought Alex was a good bloke. He can see now that he's a cock. I am relieved, in more ways than one. In fact, if we hadn't been at the urinal, Andy's prodigal return to my team could have been worthy of a man-hug.

The art of the man-hug

Used correctly and sparingly, a man-hug can seal a powerful, emotional bond between close male friends. Under no circumstance should a man-hug become a standard form of greeting among men who see each other regularly in work and/or social situations. That's what hand-shaking is for.

Situations which may warrant a man-hug include: the return of a best friend from a stay overseas of not less than eight months (two weeks on a Greek island is not sufficient); life-changing good news (e.g. engagement/impregnation of wife/arrival of first-born son, but not pay rise/house purchase/successful completion of kitchen conversion); life-changing bad news (e.g. divorce/family bereavement/limb amputation, but not marital dispute over new type of wallpaper/failure to win lottery); significant national sporting victories (e.g. England winning the Rugby World Cup) but only if in a pub, not if in a living room; and the meeting of minds after a long-running disagreement (e.g. Andy thinking Alex was an acceptable human being).

Man-hugs should be brief.

Hands should only be used to back-pat; not, under any circumstances, to rub or squeeze.

Chests should touch but nothing else.

Thursday 6 October

Denise has completely lost interest in me and I miss her sadistic taunts. Furthermore, I now have to move the weight key thing at least ten notches up rather than down after no-longer-sweaty-or-fat guy has been there. It's utterly demoralising so I tell Denise I don't think it's working out. She half-heartedly suggests 'we' join a class. How about aerobics? It's for girls. Or boxercise? It's for lesbians. Or spinning? I think I'll just leave actually. 'Okay,' she says. 'Sign here.' Don't care. Thursday is the new Friday. Off to Stockholm tomorrow after Isabel spotted Ryanair flights for 99p.

'It will be like a second honeymoon,' said Isabel.

'But darling, we're unlikely to get diarrhoea, jet lag, altitude sickness and heatstroke in Scandinavia. At least, not all at the same time. How can it possibly be as good as our first honeymoon?'

Friday 7 October

A bad start to our spontaneous second mini-honeymoon. Because our flight leaves Stansted at 6.05 bloody a.m., we have to get to Stansted at 4.05 a.m. which is before the Tube starts so we have to get a taxi which costs £46 or more than twenty-three times as much as it's costing us to fly to Stockholm. It also means we had to wake up at half two, which is effectively the night before, which is just horrible.

At the airport, whole families of aggressive holidaymaking yobs, all dressed head to toe in England football kit, are already drinking pints of lager and fighting with each other, even though they would normally be tucked up in their beds at this hour. Then they all get on our flight before us through a mixture of threats, elbowing and well-timed sprints, so Isabel and I fail to find two seats next to each other. I pay about forty quid for a soggy sandwich and try to improve on the two-and-a-quarter hours' sleep I've had while the hyperactive child behind me uses my headrest, then my head, as a punchbag.

Obviously, we didn't fly to Stockholm at all. We flew to Stockholm-Skavsta, which really means we flew to Skavsta-Stockholm, which really means we flew to *bloody Skavsta*. Stockholm is fifty-five miles away by coach, the first of which we just miss because the flight was late in and all the hyperactive families elbow their way off the plane before us and we were half asleep and bloody hell … So we wait for the midday coach and an hour and twenty minutes later we're in Stockholm. By the time we reach the hotel, it's nearly three. It feels as if we've been travelling for twelve hours, mainly because we have. So we decide to have a quick siesta. I wake up nine hours later thinking I'm in a small cell block in southern Turkey. Isabel is equally disorientated when I shake her awake.

We're both starving and our hotel doesn't do room service after 11 p.m., so we walk out into the Scandinavian night to forage for something to eat. It's one in the morning and our part of Stockholm has shut. Our only option is to drink vodka on the streets with bored Swedish teenagers or buy a donkey-lip kebab from the only food-seller who forgot to go home. Like starving Andean plane-crash survivors who decide to start eating one another, we opt, in desperation, for the kebab.

Sunday 9 October

Have spent the rest of the weekend trying and failing to recover from peculiar Ryanair short-haul jet lag. Up at 5 a.m., bright-eyed and bloody bushy-tailed, roaming the streets in an attempt to find anything that's open before eight; then, flagging, can hardly stay awake past 7 p.m.

Cruelly, our flight back from Skavsta-Skavsta didn't leave until 10 p.m., hours after our Ryanair bedtime. At least, with the help of an axe and two hand grenades with the clips off, I managed to get us two seats next to each other. But then we landed at Stansted four or five seconds after the last train left. Tried to get a coach but they were on strike so took another cab, this time with an hour-long wait and a special airport premium. Sixty quid later ('Take it or fackin' leave it, guvna, there's a whole fackin' queue a people going a lot fackin' furver than Finsbury facking Park who'll take it'), our no-frills adventure is over. I feel as if I've been to Peru and back in a weekend, which probably would have been quicker and less stressful.

At least Alex didn't pop out coincidentally from behind the plastic tree in our hotel foyer with a: 'Hi, babes, fancy seeing you here. I'm still missing my Moroccan girlfriend, babes, so I thought I'd have a weekend in Stockholm to cheer my poor little self up, babes, babes, babes.'

Monday 10 October

'Thanks for the note. You're very naughty.'

Saskia is standing in the hall in her pants and nothing else, trapping me in full stealth-burglar mode between the letter boxes and the front door. I am speechless long enough for her to say, 'And don't worry, I understand.' Then long enough again for her to walk right up to me, open her letter box, take out her letters, turn around and walk back into her flat.

Isabel is making toast upstairs. She is also only in her pants and nothing else.

'What's wrong?'

'Nothing's wrong. Why would anything be wrong? How could anything be wrong? Who would anything be wrong?'

So now she knew something was wrong.

'I just like it when you make toast in your pants.'

I am now lying to my wife. Or at least concealing the truth. I do like it when she makes toast in her pants, especially when she follows the Marmite recipe properly. But I didn't tell her about Saskia being in her pants. So that's lying by omission. Which is tantamount to adultery. And what note? What bloody blinking note? I didn't send Saskia a note. Why would anyone who's been married to the girl of his dreams for five blissful months and eleven quite fraught days send a 'naughty' note to the girl of his nightmares?

Emergency pub meeting. Johnson says it's the six-month itch when I tell him what happened this morning. I re-explain what happened this morning, emphasising that I did nothing, but he sticks to his theory. 'It's the six-month itch come early,' he expounds. 'You've heard of the seven-year itch? Well, that's outdated in the computer age. Everything happens much faster these days: speed-dating, speed-shagging, gunshot weddings, quickie divorces. There's no time for a seven-year itch. That's why there's a six-month one.'

'It's shotgun, not gunshot, and I am not itchy. I haven't done anything.'

'You don't have to do anything. It sounds like this girl can do it for you. You can be a perfectly innocent bystander and along comes some harlot, some wanton woman, and before you can say, "Back off, bitch, I'm a happily married man," she'll lure you.'

'I won't be lured.'

'She'll lure you.'

'I won't be lured.'

'Okay, fine, but take my advice. Whatever you do, don't scratch the itch. It's okay to have an itch but you must not scratch it. Not even a little bit. If you scratch it, it will only itch more. Before you know it, that itch will have you back to bedsits and pizzas and sad, lonely, pathetic, meaningless late-night masturbation, my friend.'

Andy is equally helpful. 'Wow, it's pretty karmic, don't you think? Saskia could have moved anywhere in the world, anywhere at all. China, Luxembourg, French Guiana. But she moves into the flat below yours in Finsbury Park, London, England. Perhaps it's a sign. Perhaps you're meant for each other. I mean, you and Isabel are meant for each other, but maybe more than one girl was meant for you. Like in Mormon culture. Like you have two kindred spirits.'

'I thought you were supposed to be moving to Geneva with your latest kindred spirit?'

'It didn't work out. Couldn't get a transfer. But wait until you meet Alessandra.'

Wednesday 12 October

To Andy's with Isabel to assess Alessandra, an Italian-Mauritanian who only speaks Italian and Hassaniyya Arabic, neither of which Andy speaks (though he can say, 'I think your country is beautiful,' in Swahili). Unfortunately, the assessment process was interrupted by my spending a night in a cell in Brixton Police Station.

How I ended up in a police cell in Brixton

'Help, help, help.' That was how it started, right in the middle of a game of stuttering, desperate, only-way-to-get-through-the-evening, multinational Monopoly, someone getting mugged in the street outside. 'My Filofax, my lipstick. Help.' Or words to that effect.

Before I had time to think, 'It's raining, put your shoes on,' I was out on the street. Andy must have been doing double knots because he arrived ages later. By that time I was already in pursuit.

'Look after the girl, I'm going after them,' I shouted, before wishing I hadn't because no matter how heroic you're being, you really don't need to sound like you're in *Baywatch*.

Still, this was it. This was my chance. With each step I took, I felt the chains of emasculation fall away. As I gained on the muggers, I was proving that I was a man, not a big girly girl. I was alive at last.

And I really was gaining on them. Quite quickly. They were a hundred yards ahead, then ninety, then eighty, then … then they stopped running.

My shoeless pursuit was so quiet that they hadn't even noticed they were being pursued.

'Now I have them, the fools,' I thought. 'Those foolish muggers. Those two stocky, hooded, foolish muggers who might well be carrying concealed weapons or other sharp objects. Being caught by me, not stocky, with no concealed weapons or other sharp objects. I've got a napkin and a silver dog but that's about it.'

So I stopped running as well because there's being brave and being so stupidly brave you get cut up into lots of little pieces on the mean streets of Stockwell.

I was left with the cowardly option: to follow them at a discreet distance. So I followed and followed and followed all the way back to their lair in Brixton, wishing with every wet puddle that I'd put my shoes on. I could have tried a citizen's arrest. That might have worked. The muggers might well be the sort of muggers who would accept my right to use reasonable force to prevent crime or arrest offenders or persons unlawfully at large under the Criminal Law Act 1967.

They might well not be.

And so, having memorised their address, Jessica Fletcher-style, I started running back to Stockwell to get help, but halfway there, a police car, sirens wailing, screeched to an incredibly dramatic halt beside me.

'Been chasing muggers, have we, sir?'

Isabel had called in my description.

It's my first time in a police car and it's pretty damn exciting going through red lights and stuff. The sergeant kills the siren as we arrive at the flats. Back-up arrives from the other direction in case things turn nasty. Descriptions I've given are walkie-talkied back and forth, and then it's time for the bust. We all exit our vehicles at the same time and cross the road like Dempsey and Makepeace and Cagney and Lacey and the Professionals and the Avengers and Steve McQueen in *Bullitt*. Unfortunately, I've only got the theme tune from *The Bill* in my head, but I'm also thinking, woo-hoo, I'm going to be in a bust.

'Sir, wait in the back of the vehicle, will you?'

I'm not going to be in a bust.

At Brixton Police Station everyone is calling me either Zola because I am not wearing any shoes or The Guv'nor because I instigated a successful arrest. None of this changes the fact that Brixton Police Station is such a dangerous place at one in the morning that the safest place to keep me while I wait to give my witness statement is in a cell. It takes three hours for them to get to me – I am released an hour after the muggers, which is enough to make me vow never to half chase anyone half heroically ever again.

Back in Stockwell, Isabel, Andy, his Italian-Mauritanian wife-to-be and the mugging victim have all stayed up waiting for me, which is nice, but are all so drunk that they sing 'I need a hero' when I walk in, which isn't.

Thursday 13 October

After two hours' sleep, I had to go to Penge, of all places, for the anger-management course. Everyone else on the course has a look of sinister calm, like they might explode at the slightest provocation. I wonder why they're here. They all look like completely normal, respectable businessmen. Scratch the surface and I bet you'll find wife-beaters, bullies, sadomasochists and the middle-class ringleaders of football hooliganism. These are the sorts of people that pulled the wings off flies when they were children. All I did was throw a (cold) cup of tea over a work experience.

We begin with a sort of anger amnesty. The organiser asks each of us to introduce ourselves and reveal what makes us angry. In response, she gets a barrage of irritations: switching broadband provider; the Microsoft Office Assistant staple; the French; people without any noticeable disability using the special parking areas at Tesco, and so forth. One guy goes puce describing his hatred of cyclists who fail to observe the rules of the road. The next guy, already puce, proclaims himself a cyclist who loves failing to observe the rules of the road but hates inconsiderate drivers. Then they both add each other to their angry lists and have to be physically restrained.

When it gets to my turn, I decide to be perfectly honest and list anger-management courses I don't need to go on because all I did was throw a (cold) cup of tea at an obnoxious work experience. I am told that I am not being constructive so I say that's not surprising because I spent last night locked up in a cell in Brixton for a crime the people I was chasing committed. In response, the organiser, a dowdy woman with a neat bob and thick-rimmed glasses, writes something down in her file. I ask what she has just written and she shows me.

'Has denial issues,' it says.

Astounded at the injustice of it all, I tell her I also get angry when people make sweeping judgements about people they have only just met. For instance, I say, I have a good idea that she's a dowdy woman with a spurious career who should have been a librarian because she bloody well looks like one. However, I continue, it would be unfair to draw such sweeping conclusions because we have only just met.

Well done, William. I now have to attend a course of six more anger-management sessions. I hold Ryanair responsible, and Alex and Saskia. I haven't slept properly for days. It's not denial, it's the truth.

Friday 14 October

Because of Ryanair and the three hours in a police cell with wet socks, I now have the 'flu. Still struggle into work just to check I haven't been sacked for upsetting the anger-management librarian. Although I almost certainly have a temperature, no one at work is remotely sympathetic. I am too ill to work so I surf the Net for information about sneezing. Then I go home, taking care to sneeze on all the bastards on the Tube who have their iPods on too loud.

FOUR FACTS ABOUT SNEEZING I LEARNT WHEN TOO ILL TO WORK

1. The material spread by sneezing can travel up to three metres at one hundred miles per hour.

2. There is some debate over who holds the world record for the loudest sneeze. It is either Yi Yang of the People's Republic of China at 176 decibels or Bill Page of South Australia at 186 decibels. For perspective, Maria Sharapova grunts at 101.2 decibels, scoring a home goal in a football stadium generates 115 decibels and a jet takes off at 140. Anything above 80 decibels can damage hearing, another good reason to sneeze all over Tube iPod-ers.

3. As reported in the *Lexington Leader*, serving the people of Lee County, Texas, Bobby Ruthven of McDade suffered severe injuries in a one-car automobile accident last Thursday at approximately 3 p.m. He was travelling westbound driving a beige 1988 Ford Mustang convertible when he suffered a

sneezing attack and veered off the road. Emergency personnel had to use the Jaws of Life to remove him from the wreckage.

4. There is a disturbingly large group of people in cyberspace who find sneezing sexually exciting. It's to do with lack of control. Note to self – don't ever follow any sneeze fetish links again.

I'm near death's door when I get home. Mercifully, Saskia is not there waiting in her pants. Isabel is already home. She isn't in her pants either but she's looking tired and needy. This is bad timing. It's my day for looking tired and needy.

Before I can convey to her how needy I am, she tells me she's had a bad day. *She's* had a bad day? She doesn't know the half of it. And I doubt very much that her day could have been as bad as mine. Except hers was: a whole country has pulled out of an aid programme she'd been organising for months.

Still, that's a work thing. I'm dying here. So I tell her, because she's not asking, that I'm ill. That I have flu.

She says it's not flu, it's just a cold.

We have been through this before.

'I have a temperature,' I say.

'No, you haven't,' she replies, holding my forehead, which is a bad way of judging unless you're a mum and we haven't got a thermometer to prove it either way.

'I have a sore throat, a dry cough, a really, really itchy nose and no appetite, which is flu,' I say.

'That's a cold,' she repeats. 'But I'm going to get you some hot lemon and honey, some Marmite toast and a hot-water bottle.' And now I feel guilty because all I have is a cold and I could, frankly, have been more sympathetic.

Saturday 15 October

Ugh. Actually, I am really ill. My cough is like something from the Crimean War. Possibly laryngitis? Whooping cough? At least Isabel has become Florence Nightingale: even told Arthur Arsehole I was too ill to have anyone see the flat. Shame, I would like to have infected an estate agent.

In the afternoon, an aid parcel of soups and Lemsips is waiting outside our door, with a note reading, 'Heard you needed cheering up. Get well soon, Nurse Saskia, xxxxx.'

'I told her you only had a cold.'

'It's not a cold, it's flu. She's just being nice.'

This was the wrong thing to say. In the fog of illness, I had momentarily forgotten that Saskia was the Destroyer of Relationships. Why would I side with her? I backtracked quickly but days of careful diplomacy have been unravelled with one stupid pro-Saskia comment.

Monday 17 October

Typical. Just in time for work, I can blow my nose straight through. Not the deeply unsatisfying one-nostril-blocked whinny but a full glug-glug-glug, tissue-filling neigh, leaving both nostrils clear for a marvellous few seconds. Filled three whole tissues on the Tube, causing the person next to me with two ghetto blasters strapped to his ears to tut. Unbelievable cheek.

Spontaneously order a folding bike on the Internet. Looks very cool and costs a quarter of the price of the boring Bromptons that everyone else has. While we are still trapped in Finsbury Park, I will be able to avoid the Tube. When we move to the country, I shall take it on the train. Perfect.

Wednesday 19 October

Folding bike already at office when I arrive. Very quick delivery, which is obviously because they're not inundated with orders. It is smaller and yellower than it looked in the photo. When I pedal, my knees hit the handlebars. It does fold nicely and it was cheap so I decide to cycle home on it. By pointing my knees out, I can pedal unhindered but look like Dick Van Dyke. Even though it's bright Day-Glo yellow, buses and taxis seem to be targeting me rather than avoiding me. The wheels are tiny. It is very hard not to wobble.

Miraculously, I am still alive by the time I reach the Holloway Road where some hilarious drunk waiting in a bus queue runs up behind me and piggybacks me. I stop and ask him what he thinks he's doing. 'Sorry, mate,' he bellows, for all the bus queue to hear, 'I thought you were the Number Ninety-seven.'

I walk the bike the rest of the way home, resolving to stick it on eBay at the earliest opportunity.

Thursday 20 October

Dreamt I was in the Tour de France last night and, with just twenty minutes until the start of the most precipitous Alpine section, the team realised they'd forgotten to bring my racer. A frantic call for assistance goes out and eventually some Provençal peasant produces a yellow folding bike. Then we're off. Everyone just vanishes in the first minute, leaving me and thousands of French people with cowbells. I woke as humiliated as when I went to sleep.

Got the Tube to work because it should be marginally less awful than cycling. Except a girl sitting opposite me breaks the cardinal Tube rule (Thou shalt never talk to another person on the Tube) by saying, 'Hello, William, how are you?'

I know her. I'm sure I know her. But for the life of me I can't remember her name. Normally, in this kind of situation, I would try to bluff my way through with lots of ambiguous questions: How are you? How's things? What's happening? Crowded on the Tube today, isn't it? But before I can take the sensible route, a small voice says, 'Just be honest. She's probably a girl you once met at a magazine party. It would be much politer just to say you're terrible with names and you're sorry you've forgotten hers.'

'I'm sorry, I know we've met but I'm terrible with names. And I've forgotten yours.'

'It's Lucy. We went to university together. We shared a house together. You once tried to have sex with me in Paris. I came to your thirtieth birthday party last month. We chatted about how important it was to stay in touch with old friends. You're coming to my wedding on Saturday.'

Despite explaining I'd just had a severe bout of influenza after foiling a mugging, she got off at the next stop and I was left alone in a carriage of smirkers. When I tell Isabel, she says I've probably got prosopagnosia. From the Greek, *prosopon* meaning 'face'; *agnosia* meaning 'ignorance'. According to some magazine she was reading only yesterday, a housewife in Boulder, Colorado, couldn't even recognise her own face. Whenever she was in a busy restroom, she had to twitch to know which face was hers.

Either that or I'm an idiot.

Saturday 22 October

Last wedding of the season. I manage, between service and reception, mid-confetti as it happens, to smooth things out with Lucy. I mention prosopagnosia. And also that, judging by how beautiful she looks today, I'm not surprised she didn't have sex with me in Paris. Lucy seemed to appreciate this but Isabel, who of course overheard, didn't. I think the whole Saskia thing has made her lose her sense of humour. Anyway, the wedding was surprisingly good, avoiding, as it did, all the usual pitfalls of weddings (e.g. making up your own vows, holding the reception at a golf club, fainting).

38/40, two better than ours. Hope their marriage is a disaster.

Tuesday 25 October

Bike sells for only twenty quid less than I bought it for and Isabel thinks I'm looking quite fit, despite leaving the gym.

Wednesday 26 October

Some nice people came to look at the flat. Loved it, said Arsehole. They'd like to make an offer.

Friday 28 October

Have to fly to New York tomorrow to interview Hillary Clinton for next month's cover story because all the senior interviewers and correspondents at *Life & Times* are either sick, busy or recently deceased. Hillary Clinton never did interviews with *Cat World*. Johnson reckons this will be my big break. Will completely make up for killing Sandra and dunking workie. I actually manage to laugh.

Isabel not delighted but understands sudden and unexpected career opportunity, particularly in wake of tea-throwing debacle. It means, she says, that we'll have to cancel lunch with our respective parents.

Can't see how this week can get much better.

Saturday 29 October

Upgraded!

I have a flat bed. I have proper cutlery. I have the choice of a thousand films with explosions, a thousand cocktails and a thousand different ways to adjust the lumbar in my seat, whatever that is. Even the toilet is completely different: there are moisturisers, aftershaves and a small but tasteful bouquet of orchids rather than strewn tissues, toothpaste spit and an unflushable memento from the previous occupant's visit.

Still can't see how this week can get much better, although the last time I said that it did, so I'm going to stop saying it. Perhaps Clinton will reveal that she slept with an intern exclusively in my interview? Or my hotel will know who I am and upgrade me to the presidential suite? Or I'll notice a waitress has dropped her lottery ticket, pick it up for her, accept her invitation for a coffee during which she'll check her numbers, realise she's won the interstate jackpot, and give me half? Although that might be difficult to explain to Isabel.

I wish Isabel had been able to come with me – she'd love it.

When I reach the airport taxi rank, I shout 'Taxi' excitedly, even though it's my taxi anyway. And when I get to the hotel, I can't resist an 'Any messages?' Then a 'No, okay, I'm expecting a call from Hillary Clinton's people.' But the receptionist is like, whatever. So I'm like, like I care. So he's like, waddayougonnadoaboudit? So I'm like, talk to the hand, buddy. I love it.

My room is on the fifty-third floor but the lift – sorry, elevator – only takes four seconds. This is all just brilliant, I'm thinking as I walk down the corridor to my room. I'm in New York. On assignment. And I'm going to go out and order the biggest hamburger in the whole of Manhattan. And gosh, I recognise that bottom and oh God, that's because it belongs to Saskia.

She Who Destroys Relationships.

'What are you doing here?' As well as being completely flabbergasted, I'm very angry, not because I have an anger-management issue but because there have been too many surprise turnings-up in the last couple of months.

'Hello to you too.'

'Yes hello, but what are you doing here? Are you following me?'

'What do you mean?'

'Well, here you are in the room next to mine in New York a month after you miraculously turn up in the flat downstairs from me in Finsbury Park.'

'I'm here for my best friend's twenty-fifth.'

'Oh, right.'

Her turn to look furious. 'Anyway. As you may have noticed, this is my room, I arrived first and therefore you are following me. So what are you doing here? And why the hell would I follow you? Just because we had sex a million years ago, you automatically assume I'm some bunny-boiling maniac who's decided the best way to spend my time is by following you around the world? You prick.'

'But —'

'But what? You think I'm so desperate? You think I don't know you didn't go to East bloody Timor to hunt for snake-eating orchids? Huh? You are a pathetic, snivelling bastard. You are a prick. A prick. A *prick!*'

And with that, she slammed the door. Which would have been a perfect, perfect way to leave things. Saskia hating me; Isabel loving me: that's absolutely the way it should be. Simply leave the DoR fuming safely in her room and go and order that enormous burger.

Except she was right, I had been a prick. It wasn't her fault she'd picked the flat I lived above. It wasn't her fault we were both in the same hotel in New York. She'd been friendly, I'd been a prick.

I went into my room and tried to admire the amazing view of Manhattan, but I couldn't. I felt bad. It was a million years ago, the sex. She's had lots of sex since then, all of it probably just as exciting, possibly even more so. And it was me that finished the whole thing. I cheated on my girlfriend. Then I finished with Saskia. All pretty callous.

Of course she did phone Elizabeth and tell her everything.

But that's just the sort of girl she is: spontaneous, strong, good at getting what she wants. Back then, she wanted to get even. Now, she wants to be friends.

I knocked at her door.

'What?' Still furious.

'Sorry, I was shocked.'

'Apology accepted. I'm just ordering drinks. Scotch and dry, right?'

Bugger.

Monday 31 October

It all happened incredibly fast.

First, I did accept the drink, but wrapped it up nice and fast.

Second, Hillary's people called my people, well, me, to cancel the interview and my office booked me on the Sunday night flight home.

Third, I flew home un-upgraded, telling myself all the way across the Atlantic that the Saskia thing was just another unfortunate coincidence, that I had nothing to hide and that I should be completely honest with Isabel.

Fourth, Isabel was there to meet me at the airport at the crack of dawn to cheer me up because the interview hadn't happened.

Fifth, her being at the airport meant I hadn't had time to psych myself up to tell her I stayed in the same hotel as Saskia and that I had a drink with her so I didn't tell her anything at all.

Sixth, I went to work kicking myself for being such an idiot because now I wouldn't ever be able to tell her because why, then, hadn't I mentioned it immediately?

Seventh, I called Saskia and told her not to mention New York if she was to bump into Isabel.

Eighth, she said sorry, she already had bumped into Isabel and had mentioned New York because she hadn't thought of any reason not to.

Ninth, Isabel's mobile was switched off.

Tenth, by the time I got back from work, Isabel was gone.

NOVEMBER

'Marriage may often be a stormy lake, but celibacy is almost always a muddy horsepond.'

THOMAS LOVE PEACOCK,
Melincourt (1817)

Tuesday 1 November

I don't think anyone can truly understand the meaning of being in the doghouse until they have been married for six months, gone to New York for the weekend by accident with a woman they once had sex with on Hyde Park Corner, and then tried not to mention it.

Isabel strode in at one o'clock this morning after presumably getting a pep talk from the bridesmaids. I left the requisite number of explanatory messages (eight) and thought it would be a good, martyrish idea to stay up, despite the overnight flight and long day at work. When I heard her unlocking the door, I adopted a haggard pose on the sofa, then looked over mournfully, ready to begin my apology. Before I could start, though, she fixed me with a paralysing glare, much like a python fixes a guinea pig. In low, monotonic tones, she spelt out the cruel size and shape of the doghouse: 'I've listened to your messages and I'd like you to sleep on the sofa.' For a delightful second, I thought she was joking – 'Get me a cup of tea or you're sleeping on the sofa' was her favourite line when we were playing at newlyweds. When she stormed into the bedroom, a sheet and pillow flying out soon after, all turned to despair again.

I but-, but-, but-ed through the door for a bit then decided to accept my lot and bed down for the night in the living room.

It took hours to get to sleep. When I woke, she had already left. A text message declared that she would be out again tonight.

Wednesday 2 November

A second night on the proverbial and actual sofa. My tactic tonight was to be asleep on her return because I was bound to look uncomfortable, she was bound to feel sorry for me and she would wake me up. It failed. I woke at 6 a.m. and the bedroom door was resolutely closed. So I decided to play hard to get and left before she woke. This meant great personal sacrifice – I had to wear the same clothes as yesterday, but it would be worth it just to be able to talk to her.

It worked. Well, it did and it didn't. For the first time in three days she called, which is good because it means the silent treatment is over, but bad because she was just calling to say she was staying with the fat bridesmaid tonight, that she would be away for the weekend and did I have a problem with that? I said I didn't but we really should talk. She said, 'What, about you and your floozy? I don't think so,' and hung up.

Saskia popped her manipulative, twisting, untrustworthy head out of her unbelievably badly located front door to ask, in a butter-wouldn't-melt purr, whether everything was all right.

'Fine, thanks,' I lied.

'Anything I can do to help?' she offered, unhelpfully.

'No thanks. Isabel still isn't talking to me because of whatever it was you helpfully said last time.'

'All I said was that it had been a nice surprise to meet up in the Big Apple and catch up on old times.'

'Oh, great. No wonder she's so angry with me.'

'She's very uptight, isn't she, your wife? Doesn't trust you an inch.'

'Well, that might be something to do with you. You put other women on edge. You're that sort of person.'

'Thank you, darling. You know where I am if you need or want anything.'

I hadn't meant it as a compliment, and what I want you to do, you treacherous evil harlot with your legs and your blonde hair and your skirt and your legs, is to go and live on the southern end of Stewart Island, where even you couldn't ruin a perfectly decent relationship. Unless of course you manage to upset some penguins.

Upstairs, I put my sad-lonely-bastard pizza in the you-idiot-what-have-you-done oven, and settled in for another evening alone.

Thursday 3 November

Day three of attempt to escape the doghouse, this time with Steve McQueen-on-a-motorbike panache: romantic dinner à deux to greet Isabel when she gets in from work. Left work early, fought lots of fellow panic-buyers to the rocket salad, garlic bread, salmon roulades and filet mignon at Marks & Spencer, then raced home to tidy flat, draw a big sign saying 'I'm sorry', put on soothing, unantagonistic music and scatter lots of tea lights.

Isabel arrived just as one of the candles ignited the 'I'm sorry' sign, which in turn set the highly flammable plastic magazine files on the sole surviving highly flammable bright-blue bookshelf on fire. I ran from the kitchen and began patting the uncomfortably large flames with my hands. Patting, I quickly realised, is the same as fanning, so I stopped and looked around for Isabel, who had just vanished. As the smoke alarm belatedly kicked in, I yelled out to her, 'Call the fire brigade.' At which point she emerged from the bathroom with a soaking towel and threw it over the bookcase. The fire was extinguished, the flat saved and I was still in the doghouse.

Friday 4 November

A horrible night. I'd been allowed back into the bedroom after a fairly edgy supper but Isabel had cold-shouldered me from the outset. In many ways, the in-bed cold shoulder is worse than the sofa cold shoulder. On the sofa, you can accept your fate and go to sleep. In the same bed, you are reminded with every breath and fidget of the trouble you are in. Is she asleep? Is she awake? Should I pretend to sleep? Should I pretend to be awake? Should I try to put an arm across her arm? Should I roll sleepily across and hug her? No, obviously not.

In the morning, while she is brushing her teeth, I decide to broach the subject again. I opt for a speed-talking approach. 'Look, I'm sorry about New York. I went for a drink with Saskia because I'd been rude to her. I was going to tell you but —' And dammit, she interrupted there, halfway through the tooth-brushing, just when it still sounded all guilt-ridden and excuse-y rather than honest and record-straightening.

'I am gow going away for ger weekend. I want you goo gink garefully agout what you gink gis garage geans gooyou. Now geegme alone. G.'

So I left her alone, even though I already knew what this marriage meant to me. I would spend the weekend pretending to re-evaluate. Then everything would be all right on Monday.

Saturday 5 November

After a tedious morning repainting the burnt bit of the ceiling, throwing out the crappy bright-blue bookshelf (whose manufacturers really should be reported to Health and Safety) and putting the unsinged books into storage, I go to the pub with Johnson and Andy. Johnson applies reason and judgement to my marital difficulties and concludes that I am not at fault and it is Isabel who is being unreasonable.

WHY ISABEL IS BEING UNREASONABLE: A MATHEMATICAL ANALYSIS

I did not know Saskia was going to be in New York +1

I was initially confrontational with her +1

I then apologised and accepted a drink –5

I had the drink and left without being lured +5

I didn't tell Isabel about the drink –5

I called Saskia and asked her to cover up –2

I slept on the sofa for two nights +5

I made dinner with candles and a sign +2

I nearly burnt the flat down –3

I have had to handle all the solicitor's house-move stuff on my own +2

I have been in the doghouse for five days which is ages considering I was not lured +5

TOTAL +6

Andy doesn't apply reason or judgement, choosing instead to remind me of his suggestion to hole up on a tropical island with Isabel. I leave the pub for once convinced that Johnson is right. New tactic: a big fight.

Sunday 6 November

When Isabel gets back, I tell her she has been unreasonable. She explodes. I explode back. I explode that she gets mad when I even so much as allude to the possibility that Alex might have designs on her but that they go out all the time. She explodes that that's because they're friends and didn't have sex on Hyde Park Corner. I explode that there was some covering up of breast-touching and whatever else. She explodes that at least Alex isn't a slut. I explode yes, but he is a stalker who keeps following me and heavy-breathing down the phone.

We retreat to the red and blue corners of our flat. Then yet another night of in-bed silent treatment. I am beginning to wonder whether I should have been unfaithful anyway. Couldn't possibly be any worse than this.

Monday 7 November

Just as I am deciding whether it would be easier to get the Tube home or jump off Tower Bridge, I see Isabel across the street from my office. She is smiling in a nice way, not a white-with-molten-burning-cutting-off-testicles-rage way, and she is also holding a gleaming new mountain bike with a ribbon wrapped around it.

'I'm sorry. You were right. I overreacted.'

Spot the trap, William. Don't fall in it. Don't agree with her.

'No, you didn't. I was wrong. I'm sorry. It's all my fault. I was an idiot.'

'It was just a shock. It seemed so implausible that you should be in the same hotel as Saskia.'

Another trap. Keep going.

'I should have said something. I was going to say something. I'm an idiot. I'm such a big idiot. I'm such a big, fat, stinking idiot.'

That's enough. Don't over-egg the self-flagellation pudding.

'Anyway, I've got you a little present: part-apology, part-country-house-warming.'

Like a phoenix from the ashes of the world's hairiest doghouse, I rise again. Forgiven. Apologised to. An owner of a very cool mountain bike.

I shall never try to hide anything from Isabel ever again.

Tuesday 8 November

First of six monthly anger-management meetings. Too happy to let the pointlessness of it get to me. I say everything they want me to say and nothing more.

Wednesday 9 November

To dinner with Lucy, who I'm still having to pretend to be best friends with after the whole forgetting thing, even though we went to her annoyingly perfect wedding. She is up from Marlborough for the weekend with her new husband, Tarquin. He is an archaeologist with a special attachment to Stonehenge. She is an expert in Chinese art at Sotheby's. Which means that, unlike me, they have found some way of applying their degrees to actual life. That, again unlike me, they are making some use of their brains. I don't mind being married to someone who has to make use of her brain, but I don't want to be friends with people who do as well. It is too much.

And at least Isabel doesn't read academic books to further explore the subjects she studied at university. 'It's amazing how much more interesting everything is now you know you don't have to do an exam at the end of it,' enthuses Tarquin. 'Yes, it's a true delight. Truly,' agrees Lucy. They both chortle as only smug, nauseating people can.

Back at home, I panic-Amazon the following books:

1215: The Year of Magna Carta

The Evolution of the British Welfare State

The Long European Reformation: Religion, Political Conflict and the Search for Conformity, 1350–1750

Cook with Jamie: My Guide to Making You a Better Cook

Thursday 10 November

Got the survey for the house today. Waste of bloody money. Ten pages of fence-sitting, arse-covering, commitment-phobic mumbo-jumbo.

'It was not raining at the time, so we were unable to comment on the effectiveness of the rainwater fittings.'

'No comment can be made as to the adequacy or otherwise of the roof structure or roof timbers without the opening up of the aforementioned timbers.'

'The walls may fall down, the roof may leak, the foundations could be made of jelly, the whole thing could be a disaster. We're not sure because we couldn't lift up the carpets. That'll be £840 please.'

Our solicitor says we should relax. The buyers of our flat are so excited to be moving to Finsbury Park that they had no complaints about their survey either. Presumably it didn't say, 'Tossers upstairs, nymphomaniac downstairs, murderers, rapists and dog-nappers outside.' Looks like we'll exchange tomorrow.

Friday 11 November

Can't exchange today. Someone at my mortgage company forgot to sign something although we're not sure who or what. Books have arrived, but too stressed about house to read them.

Monday 14 November

Still can't exchange. The thing someone was supposed to sign has been signed by the wrong someone so we have to get another thing altogether and get it signed by someone else.

Tuesday 15 November

Called the assistant allegedly handling the process of getting the someone to sign the something at the mortgage company.

'Carmen, it's William.'

'Hello, William,' giggle giggle. 'Can I just take your surname?'

'It's Walker. I'm the person who called you seventeen times yesterday.'

'Can you spell that?'

'W-A-L-K-E-R.'

'Oh right, yes.' Giggle. 'Was it about a mortgage?'

'Yes, we're waiting for someone to sign something.'

'Oh right.' Giggle. Long pause. 'Well, have they?'

'I don't know, that's why I'm calling.'

'Oh right. Silly' – giggle – 'me. Hold on a sec. I'll find out.'

Cue *Eine Kleine Nachtmusik*. Five minutes.

'Hello?'

'Who's that?' It's a man's voice.

'William Walker. I was talking to Carmen.'

'Oh sorry, sir, I must have picked up the wrong line. I'll transfer you back.'

Eine Kleine Nachtmusik. Five minutes. Then cut off. I call back.

'Can I speak to Carmen?'

'Sorry, she's just had to pop out to lunch. Canyoucallbackinan-hourandanarf?'

Wednesday 16 November

Started *1215: The Year of Magna Carta* but only reached page four. Then dreamt of petrol-bombing Carmen's mortgage office, her house, her parents' house and all her friends' houses, shooting anyone who tried to escape.

Thursday 17 November

Exchanged. We're moving on Saturday. Got to page eleven of *Magna Carta* and fell into such a deep sleep that I woke with a shock at eight, face down with my arms crossed underneath my body. Both of them were completely dead so I had to rock myself back and forth with my nose and my knees until they started coming back to life. Isabel thought I was having some sort of stress-related fit.

Friday 18 November

The Destroyer of Relationships is mercifully away for the weekend but kindly left a note under the door for either of us to find.

> *Dear William,*
> *It's been fun sharing the same house with you but not as much fun as it could have been. Enjoy your tweedy life in the countryside and call me if it gets too boring.*
> *Saskia xxxxxx*

What is wrong with the woman? Thank God I got back before Isabel did.

Saturday 19 November

'We don't need any removal men. We'll hire a van and do it ourselves.' That's now top of my list of Words That Will Come Back to Haunt Me, marginally ahead of 'I'll never get pickpocketed, darling. I'm too alert,' and, 'We don't need waterproofs, the forecast is sunny and, besides, a bit of light rain on an alpine trek won't kill us, now will it?'

Andy was the first to be injured, falling harder than he would have done if he hadn't been determined not to smash the vase he was holding on the way down. He really is a loyal friend again. A loyal friend with a nasty gash on his arm.

Then I lifted with my arms not my knees and people three streets away heard my back snap. It was agony until Isabel dropped her end of a chest of drawers early, causing a second snap. After that, it didn't hurt any more and I can now turn my head right around, like an owl.

I don't know how we got the sofa up the stairs but we sure as hell couldn't get it down again. So we decided to take the bay window out and lower it onto the street – only the sheer terror of lowering a sofa out of a first-floor window caused us all to become momentarily hysterical. It fell the last two metres and we now have two armchairs instead of one sofa.

Other casualties included three of the twelve wedding plates, one of the four whisky glasses, all of the champagne flutes and, when no one was looking, accidentally on purpose, a horrible crystal sculpture of a unicorn sent by one of Isabel's distant Polish relatives.

During the whole exhausting, arm-stretching, unending nightmare, Isabel managed to say 'I told you so' only fourteen times and, by one in the morning, a mere nine hours behind schedule, the flat was empty, all our wordly goods were in a battered old van and we were off to Kent like a couple of hobos.

Monday 21 November

Ahh, a fresh start. A new dawn. A proper marital home at last. I can't remember much about yesterday except that I had arms like Mr Tickle, that there are no traffic wardens patrolling our new road and that Isabel was actually squealing with delight because we had a spare room and our own private, non-communal stairs and a garden rather than a park full of used condoms and syringes. Oh, and that Isabel's mum came around twice for no reason whatsoever.

Today was great. After a first night in the new house we weren't woken by dance music, screaming or Saskia's high heels clicking away down the street. We were woken by birds tweeting, trees rustling and the sound of trickling water. The boiler, described in our survey as 'possibly all right, possibly not, can't tell 'cos it wasn't a Friday when we did the inspection', had sprung a fairly significant leak and water was trickling, like a romantic rural stream, down our bathroom wall.

We soon staunched the flow and embraced each other happily like we were doing a remake of *The Good Life*. After all, we were in the country now: a few teething problems were inevitable. We had breakfast on the patio because we'd never had a patio before, then went in for a hot bath together because it was a crisp November morning and our alfresco breakfast had given us hypothermia. Even Isabel will have a hot bath sometimes.

The commute was fine; no, really it was. Door to door, it only took an hour or so. Well, an hour and a half. But that's because I had to buy a ticket and I just missed the 08.24 and the next one wasn't until 08.47 and that was running late. I reckon I can get it down to under an hour. But even an hour and a half is fine because it gives me a chance to read. Really getting into the *Magna Carta* book now.

And I should normally get a seat. I hadn't understood why all the regular commuters were standing in small bunches on the platform. Turns out it's because the train doors always open in the same place. If I'd been in a bunch rather than in between two bunches, I would have stood a chance of a seat. So it'll be fine. I'm sure of it.

This evening, the neighbour popped around to introduce herself and tell us that our car was parked pointing in the wrong direction. She was hopping from one foot to the other, said her name was Primrose and that she got very twitchy when cars were pointing the wrong way even though she knew it was irrational. I said my name was William and that she was right to describe it as irrational because this was a quiet residential street and we could park the car whichever way we wanted. She said she wasn't trying to be difficult, it was simply that she needed the cars to be all lined up. I suggested that, perhaps, in the grand scheme of things, she was overreacting. So she put her hands over her ears and started hopping more urgently. I tried to explain some more but she just hopped faster and started humming, then umming, then screaming, '*It's the wrong way. It's the wrong way, it's the wrong way!!!!!*'

Isabel ran to the door with a paper bag, which Primrose proceeded to blow into, then tear up, then eat while we both tried to calm her. I agreed to turn the car around and her mood immediately brightened. Still chewing the paper bag, she repeated her welcome to the neighbourhood, told us to watch out for the people at number 24 and then walked off down the drive, taking care to only stand on cracks.

Tuesday 22 November

One hour twelve minutes but still didn't get a seat. A woman with a scarf on her head beat me to it. Isabel did the commute in fifty-six minutes, but that's because she's leaving an hour later when the rest of the world has already travelled.

Wednesday 23 November

Isabel does her commute in two minutes this morning on account of the fact that she has wangled Wednesdays and Fridays as 'working from home' days. I, on the other hand, am back to an hour and a half. 'We apologise for the late running of this service. This is due to the late running of an earlier service.' I want an apology and reason for the late running of the earlier service then, but none is forthcoming.

I am beaten to the last seat by the woman with the scarf again, so I take more notice of her. She is at least sixty. She has the look of someone who has spent her life being mean and self-serving. She is incredibly particular about how she folds her paper and how she lines up her glasses case on the flip-table. Her wispy, thinning hair forms a perfect, gravity-defying orb several inches around her head, protected from gusts of wind by the paisley scarf. At home, her tidy pink bathroom with shell motifs will be overflowing with big gold hairspray cans. We owe at least a third of the hole in the ozone layer to this woman.

Thursday 24 November

An hour and five. Scarf woman got the bloody seat again. I think I've worked her out: she's a barger. Everyone else dashes for a seat in a very polite, commuterish way, including me. But she barges. She also yelps if anyone touches her, which gives her an element of surprise. When a man put his briefcase on her shoe, she yelped as if it was a ten-pin bowling ball. He stepped back in shock; she nipped onto the train before him. I could try a different carriage altogether but that would be what she wanted. And who's to say there isn't a bescarfed monster on every carriage to London? Tomorrow, I will try a new strategy.

Late-night Ikea visit because Ikea on a Saturday is even worse than a shopping centre on a Bank Holiday Monday. It is still a Swedish vision of hell, with meatballs on the side. Stupidly, I hadn't eaten beforehand so I get hunger-anger before we even get through beds, and become unbearable. Isabel sends me off to the hotdog area early.

The 50p hotdog is always my Ikea highlight. It is something to look forward to, to focus on, to keep me strong as I battle the urge to fall to my knees in the middle of the Ingenious Foldaway Space-Saving Shelf Section and beg for a quick and painless death. Because it is a delicious hotdog and it only costs 50p. By having the hotdog prematurely, I am left with nothing to look forward to except more time in Ikea.

Trudging back, I cause worried looks and mutterings from other shoppers – 'Look, Dad, he's going the wrong way! He's not following the arrows. What will happen to him, Dad?' – and it is like being in *Nineteen Eighty-Four*. Except in *Nineteen Eighty-Four*, the Thought Police didn't wear yellow.

Isabel has found a shelf system called something ridiculous and we spend maybe seven or eight hours debating whether it would look less Ikea-ish in birch, beech or just white. We go for beech and trek down into the bowels of the not-at-all-super-store to try to find the flat-pack version. Isabel is convinced it will fit in the Corsa. I am not.

Then we pick out some plastic things, some glass things and some balsawood things, all of which we will regret buying as soon as we get home. We buy a wacky coloured rug after convincing ourselves it looks as if it's from the Conran Shop, which it doesn't.

They don't let you out of the loading bay area with your trolley. Oh no, that could cause a revolution. So I go and get the car. It's all becoming too much now – even Isabel is getting irritable. And the flat-pack doesn't fit. I knew it wouldn't and so, while people honk their horns and fight for spaces in a swirling Ikea maelstrom all around, I adopt the I-told-you-so position (arms crossed, motionless, slow shaking of head).

'Now we're going to have to walk home, along the hard shoulder of the M25, with a stupid flat-pack I knew wouldn't fit in the car.'

In a strange role reversal, Isabel becomes the flogger of the dead horse.

'Try putting the front seats forward a bit more.' Doesn't work.

'Try taking the headrest off.' Doesn't work. Breaks the headrest.

'Try jogging it up and down a bit.' Doesn't work. Just makes me sweatier.

'It's only an inch out. Try shoving it one more time.'

There is a loud crack as the shelves push into the rear-view mirror which works like the tip of a spear and drives straight through the windscreen. We both stop and look at the finger of cracked glass spreading down towards the wipers.

'I told you it would fit,' says Isabel.

Friday 25 November

The plan worked like a charm. By standing right next to her and adopting a brace position when the train door pulled up in front of us, I was able to repel her barging without actually looking as though I was barging her back. Because I had started off so close to her, she simply couldn't get any momentum up. And she couldn't yelp at me because I hadn't moved. She had nothing to protest about.

Unfortunately, I was so busy blocking that neither of us got a seat so we had to stand facing each other the whole way to London Bridge. Judging by the cold, cruel twinkle in her eye, she now knows she has an adversary.

Saturday 26 November

Our first weekend in the country and the prospect of a lie-in is ruined by the 8 a.m. arrival of Isabel's mother, a reluctant husband in tow. She has failed to observe the imaginary barrier that must not be crossed by parents before 10 a.m. I shall have to put up a real one, ringing the house with a high-voltage fence, barbed wire and dog patrols.

'Morning, all. Thought you'd be up by now, goodness, kids these days. I've brought some stew and some cake, and some Mr Muscle. We're going to get this kitch— *Oh my God, what's that?!*'

She had noticed the new scarecrow in Primrose's garden.

'It's the neighbour's new scarecrow,' I say, reaching for the kettle.

'What does she need a scarecrow for? Her garden's the size of a postage stamp.'

'It's because she has an irrational fear of pigeons. She doesn't like the way they look at her.'

'What's it made of?'

'Chicken bones.'

By mid-morning, it is clear that I am getting in the way so I escape by mountain bike into the surrounding hills. The minor irritations of life in the country are all worth it for this. Fresh air in the lungs, quiet country lanes, healthy exercise. No Avocado, no Denise, no £70 joining fee. You can't beat it. We've definitely made the right decision.

Sunday 27 November

We definitely haven't made the right decision. Isabel has gone mad. Today, before I was even properly awake, she announced a new raft of measures designed at countrifying our lives. I thought I had suffered enough with the whole temporary hot-bath clampdown and the goat's-milk episode. But now, in addition to resolutions 2314 through 2618, three more: we shall be ordering a vegetable box from a local farm each week, we shall no longer be using washing powder, and I am to build a compost box in the garden.

By the time our friends come down for the house-warming, we'll be living in the woods and eating worms.

Monday 28 November

Got a seat. Scarf woman furious, which made my day, but then the person sitting next to me started barking down his mobile phone, which didn't. I'm only on page sixty-two of *Magna Carta* and it's tough going at the best of times. With the barker barking in my ear it was impossible. I can't understand how some people have failed to realise that on-train barking is socially unacceptable in civilised society.

'Ted. S'George. Ya. Ya. What's the latest? Ya. Ya. Ya. Ya. Ya. No. Ya. Ya. How many did you get? Ya. Ya. Ya. Ya. What are we going to do with them? Na. Na. Na. Na. Yes, I would.'

Then, more annoying still.

'Sorry, Ted. Bloody tunn—... sorry, Ted. Another bloody tunn—... sorry about this, Ted, lots of bloody tunn—'

Isabel all excited because she spoke to a real, live farmer and ordered real, live vegetables, which will be arriving, milk-float-style, tomorrow. I'm very excited because the broken car windscreen is covered by our insurance.

Tuesday 29 November

It's all sodding turnips. Six of the big, flavourless bastards. And a tiny bit of broccoli, one courgette and some unfathomable beige things – half carrot, half dead man's fingers.

'It's organic. It's real,' squeals Isabel. 'We eat what's in season and, obviously, turnips are what's currently in season.'

'And beige fingers?'

'It's not all going to look perfect. This is called nature.'

'It doesn't look like anything I've ever seen before.'

'You're just brainwashed by the supermarkets to think everything that grows in the ground comes out washed, chopped and ready to boil. Well, they're all full of pesticides and hormones and strange genetic modifications and these,' she holds up the curled beige fingers, 'these are real vegetables.' All I can think of is the time I saw my great-aunt's arm drop from under the cover of a sheet as her body was carted off to the mortuary.

We have turnip soup for dinner.

Wednesday 30 November

Because the week is the new weekend, because we're cool and hip but primarily because there are no late trains back to London on the weekends, we hold our house-warming on a Wednesday. It is a decidedly civilised affair, as befits a happily married couple celebrating a smart move to the idyllic countryside. I don't care that we aren't going to wake up tomorrow in pools of our own vomit, with red wine stains on the carpets, walls and ceilings, bodies of unknown crashers strewn throughout the halls and illicit copulators still barricaded into bathrooms, bedrooms and larders. I can live without the police bashing the door down at six in the morning to ask if we wouldn't mind turning the music down. Or someone thinking it would be funny to demonstrate their suggestion of an open-plan kitchen-dining room by knocking through there and then. No, a nice soirée with champagne, canapés and good friends will do me.

It was a shame then that at eleven, just as our friends prepared for the mass exodus back to the grimy, smoggy, polluted streets of London, leaving me and my beautiful wife to our new-found semi-rural bliss, Alex announced he was thinking of moving out in this direction too, Saskia sent me a text message saying she'd heard I was having a house-warming and she was upset that I hadn't invited her, and Primrose decided to kidnap Isabel.

DECEMBER

'I have found the paradox that if I love until it hurts, then there is no hurt, but only more love.'

Mother Teresa
(who did not marry)

Thursday 1 December

Isabel has been released. After Primrose pushed her into her house, shouting, '*I've got a knife and I'm not afraid to use it*,' I thought, for a moment, that that was it. After surviving Finsbury Park, Isabel was going to be killed in a Kentish village. Then she came out again, Primrose's fuchsia-coloured front door slamming behind her.

'Bloody hell, she is properly mad,' is all Isabel had to say.

The policeman who arrived an hour and a half later said he wasn't going to take any further action against Primrose because it wasn't really a kidnap.

I explained that surely borrowing someone against their will was kidnap.

He said it was more of a domestic.

I said it was not a domestic because Primrose is a neighbour. Don't you have to be part of a family for it to be a domestic?

'Now you're being unreasonable, sir,' he replied. 'Ms Charterhouse is not known to us.'

'What about the weapon?'

'A cake slice is hardly a weapon, sir, and besides, sir, it's your word against hers. She says she just popped round to ask you to keep the noise down because it was half eleven and it was a weekday.'

'It was half ten. I phoned you at half ten. She kidnapped Isabel.'

'Calm down, sir', said the policeman. 'Ms Charterhouse points out that you are intoxicated and she isn't. She also said it would be pointless to kidnap a neighbour, then release them again five minutes later. It's just not the sort of thing we do in this village.'

'Are you really suggesting we imagined the whole thing?'

'I don't know, sir,' said the policeman. 'Are you sure you've only been drinking, sir? No other … substances that might … affect your judgement?'

'Don't be ridiculous.'

'Because, sir,' he continued, 'that sort of thing might go on in Primrose Hill or wherever you've come from, but down here, sir, we take a dim view. A very dim view indeed.'

'She has a scarecrow made of chicken bones in her garden, officer,' I respond, but he says that given the time of night and the lack of evidence of anything other than a bit of late-night prankery, he isn't about to go banging on her door again demanding to investigate the possibility of a scarecrow made from chicken bones, which isn't illegal anyway. He suggests we get a good night's sleep and buggers off, leaving us to clear up the party and wonder whether Finsbury Park was safer after all.

Isabel had remained silent throughout my interrogation. And then she said, 'It's okay, William. Let's just go to sleep. I think she's harmless.'

'Harmless?'

'It was only a cake slice.'

After a fitful night, we are woken at seven by an insistent ice-cream-van melody. Scribbling out yet another mental Post-it note to change the doorbell ring of the previous occupants, I arm myself with the most dangerous thing I can find in the wardrobe (a rollerblade, though I'd have preferred an ice skate), and answer the door with an aggressive swoosh. It is not Primrose, here to finish what she inexplicably started. It is a delivery man clutching a large cardboard box.

'Easy, mate,' he says, handing me the box and backing away nervously.

The mind boggled. Was it a horse's head? A fishbowl full of flies? A black spot?

Worse, Alex has sent us a house-warming present: two horrible stained-glass bedside lamps which emit various levels of bright ness depending on how many times you stroke them. Inevitably, Isabel loves them. Says she always wanted them, which is ridiculous because no one would have something so awful and twee on a wish list. It's like always having wanted a large porcelain cat or an ashtray made out of that purple kryptonite stuff.

I suggest they might look nice in the garage.

She suggests that, given that she was kidnapped by our neighbour last night, the least I could do this morning is be supportive.

I suggest that the lamps and the kidnapping are entirely unrelated and she gives me a look which suggests I have learnt nothing from seven months of married life.

Five minutes later, the bedside lamps are ruining our nice new bedroom and I have to accept that, from now on, the last thing I will see at night, not to mention the first thing in the morning, will be a tacky reminder of Alex. And Isabel stroking it.

Dinner: turnip surprise. The surprise being there really is nothing but turnip. No meat. No other vegetables. Just some sort of turnip-based sauce.

Friday 2 December

The doorbell goes at 9.30 p.m. It's Primrose, just when I'd put the rollerblade away again. This time, though, she is wielding a cake rather than a cake slice. She has made it by way of apology for the kidnapping she told the police never happened. She says she's sorry, it's just that the parked cars make her panic and do silly things. Isabel says it's fine, I say yes, absolutely no problem, and we usher her out of the door with a communion of smiles.

Isabel and I then argue for about an hour over whether she should have said something or whether I should have said something along the lines of don't ever come round here again, you maniac.

The doorbell goes again at 10.30 p.m. It's Primrose with another cake she has made by way of apology. She appears to have no recollection of the first cake. Again, Isabel says thank you and I say no problem, always good to meet the neighbours, and we usher her out the door. Again, there is heated argument about who should have said what to the lunatic bringing cakes round at God knows what hour.

I throw both cakes in the bin because they're probably made with cat food and bleach and toenail clippings and eye of newt, and we go to bed. It's hours before either of us can sleep for fear of more apologetic cakes.

Dinner, by the way: turnip soufflé. The cakes, regardless of ingredients, would have been nicer.

Sunday 4 December

Isabel strikes up a conversation with the neighbour on the other side who can't understand why we've got a problem with Primrose. Apparently, she's always been perfectly decent with them. A real pillar of the community. Never complained about the parking, never kidnapped anyone, however briefly, and certainly never been seen marching naked up and down her garden, knitting, at 4 a.m. (like she was last night). But, said the neighbour, she's not our neighbour. She's yours, so maybe you see more than we do. Or maybe you did something to upset her.

Isabel's mum says it will probably blow over, although she once had a neighbour in Poland who started acting crazy, and everyone said it would blow over, and one day the person killed nine people with a hammer, but that was Communism for you so it's bound not to happen here.

Dinner: you'd have thought we would have cleared the turnip backlog, but there is still some work to be done, so it was turnip soup followed by turnips with chicken followed by what, if we'd had pudding, would no doubt have been turnip sorbet.

Monday 5 December

I have a quick look at houses for sale in north London before (a) realising what I'm doing and (b) concluding that the only area we can afford is Finsbury Park and, thanks to the huge chunk of cash Arthur the Thieving Arsehole took, we can now only afford a studio flat. Even given Primrose, moving back to a smaller flat (without fitted shelves) in the place we've just escaped from would be ridiculous.

At least it's the start of the party season. Anything, frankly, to get us out of the house and not eating turnip. I start gently because this is the first Christmas I've had to cope with since becoming middle-aged: a night in my old local with Johnson and Andy. Having wasted most of the day trying to compose a text to Saskia explaining why she wasn't invited to the house-warming party in as inoffensive yet final yet uninvolved yet undismissive a way as possible, I ask them to help. Several pints in, they conclude, as I already had done, that it just isn't possible with only 149 characters. It's just like trying to dump someone nicely, which is impossible.

THE ONLY TWO STRATEGIES FOR DUMPING GIRLFRIENDS, NEITHER OF WHICH IS PREFERABLE

By email/letter (not hand-delivered, too risky)

Pros: you aren't there during tears and vase-throwing, and you can say what you really mean, not what will make the tears and vase-throwing go away (e.g. it's not me, it's you; I've met someone who is much less annoying; I want to have a takeaway when I feel like it, not when you say I can; it's over, goodbye).

Cons: everyone thinks you are a bastard because you didn't even have the guts to do it in person.

In person

Pros: everyone thinks that, although you're a bastard for dumping your girlfriend, at least you did it the right way.

Cons: you are there for the tears and the vase-throwing, so you have to say what you don't really mean (e.g. it's not you, it's me; no,

I just want some time on my own; please, stop crying, I'm not dumping you, I just think we could both do with a break; sure, we can go for a drink to discuss it).

Johnson says the only way to do it is by getting them to dump you. Pick your nose at dinner, spray the toilet seat then leave it up, don't just ogle other women, stop in the street and say *Wow!*, forget all anniversaries, talk only about sport. It takes about a week and you're home free.

Andy says he wishes he could get to the stage of being dumped more often – rather than having immigration officials do it for him.

Johnson says the only reason he's married is because Ali doesn't mind that he talks only about sport.

Tuesday 6 December

Another angry text from Saskia. Am thinking silence is perhaps the best option.

A boring work-related party coincides with Isabel's boring work-related party, so we agree to meet on the last fast train home, which I miss by three seconds because it left one minute, four seconds early. I remonstrate with the platform assistant who points at a sign explaining that trains are prone to leave a minute early and I'm about to point out that it left even earlier than that when I realise there is nothing, absolutely nothing, to be gained.

My phone rings and it's Isabel saying where am I because she's got me a coffee and a seat so I explain how the train left early and she says there's a sign saying it leaves early.

I retreat Zen-like into myself and wait for the last-not-fast-really-really-slow train.

Fifty minutes later, the Zen thing has worn off. The train is late and I am surrounded by a carnival of late-night out-of-towner horrors.

A benchload of teenagers are trying to eat each other's faces off like extras from a zombie movie.

A girl in a trouser suit is actually howling like a wolf because her boyfriend/husband has, quite understandably given the state of her inebriation and her mascara, abandoned her at Charing Cross.

A couple with myriad facial piercings are punching each other really hard in the facial piercings while police try pointlessly to prise them apart.

A football enthusiast sets off a klaxon – as if a distraction is necessary – while his mates try to steal the station clock.

And three women are dragging an unconscious man across the concourse, perhaps to a basement cell to be used as a sex slave, perhaps just to bed and a terrible hangover in the morning.

It's like Custer's Last Stand, and then the train finally arrives and all these people board it with me.

I crawl into bed at 2.15 a.m., nearly two hours after I would have done if the train hadn't left four seconds earlier than a minute earlier than it bloody should have bloody done bloody bloody.

Wednesday 7 December

Seven a.m. doorbell. Primrose. Why have we thrown her cakes in the bin?

How does she know we've thrown them in the bin?

Because she's been through our rubbish.

Too tired to deal with this, so I explained we have a gluten allergy.

'What, both of you?' she said, putting her foot firmly in the closing door.

'Yes, Isabel caught it off me.' The reply took her by just enough surprise to allow me to say goodbye and shut the door before becoming further embroiled.

It was going to be a good day.

Until I missed the train home again, this time because it went from a different platform. I actually cried a bit in frustration. Then sat through another two hours of exactly the same people doing exactly the same things: face-eating, fighting, passing out, vomiting. It's all so festive.

Thursday 8 December

Work party. Horrible. Already exhausted by previous three nights out and missing of trains. Isabel annoyed that I can barely speak to her due to fatigue which is all my own fault because I 'keep partying' even though it isn't because it's the train's fault.

To compound everything, Anastasia the Work Experience I Threw (Cold) Tea Over has been invited. She jetted back from New York especially for our little party. (Who jets? You don't jet, you fly.) Anyway, how sweet of her to show such disregard for the size of her bulging carbon footprint by jetting over especially. How simply marvellous. And what, pray, is she doing in New York? Currently, feature writing at the *New Yorker* but soon to be launch editor of a top-secret new section of the *New York Times* as of 3 January. She can't tell us any more or she'd have to kill us, except to say that it has been a lightning year and it's all thanks to us; well, most of us (cue withering look in my direction), and now she must be leaving because she can't, simply can't, miss the redeye back to the Big Apple. Mwa mwa. *Adios*. Spew.

Despite arriving half an hour early and listening bat-like for any platform changes, I miss my own redeye because it simply doesn't arrive. My friend the platform assistant, in a brief and uncharacteristic display of humanity, says, 'Sorry, mate, they don't tell me the whys and wherefores, but it isn't good enough, is it?'

Despite the usual cacophony of screaming, swearing, fighting and sucking, I fall into a near-coma and wake up one stop beyond home. The doors were open and if I'd made a dash for it, I could have got off in time and got a £10 taxi home. But I was damned if I was going to have a big been-asleep, missed-my-stop panic and amuse everyone still left on the train. So I just yawned and stretched as nonchalantly as possible and had to wait twenty minutes for the next station. And got a £45 taxi home.

Friday 9 December

To Penge at the crack of dawn for the anger-management course where I initiate a long discussion about whether it is our anger that requires management at all. What if, I argue, our anger was perfectly justified and it was society's consistent ineptitude that needed the managing? The same woman as before twitched slightly at this perfectly valid argument, but rather than respond with a sensible/erudite/enlightening answer, she just made more notes.

I wasn't going to give her the satisfaction of becoming angry this time. I could beat her at her own game.

Got the third-from-last fast train home, with a wink from the platform assistant. In bed by 9.15 p.m.

Saturday 10 December

A momentous decision. I am not going out ever again in London. I don't care what anyone says, I refuse to socialise in the capital. I am too old. I am too tired. I don't like drinking, I don't like staying up late, I don't like hangovers or trains or hassle. Consider all engagements cancelled.

Isabel accepts this 8 a.m. pronouncement with enthusiasm. Anything, she says, to stop the whingeing. And she happily agrees to cancel everything too. We shall spend the next two weeks in out-of-town bliss, apart from, of course, having to commute in every day for work but that's fine because I know how to beat that scarfed woman to my seat.

Monday 12 December

This is much better.

A lovely weekend of pubs and winter walks and fruit crumbles and mulled wine and lie-ins and sex and backgammon. Even the turnip mountain has been conquered.

Tonight, I picked my way through the early evening office-worker revelry, happy in the knowledge that I shall be tucked up in bed fast asleep in my village and that all these idiots will be missing trains and slipping on vomit and sleeping with strangers who will appear far less attractive in the morning.

Wednesday 14 December

Even a missed call from Saskia cannot dent my spirit. I just can't understand why people who are already in relationships bother going out and getting drunk and chatting. There's nothing in it. Just pointless conversation, unnecessary outgoings and a hangover.

Staying at home is the new going out. Home has all the advantages of a bar (alcohol, seating) with none of the disadvantages (other people, loud music). Plus you can still have sex.

We appear to have upped our average to just under once a day, which is a relief given the latest shock survey in the papers this morning. The French say they do it nine times a week compared to the Germans who only do it four times. The English, more importantly, given that one must always judge oneself against one's peers, do it just eleven times a month, so I'm ahead. By 0.12 intercourses per day.

I am in the upper quartile.

Saturday 17 December

Isabel and I had a long conversation last night about how good marriage is, how lucky we are to have found each other, how the first few months were bound to be difficult because our lives were in a state of flux.

If I'm honest, which I wasn't at the time, it was quite a boring conversation; one of the ones you have to have from time to time when you're sitting on a sofa with your wife and it's pesto pasta night and there's nothing good on TV. My refusal to attend Christmas social events has been met with scorn at work – I cannot walk into a room without someone humming the theme from *Terry and June* – but I refuse to give up my comfortable, suburban, pedestrian, enjoyable existence.

Sunday 18 December

Whole day in bed. No Primrose. No texts. No violent carol singers. Only the strokeable bedside lamps intrude on an otherwise perfect day. Isabel calls me a stud and this time she wasn't even being ironic. I don't think. You can never be sure.

Monday 19 December

It would appear that my thirty-day, money-back-guaranteed Viagra trial has begun. I know this because a box of little blue pills has arrived in the post addressed for 'M. Walker', which Isabel has opened. The company, based in Florida, has my credit-card details, which they have already used to withdraw an initial down-payment of US$240.

Isabel is speechless.

Well, she's speechless for about twelve seconds before she asks why I think I need Viagra and whether it would have been sensible and appropriate to discuss this sort of thing with her, or perhaps a doctor, before signing up to some dodgy American therapy programme. And spending a large proportion of our marital budget on sex pills.

I had only been expecting a cup of tea (which, by the way, is now standard-issue goat's milk *sans* sugar, which I have, as an adaptable husband, grown to quite like). Now I'm getting the Viagra Monologues.

Only when Isabel pauses for breath can I focus enough to point out that I know nothing about it.

Only after forty-five minutes of *Eine Kleine Nachtmusik* do I find someone at my credit-card company willing to believe that I do not need Viagra.

'So, Mr Walker, you definitely didn't give your details on any adult website?'

'No.'

'And there's no way anyone using your computer in your house could have accessed an adult website, typed in all your personal details and signed up to some sort of eighteen-plus sex site?'

'No.'

'Because lots of people, when they get found out by their wives or girlfriends or cohabiting partners, claim this sort of thing is fraud rather than admit they have been on adult-content websites.'

'Yes, okay.'

'Yes, okay, as in, Yes, okay, you have been on adult-content websites?'

'No, yes, okay as in, "Yes, okay, I understand but can we get on with this … I know nothing about this, I have not signed up for a Viagra trial and I don't need a lecture. I just want you to find out what happened and get my money back."'

'Yes, okay.'

I am going to write a letter of complaint to my credit-card company.

Tuesday 20 December

Isabel apologetic today about Viagra misunderstanding. I forgive her quickly because we are blissfully, rurally in love until I realise why she's being nice. Bloody Alex is coming to bloody Christmas bloody lunch at her bloody parents' house.

'What?'

'Alex has been invited to join us for lunch. My parents only just mentioned it.'

'Why?'

'Because his family are in Montreal with his sister.'

'What?'

'He told them he'd be on his own for Christmas.'

'How?'

'When he spoke to them.'

'When?'

'On the phone a couple of days ago.'

'Why?'

'He still calls them every now and again. Just to keep them up to date.'

'Why?'

'I don't know. I guess he just likes them.'

'Why?'

'What do you mean, "Why?" Are you saying my parents are difficult to like?'

And so on.

So my first Christmas as a married man is ruined even before it's begun.

Thursday 22 December

Must buy Isabel present, despite Christmas being ruined. Missed last orders on Amazon. Went to John Lewis on Oxford Street and saw two women fighting over the last pair of Rudolph the Red-Nosed Reindeer Y-fronts which was such an unfestive and depressing sight, I had to leave with nothing but a set of cheese knives for the in-laws. Liberty just seemed silly – £180 for a scarf? Unsure of myself in Agent Provocateur what with all the super-confident, super-buxom staff walking around in lingerie. Just gone too far in Ann Summers. Just as wrong but for all the opposite reasons in Dorothy Perkins. And she's not going to appreciate anything from the Gadget Shop (not even the remote-control indoor helicopter I only just manage to convince myself not to offer as a novelty present).

Why can't they have a shop selling things women want rather than lots of shops selling things men think women want? Why can't I just give someone some money in return for an appropriate and preferably pre-wrapped present?

I decide to phone a friend – aka Johnson – who puts on Ali who tells me I've left it quite late before giving me a brief but instructive lesson on successful present-purchasing for women.

WHAT WOMEN WANT

Men to guess miraculously, by some divine inspiration, the exact obscure thing they've been wanting all year even though they don't even know what it is themselves.

Sexy but at the same time flattering but at the same time comfortable lingerie. Which, like the above, doesn't exist.

Tickets to something girly like the ballet or a musical, not a rugby match.

Someone else to take them away from all this.

WHAT WOMEN DON'T WANT

A threesome.

An ironing board.

Sports biographies, iPods, laptops, remote-control helicopters or anything else that is clearly for the man, not the woman.

Slutty lingerie (e.g. crotchless and/or edible panties, nipple-revealing bras, suspenders), whips, handcuffs, French maid outfits or anything else that is clearly for the man's benefit.

Ali then puts Johnson back on so I can tell him what she just told me. I like the way their marriage works. It's practical.

Saturday 24 December

To my parents for a sorry-we're-spending-Christmas-with-my-wife's-family-and-psycho-ex-not-you lunch. Mum is in denial. She has made roast turkey.

Sunday 25 December

Christmas is supposed to be a time of peace, love and understanding. No such luck, through no fault of my own, for me.

Rubbish Christmas, part one

Despite my best efforts, the present-giving went horribly wrong.

She went first and absolutely loved the thoughtful theatre-and-dinner tickets, the non-slutty lingerie and the wheelbarrow full of perennials I'd left wrapped with a bow in the garden. I went second and didn't look suitably excited by the socks (labelled with the days of the week so I can pair them more easily) or the book (titled *It's Not Easy Being a Man: 25 reasons why you really are always right and she really is always wrong*).

'It's just a joke.'

'Hahahahaha. A joke book and another nag about how I never pair my socks. Thanks.'

'Well, we did say we weren't going to do big presents this year, what with the house move.'

'Yes, I know, but we always say that. You're not supposed to take it seriously.'

'Well, it's silly to spend a fortune on presents we don't need …'

'Please don't say "… what with the starving Africans."'

'… What with the starving Africans.'

'Okay, I'll send the pants and the theatre tickets to Africa.'

'That's not funny.'

'Well.'

'And I thought you'd like the socks. You can walk around with Monday on one foot and Thursday on the other. You like being a rebel.'

Rubbish Christmas, part two

Alex is already there when we arrive, hogging the sofa next to Isabel's mum who is showing him a photo album.

'Hi William, Merry Christmas. Come over here and look at these amazing pictures of your very glamorous parents-in-law.'

I approach warily and before I can run screaming from the room, the house, the village, the whole goddamn planet, I find myself looking at porn.

'You really were very striking when you were younger, Mrs B,' says Alex as we look at a picture of Isabel's parents clutching each other, pendulous breasts and swollen pudendum on show for all to see.

'Thank you, darlink,' she replies. 'Look how firm Henry was back then.' I fight back the sudden urge to die in a pool of my own vomit and acute embarrassment.

'Oh Mum, not that album again, it's disgusting,' says Isabel, but doesn't do any more in the way of coming to my rescue.

'Don't be silly, darlink. Stop being so conservative.'

Over the next twenty pages, I am subjected to a barrage of images that would shock the most liberal of thinkers. It's art, apparently: a wedding gift from some Sixties photographer friend of theirs.

Why wasn't I warned?

Consecutive turkey lunches are hard work in any circumstances but with the added parental nudity, I have no hope of finishing my meal. Isabel's father – who I can now only picture naked and ecstatic under a younger, firmer version of Isabel's mother – is, of course, highly disapproving.

Rubbish Christmas, part three

Alex has also bought Isabel's parents a set of cheese knives for Christmas. Except mine came from John Lewis and his came from Fortnum's. Mine are accompanied by nothing ('Because,' said Isabel, 'my parents don't like ostentation'). His are accompanied by a whole wheel of Stilton from Neal's Yard. And a book on great cheeses of the world. And some chutney he made himself. Six bottles, each a different level of spiciness.

'Because I know you like it spicier than Mr B, Mrs B.' The two of them laugh conspiratorially. I've never laughed conspiratorially with my mother-in-law. I've never called her Mrs B either.

Mr and Mrs B love ostentation. They hug him and say you shouldn't have, marvel at how he managed to find time to make chutney, then unwrap my shitty cheese knives and everyone looks blank. Eventually, there are muted thanks, suggestions of perhaps taking one set back (I wonder which), then me saying I've still got the receipt, then Alex saying what a silly coincidence, then me replying, yes, cheese knives are like buses, and then no one laughing.

They use Alex's knives to cut Alex's Stilton. I use mine to cut him into tiny little cheesy pieces and serve him on cocktail sticks with pineapple. Until someone spoils my fantasy by asking me to pass the chutney.

'I'll try number five. Number four was good but I'm ready for the hard stuff.'

Someone kill me.

Rubbish Christmas, part four

You really would have thought that that was enough for one season of glad tidings but then, on the miserable post-lunch walk through high winds and sleeting rain, I find myself stuck at the back with Alex. The real Alex, the bastard who's in love with my wife.

'Shame about the cheese knives,' he begins, a big grin on his stupid face.

'Yes, devastating,' I retort rather pathetically.

Stony silence.

'How are the lamps, by the way?'

'Great, really great.'

'Really? Isabel didn't give me that impression. Sounded like they were more up her street than yours.'

'No, they're up both our streets. We're on the same street. So thanks, I like the lamps. Very … tactile.'

'Oh, okay. Well, that's good.'

Even longer stony silence.

'And I'm glad to hear your marital difficulties are over.'

'What marital difficulties?'

'You know.'

'Look, mate, it's none of your business, but for your information there is no marital difficulty …'

'Yes, but Isabel's my friend and I'm just saying I'm glad everything is back on track.'

'Hang on a —'

'And that all is well in the you-know-what department.'

'No, I don't know what. What are you talking about?'

'Nothing. Hey, do you fancy going paint-balling sometime? I've never done it but it's supposed to be great.'

'Not really, no.'

'Oh, okay.' And with that, he climbed a stile and went running off after his number one fan, Mrs B.

Monday 26 December

Did you tell Alex I didn't like the lamps? No.

Did you tell Alex we were having marital difficulties? No.

Did you tell Alex I was buying your parents a set of shitty cheese knives? No.

Did you tell Alex we were having sexual difficulties? No.

Well, how did he know all that then?

Wednesday 28 December

I don't know what to think and I don't think I care any more. Like Diana, I'm in a crowded marriage. Except I don't think Diana's threesome involved actual spying.

Because the options I've narrowed it down to over the last two festive days are these: either Isabel is lying and she is telling Alex all about our private affairs and they're having a good laugh behind my back; or she isn't lying and Alex is somehow listening in on all our conversations. Neither is great.

To clear my head, I decide to go for an early morning ride on the bike Isabel bought me the last time we were being driven apart. It is dark when I leave but the blood-red orb of the sun soon breaks over the horizon and I am out of the village, racing along the lanes on a crisp winter's day. It's good to do some exercise every now and again, I think to myself. Not in a stinking gym with some Lycra-clad sadist driving you on. Out in nature, sweeping through the glorious British countryside, alone in the elements, fresh air pumping through your lungs.

'Morning,' I call cheerily to a tweedy man walking his dogs. He looks vaguely familiar.

'What do you think this is?' he shouts back, pointing to a locked gate we've both reached at the same time.

'It's a gate,' I reply, too puzzled to understand.

'You can't get a bloody horse through that, can you?' He's still shouting, although we're now no more than three feet apart.

'Probably not.' I still can't work out what he's getting at. Neither of us has a horse so it's not an enormous problem. You couldn't get a wheelchair through it either, but again, it's simply not an issue.

'It's not a bloody bridle path, so you're not allowed to cycle here,' he shouts.

'Oh, I must have taken a wrong turn. I've got an OS map here.'

'You think I can't read an OS map. You think I'm some sort of bloody idiot. I can read an OS map. I live here. I live on this estate. If you don't believe me, ask anyone.' His whole head has swollen into a red, veiny balloon. He must be seconds away from having a stroke, and that is probably a good thing.

'I'm sure you can read an OS map. Would you mind telling me where the bridle path goes, then?'

'WE'VE ALL GOT KEYS. EVERYONE IN THE VILLAGE HAS GOT BLOODY KEYS. SO DO YOU THINK I'M BLOODY LYING?'

It's quite a flabbergasting onslaught.

'No, I just want you to show me where the bridle path goes.'

'YOU DON'T BELIEVE ME? YOU DON'T BLOODY BELIEVE ME? WHERE ARE YOU FROM? WHERE ARE YOU BLOODY FROM? YOU'RE NOT FROM THE VILLAGE.'

I tell him that I am from the village and that I'd be grateful if he could just stop shouting long enough to tell me where the bridle path goes.

'OVER THERE!' He's pointing at a path covering the same ground but coming out at a stile ten yards further along. I have trespassed off it for about ten seconds. I tell him this and he goes an even redder shade of scarlet.

'I DON'T CARE. I COULDN'T GIVE A TOSS. IT'S THE GAMEKEEPER YOU WANT TO WATCH OUT FOR. HE'S NOT NEARLY SO UNDERSTANDING.'

'What's he going to do, shoot me?'

The tweedy man's face becomes inscrutable and without another word he climbs over the stile and walks off.

I shout Merry Christmas after him and walk my bike the eight yards to the correct stile, swearing to attend the next Countryside Alliance march just to throw rotten eggs at all these silly wax-jacket-wearing idiots.

I get home more stressed than when I left. I shower, I change, I jog down to the station to get the train to work. Standing next to me on the platform, as he is every morning, is the tweedy man, now de-tweeded and wearing standard-issue business suit. I knew I had seen him somewhere before.

He bids me good morning, as he always does, not recognising me without my law-breaking mountain bike.

I bid him good morning back, then spend the rest of the journey into London wishing I'd bid him fuck off instead. But by the time we come into Charing Cross, I have a plan. I walk over to his seat, hand him a leaflet from my anger-management class and suggest he joins us.

The look on his face as he puts two and two together is still not enough to cheer up a day that began with a stroke of Alex's horrible lamp.

Saturday 31 December

Firstly, let me say, dear diary, that this will be my last day of drinking for a month. I can feel both my kidneys protesting at the cruel treatment they've been subjected to over the last month/year/decade, despite my brief lapse into rural bliss. And my liver seems to have left the building altogether. Andy is also suffering acute organ failure. Johnson has been told by his wife that his pot-belly is getting a pot-belly of its own. She loved the original pot-belly, but not the new one. We are all abstaining for a month.

Which partly explains what happened later.

Because I worked all week and Isabel's more enlightened office closed for the festive period, she was left to arrange the fancy dress. Hers was therefore brilliant – Marilyn Monroe in *that* dress, complete with convincing wig and portable up-skirt wind machine. Mine wasn't so good. I would be Clark Kent until midnight, then phone-booth myself into Superman to welcome in the New Year. I didn't think it sounded like a good idea, particularly given that Isabel had been unable to find a proper Superman costume.

Still, she told me I looked sexy with my Clark Kent glasses so I went along with it. All evening, her annoying friends (why couldn't we have gone to one of my friends' parties?) asked why I'd come to a fancy-dress party in a suit. All evening I said, wait and see.

As the hour of both revealing my superpowers and abandoning drink for a month approached, I became increasingly inebriated. Isabel was wowing everyone with her billowing skirt and I was de-wowing them with my suit and speccy four-eyes.

Bong. Bong. Bong. My big opportunity.

I stepped onto the dance floor and began to strip. Empowered by vodka, I really gave it everything, flinging my blazer across the room, nearly garrotting myself as I whipped off my tie. Then shirt, then trousers. It wasn't quite Christopher Reeve, but as I stood there in my Superman T-shirt, frilly red knickers and blue tights, I expected a round of applause at the very least.

No one noticed.

Everyone was too drunk and too busy singing Old bloody Lang bloody Syne.

Except for Isabel. She'd watched the whole debacle from the kitchen doorway. After suppressing a cruel giggle, she came over and whispered, 'Let's go home, Superman, before your cover is blown.'

That wasn't even the embarrassing bit. I can't remember the Tube or the train. I can remember getting back to the village and Isabel still Monroe-ing her knickers at me. And getting into the house and her singing 'Happy Birthday' all provocatively, and me pretending to fly and hurting my knees quite badly. And then us, rather spontaneously I thought for married people, tearing each other's clothes off. Literally tearing them, so that we'd have trouble returning them to the fancy-dress shop next week – not that I was thinking about that at the time. Well, I was a bit.

And then starting to have sex.

And it all going to plan.

And then the image of her naked, postcoital mother and father, winking provocatively from the album on Alex's lap.

And then retreat. Like a snail someone just threw salt over.

And the words, 'Don't worry, we can try again tomorrow,' coming from Isabel's lips like a bullet between the eyes of a malfunctioning prize bull.

I am sexually incapable. Happy New Year.

JANUARY

'The majority of husbands remind me of an orang-utan trying to play the violin.'

HONORÉ DE BALZAC

Sunday 1 January

No one, not her, not me, says anything about my lack of performance, which means it must be a serious problem. Really need a drink but mustn't fail at that too.

Monday 2 January

Still no one's said anything about Mr Floppy. Soon it will be time to have sex again, with this unresolved. Can't believe this is clashing with the alcohol ban.

Tuesday 3 January

We're on the sofa watching Bond and a *Gardener's World* winter special (I get fifteen minutes, she gets fifteen minutes. How's that, by the way, for marital harmony?) when I decide the sooner, the better on the sex front. After all, it's exactly the same as getting straight back in the saddle after a fall. Assuming, of course, that neither you nor the horse has broken a neck.

I wait until it's Bond (no point making a move when they're digging up parsnips). Then I put my hand, which is schoolboy clammy, on her knee like we're on a grubby first date at the cinema. Unlike most of my first dates, she seems unperturbed, so I go in for a kiss. Our teeth bang, which hasn't happened in years. I retreat.

I stretch my arms up, then down, and snare her with one of them – another textbook adolescent manoeuvre. I pull her towards me, start nibbling her ear, she moves to swat me away and I go in for another kiss. Better this time. I resist the urge to ice-cream-cone her mouth out with my untrained tongue because I am not actually a teenager. We kiss gently, then more vigorously, and just as I'm going to go for second base, BANG, Isabel's naked, writhing parents pop into my head again.

I stop kissing Isabel and look back at the television to find Sean Connery just millimetres from laser-gun castration.

Wednesday 4 January

Andy is in love in Guiana and can't make himself available for an emergency pint until next Wednesday. Not that we can have a pint anyway.

Johnson is the next best bet so we meet for lime sodas in a wine bar. He has his own problems. The pot-belly's pot-belly has grown half a centimetre since he stopped drinking four days ago. He's thinking of starting to drink again.

My problem, he thinks, is that I'm thinking too much. It's better to keep it simple: every time I start overanalysing during sex, I must simply chase the thought away. It's the same principle as counting sheep.

If that doesn't work, then I must use the Sex Gears.

'Tell me about the Sex Gears, oh Grand Master,' I say, nursing my fruitless pint of fruit cordial.

'Okay, it's like what Sting does, only simpler and without the need for a Moroccan yoga tent. If you want to go faster, think of a beautiful woman you are in no way related to. If you want to go slower, think of your mother-in-law. Since we have already established that the latter has quite an extreme effect, this should be considered reverse. And you *never* put a car into reverse when you're driving.'

'You're quite pleased with this, aren't you?'

'Mine are as follows: first, Maureen Lipman; second (or neutral), the wife; third, Michelle Pfeiffer in *Lethal Weapon IV*; fourth, Pamela Anderson; I don't need a fifth.'

'You really are a disgusting human being.'

'My reverse is Ann Widdecombe.'

Thursday 5 January

I have spent the last two days not thinking about anything. Every time the idea of sex comes into my head (which, as has been well documented, is every thirty-four seconds), I count sheep. Which is taking Johnson's first theory far too literally but it seems to work.

Isabel has still said nothing about the New Year debacle followed by the billowing sex-free tundra that has followed. I can only assume it is not a problem. Or that she is confiding in Alex.

When Isabel and I both get back from work early, I decide to give sex another chance. Even as I suggest it – as matter-of-factly as possible – I can feel those disturbing images trying to push themselves into view. I count sheep but the sheep start having a Polish accent and saying 'darlink' at the end of every sentence.

I have no choice but to try the gears. Starting in third (Isabel, because there's no way she's second), I reach for fourth (Cameron Diaz in *Mask*) and all is well so I drop it back into third, and it's just like the old days, but then I slip the clutch and find myself grinding into reverse. Panic sets in, I go back to Cameron, still struggling, but I haven't got a fifth. Didn't think I'd need one. And suddenly, there it is: fifth. Saskia. The Destroyer of Relationships.

In the postcoital aftermath, Isabel says simply, 'Is everything all right? You seemed … distracted.' And I say simply, 'Yes, everything is all right.'

Friday 6 January

Johnson is shaking his head gravely by the water cooler.

He says he blames himself. He should have warned me that imagining other women while in bed with one's own wife is a big step, and not one to be taken lightly. And it is crucial, absolutely crucial, not to have any gears that are real people. Pamela Anderson is not a real person. Saskia is.

What was I thinking? Well, I wasn't thinking, that was the whole bloody point. And now I've imagined my terrifying ex at exactly the wrong moment and does this mean I find Saskia more attractive than my own beautiful wife?

Johnson says it's just a rogue gear. He slipped into Ann Widdecombe at exactly the wrong moment once: it took him weeks to recover from the terrible ecstasy.

I spend the rest of the day with a migraine that I can only assume is some sort of guilty reaction to the fact that I committed mental adultery.

Saturday 7 January

Still have a headache. Deserve it.

Another text from Saskia. Delete.

Monday 9 January

Apparently, it's the toxins washing themselves out of my system. Andy has a headache in Guiana and Johnson is out of action in Islington. His beer belly is expanding at the rate of one centimetre every four days despite the total lack of beer. It seems sensible, for our health and sanity, to give up giving up alcohol. I explain all this to Isabel, who is entirely unsupportive. She tells me that a week from now, I will feel out of this world, like a million dollars, smashing.

Then she says she's going for a drink with Alex so she might be home a bit late.

Tuesday 10 January

After the joys of December, the miseries of January. We aren't arguing like we did when we were newly married. Then, we'd have a good burst of unreasonableness followed by honeymoon-ish resolution. Now, it's low-level bickering, caused entirely, I think, by the continuing problem of Alex.

THREE EXAMPLES OF LOW-LEVEL BICKERING IN ONE DAY

'Where's the ibuprofen, darling?'

'I don't know. Where did you last have it?'

'If I knew that, I wouldn't be asking, would I?'

'You should put things back when you've used them.'

'I do.'

'You don't.'

'I do.'

'So why can't you find the ibuprofen, then?'

'So how was the drink?'

'Don't start.'

'I wasn't. I was simply asking how the drink with the guy who touched your breasts was. You know, the one who's glad we're through our marital difficulties.'

'He said he never said that. He said he just asked how married life was treating us.'

'He didn't.'

'He said he did.'

'He didn't.'

'Lentils are pretty tasteless, aren't they?'

'You just have rubbish taste buds. You can't appreciate subtle flavours.'

'I can.'

'Why do you add salt to everything, then?'

'Because I am slowly poisoning myself to death so I don't have to eat lentils.'

'Good.'

'Good.'

'Good.'

Wednesday 11 January

The tweedy heart-attack man and the scarfed hairspray woman sit next to each other on the train and it's like watching a World Championship elbowing contest. From my own bitter experience, I know that neither are the giving-in sort and by London Bridge it has erupted into full-scale childishness. The woman knocks the man's umbrella into the aisle. He retaliates by shredding her *Woman's Own*. She punches a hole straight through his *Telegraph*. He pulls off her scarf. She punches him.

The rest of the carriage refuse to get involved – we are united in our sense of pleasure – and I am in a good mood all the way to my anger-management class.

'Have you any further thoughts on our discussion last month?' I ask before the woman with the neat bob can set her own agenda.

'Which discussion would that be, Mr Walker?'

'The one about whether or not anger is justified as a response to our broken-down society. And please feel free to call me William.'

'We're not here to find reasons to justify anger, Mr Walker. We're here because you have a problem managing it.'

'Yes, but he has a point though, doesn't he?' suggests the cyclist, who seems to be back after escaping the last two classes. 'I mean, if everything is so much more irritating than it used to be, surely the rational response is to become irritated by it?'

'No, Mr Schofield,' interjects the woman, her bob twitching ever so slightly. 'Irritation is simply an emotional response. It is subjective, not objective. It is therefore not a question of it being rational or not.'

'But, Ms Prestwick,' I say. 'Or may I call you Harriet? I don't understand what you mean. If a train leaves earlier than it's supposed to, if a man in the countryside shouts at you for no reason, if a neighbour kidnaps your wife and a thirteen-year-old achieves more in six months than you have done in your whole career, surely you are entitled to be angry? If only to release tension?'

'No, please call me Ms Prestwick and yes, I see your point, but anger is a negative response.'

'Well, Harriet,' says the cyclist.

'Ms Prestwick,' corrects Harriet.

'Well, Ms Prestwick, I threw my bicycle through the windscreen of a car that had cut me up on a roundabout and I felt a lot better afterwards.'

'Yes, but that was illegal.'

'So was cutting me up on the roundabout.'

'Yes, but two wrongs don't make a right.'

'But two negatives do make a positive, Harriet,' I conclude.

'STOP CALLING ME HARRIET.'

I have won the battle, but with three more months of meetings to go, the war still hangs in the balance.

Saturday 14 January

Literally no energy. Can hardly be bothered to get out of bed. Isabel and I have yet another fight about pairing socks. Even though she told me she'd bought the days-of-the-week ones in order for me to mis-pair to my heart's content, that relaxation of rules did not extend to putting them in the sock drawer unpaired. I explain that if I spend just ten minutes a week pairing or mis-pairing socks, that's 520 minutes a year, which is two weeks of my next forty years of married bliss. They are my socks, it is my sock drawer, leave me alone.

She says they keep getting muddled with her socks.

I say I'm tired.

She says, 'Just have a bloody drink then.'

So I call Johnson to see if he's cracked yet. He hasn't but says his wife is about to leave him so it's not all bad.

Tuesday 17 January

Texts from Saskia still haven't stopped. She now seems to have got through her angry phase and is entering an everything's-perfectly-all-right one.

Yesterday's text: 'drnks, mine, tonite, W. Wld b gr8 2 ctch up x.'

Today's text: 'soz u missed drnks. dinner?'

Tomorrow's text: 'soz u missed dinner. Rabbit boiled to perfection. Brkfst?'

I risk the first text for weeks. No complicated explanation for silence, just: 'Can't meet. Super-biz. All best.'

No response. At last, she's got the picture.

Thursday 19 January

She hasn't got the picture. 'Thnks for txt. Sounds good. Look frwrd to it.'

Friday 20 January

Twenty pairs of black socks arrive at my office with a note from Saskia: 'A solution to your marital problems. Xxx'

'Saskia, it's William. Who told you?'

'Hello, William. Who told me what, darling?'

'About the socks?'

'Oh, that. Did you like them?'

'Um, well, yes, that's not the point. Have you been speaking to Johnson?'

'No.'

'Or Andy?'

'No.'

'Well, how did you know?'

'Know what?'

'About the socks?'

'Oh, I can't reveal my sources, darling. Now, about dinner.'

'I told you I'm busy.'

And I hang up, wishing it was an old slammable phone, not an unsatisfying press-the-red-button mobile, then throw all the socks in the bin.

'Throwing them away?' asks the IT geek who is walking past clutching a bag of microchips.

'Take them,' I reply, and he does.

I decide not to mention Saskia's socks to Isabel even though the leak almost certainly came from her side.

Saturday 21 January

Isabel's Christmas present (or part thereof): theatre plus champagne dinner. A whole bottle, as it turns out, but of course I can't drink so Isabel quaffs the lot, preparing her well for a three-hour Ibsen shocker at the Almeida. My legs don't fit in the seat so while I weigh up the cons of deep-vein thrombosis with the pros of hanging my feet over the shoulders of the tetchy person in the row below me, Isabel has a refreshing nap. We both refocus on the play in the last twenty minutes, thanks to a couple of unexpected gunshots. Several characters I have previously been annoyed by proceed to commit suicide and a woman in a heavy skirt says something lengthy and repetitious about a seagull.

We retire to our village, me feeling like a philistine for not getting the seagull analogy, Isabel babbling on about how Ibsen is overrated anyway.

Waiting for us on our doorstep is what can only be described as a crucifix made of chicken bones with a sort of Jesus-figure fashioned from dried chicken skin. Primrose has struck again.

As I open the door to find the phone book to call the police, Isabel takes the law into her own hands, throwing the dead chicken sculpture over the fence like she's Fatima Whitbread in the Seoul Olympics, then walking through the door and slamming it confidently behind her. I point out that this is just as ridiculous as the play. She points out that she needs to sleep, and promptly passes out on the sofa.

Sunday 22 January

The policeman is tapping his foot impatiently when I finally open the door at 7.30 a.m. the next morning. He says he is investigating reports of assault and vandalism. I say I have no idea what he is talking about, so he says I threw dead animals at our neighbour last night. I say I certainly did not and even if I did, it would only be a domestic. And he says no it wouldn't and I say well you know what I mean.

'Now look here, son,' he says, which no one has said to me for at least two decades. 'We don't take kindly to troublemakers round here. First, you slander an upstanding member of the community, then you nearly run someone down on a footpath while cycling illegally and now you attack people with dead chickens.'

'Do you have any independent witnesses?'

'I'll be keeping my eye on you from now on.'

'Good day to you, officer.'

I have a hangover even though I didn't drink anything. Isabel, diametrically, is fine. And she seems unperturbed by the fact that I now have a reputation as a troublemaker in the village even though it was she who threw the chicken crucifix at Primrose.

Andy calls to ask if I still need an emergency lime cordial and I explain that things have deteriorated significantly since then, but that the main issue has been resolved. Which is true. I am sexually competent again, although mentally adulterous.

I suggest that we should start drinking again: we have, after all, proved a point and cleaned out our systems. Andy says he plans never to drink again … his new girlfriend works for an NGO in Guiana dealing with the problems of alcoholism in the native communities. He has seen first-hand the effects of drink and he has decided to say no.

I decide to give it another couple of days. And find a new best friend.

Monday 23 January

Still hungover from all that lack of alcohol. Three weeks now. Where's the bit where I feel great? I am actually woken this morning not by the cock a-crowing or the sheep a-baaing or the neighbour a-knitting-chicken-skin, but by the sound of my own irregular heartbeat. My whole central nervous system is shutting down.

Wednesday 25 January

Anastasia has sent early copies of her new *New York Times* section to poor little us at *L&T*. I'm surprised she found time, what with the number of pages she has to edit in the world's greatest newspaper. And the number of articles she's managed to write herself. Everyone loves the section, even though it looks like pretentious nonsense to me. Even the IT geek can't hold back his enthusiasm.

'I thought you'd prefer *Computer Mart Monthly*,' I snap bitterly as he joins a syrupy conversation about how stunningly uncompromised the section's production values are.

'Oh, because I'm the IT geek, you think I can't appreciate high culture?'

'Well, I wouldn't say it was high —'

'Just because I spend all day telling idiots like you how to switch on a computer?'

'Well, now come on, that's a bit —'

'When was the last time you read Sartre, Camus, Molière, Descartes? When did you last reread *Du côté de chez Swann* or pondered the central despair in *La Prisonnière*?'

'I'm not really into the, err, French —'

'Goethe, Schiller, Brecht, Mann?'

'Or German.'

'Cáo Xuěqín, Omar Khayyám, Svarupananda Desikar, Chikamatsu Monzaemon?'

I'm more into the, err, English —'

'Trollope, Coleridge, Wordsworth, Milton, Chaucer?'

'Yes, I've read *The Canterbury Tales*.'

'When you were at school, I bet?'

'No.'

'Yes.'

'No.'

'Yes.'

'Sounds like you've got too much time on your hands.'

'Philistine.'

'Geek.'

The day deteriorates, as if that were possible …

I get another text from Saskia.

I get another mini heart attack even though, after almost a month alcohol-free, I am supposed to be feeling ten years younger.

I get another earful of domesticity from Isabel (I forgot to clean the bath but it was because, Your Honour, of the mini heart attack, but that's just not good enough, but it won't happen again, Your Honour, one strike and you're out.)

I get a whole foot wet in a trick puddle.

I get shamed out of my train seat by a pretend pregnant woman.

I get another text from Saskia.

I have a drink. Aaaaaaaaaaaaaaaaaaaaaahhhhhh, Bisto.

And another. And another. And another. And two more strong ones.

Just as I am commenting to myself on the joys of binge-drinking, two of Isabel get home, both of whom look furious.

'Hello, Isabels,' I hiccup.

'It's eight o'clock.'

'So?'

'You said you'd meet me at the restaurant at half seven.'

'Oh.'

I am escaping across a rickety bridge, but each time I reach the safety of the other side, a bungee padlocked around my waist pulls me back to the other side, the side where a girl who looks like

Saskia from behind but Isabel from the front keeps transforming into a giant spider every time I return. The harder I try to escape, the more swiftly I am bungeed back, the closer I get to the giant spider's eight gnashing jaws. Even when the desperate urge to urinate wakes me, it still takes the trip to and from the bathroom to convince myself that my wife is not a giant spider.

Thursday 26 January

'Spiders don't have eight mouths,' is all Johnson has to offer by way of dream interpretation before joining me on another lengthy celebration of the end to our month's abstinence. Twenty-two days is pretty damn near close enough if you ask us.

I wake up in the bath at four in the morning. The only reason I wake up is because the water is ice-cold and all five extremities are experiencing a strange tingling sensation. I scream quite piercingly. Isabel unimpressed.

Saturday 28 January

Andy says the girl from Guiana isn't the one, that giving up alcohol is not right and, besides, it's England v. France this afternoon, and he's got three tickets. Isabel still unimpressed.

Sunday 29 January

Buy flowers for Isabel. Isabel pretends to be delighted but I can tell she's unimpressed. Don't care. The petrol station where I buy the paper only has limited choice, plus it's supposed to be the thought that counts. And besides, I have had a tough month, what with the lack of alcohol, the sense of failure both at work and by nearly but not quite fulfilling a resolution, the realisation and acceptance of the fact that I have had an affair, though only mentally, the continued suspicion that someone is out to wreck my marriage, and so forth.

At least the reassuring signs of persistent alcohol abuse have returned: foggy memory, red eyes, kidney ache, pre-coffee nausea, post-coffee nausea, monosyllabic wife.

Monday 30 January

I have become almost resigned to grim coincidences in the marriage-wrecker department. So the fact that the day after I buy a bunch of flowers thoughtfully for Isabel, albeit from a petrol station, Alex also buys a bunch of flowers for Isabel comes as no surprise. Nor does the fact that the flowers are at least six times as extravagant as mine and have never been near a petrol station in their flashy little lives.

I have to fight my way through them just to get into my own house, which is probably symbolic of something depressing. Isabel seems to think there is no need to explain them, or the note: 'Chin up, babes, all will be well soon. Me xxx.'

'He got you a bunch of triffids. I didn't think you liked triffids.' (A swing at the ball …)

'Please don't start, William. I'm not in the mood.' (… and a miss. Strike one.)

'It's okay. All will be well soon. It says so in the note.' (Another swing …)

Total silence. (… and another miss. Strike two.)

'So are you two running off together at last?' (He swings for the home run.)

'I told him I was having a bad time at work. That's what the flowers are about, since you're obviously not going to drop it. And I told you as well, but you were too busy going off to get drunk with your stupid friends to register it. You can be really selfish sometimes. I'm going over for dinner with my parents. See you later.' (He misses, strike three, he skulks back to the dugout.)

Tuesday 31 January

Buy more flowers for Isabel. Six times bigger than the triffids. Mortgage job. Note says, 'Sorry.' And I really am. Of course she's been having a bad time at work. And when she has a bad time at work, it's really important. Because she cares about her job. I must remember that. I must remember that Isabel is doing her job for proper, altruistic, planet-saving reasons, not just for her own self-aggrandisement like the rest of us.

Still, the mortgage job flowers have been ignored, which is a bit rough. She doesn't even mention them when I call to ask if she would like to meet for lunch. She then says she can't meet because she'll be checking into a Travelodge to have sex with Alex like she does every Tuesday lunchtime.

By being rendered speechless at such a disgusting thought, I apparently get myself into further trouble.

'Jesus Christ, William. I was joking. This is getting ridiculous.'

If I'd laughed my head off at the hilarity of it all, she might not have hung up. And I might have still been on the phone to my wife when Saskia stormed into my office, which would have been even worse, I suppose.

'YOU CAN'T JUST FINISH IT LIKE THAT,' she begins, by way of hello. The production of a national magazine grinds to a halt as everyone swivels around on their stupid swivelly chairs to see who the girl with the seventeen-foot-long legs has come to kill. But before I have a chance to properly reflect on the disadvantages of an open-plan office, Saskia grabs my small plastic cup of water and throws it in my face.

For the second time in five minutes I am speechless, and for the second time in the same five minutes this is a bad idea.

'HAVEN'T YOU GOT ANYTHING TO SAY FOR YOURSELF?'

'Saskia, can you just calm down for a second?'

[Wrong again. Don't engage with her, just tell her to get out of your office.]

'CALM DOWN?! CALM DOWN!? I AM PERFECTLY CALM.'

'You aren't. You're shouting.'

[Still wrong. Get perspective here. A madwoman has just stormed into your office.]

'I'LL SHOUT IF I BLOODY WANT TO, YOU BASTARD. WALKING RIGHT BACK INTO MY LIFE, THEN PRETENDING I DON'T EXIST.'

'I'm married.'

[Wrong because now, judging by all the raised eyebrows, everyone I work with suspects I'm having an affair. And it's only aggravated her anyway.]

'YOU CAN STILL BE FRIENDS WHEN YOU'RE MARRIED, YOU KNOW? OR DID YOU THINK I WAS ONLY FOR SEX?'

[That pretty much confirms everyone's suspicions.]

'No, you're right. We can be friends.'

[Idiot.]

'IT'S TOO LATE FOR THAT.'

'It isn't. It's never too late.'

[I'm panicking now, saying any cliché that springs into my head.]

'You're a cruel man, William.'

[She's stopped shouting now but she's sobbing instead, which is worse.]

'It's not you, it's me.'

[A woman crying is guaranteed to make a man say anything, absolutely anything, to stop the tears.]

'I don't understand what you want from me.'

[What I should have said at this point is, 'Err, nothing except for you to get out of my office and never show your terrifyingly unpredictable face again, you bunny-boiling freak.' But of course I didn't say that.]

'Let's have dinner.'

'Sure,' she said, instantly happy again, as if the last five minutes never happened. 'I'm free on Friday.'

And with that she struts out of the office like she's in a shampoo advert, swivel chairs swivelling as she goes.

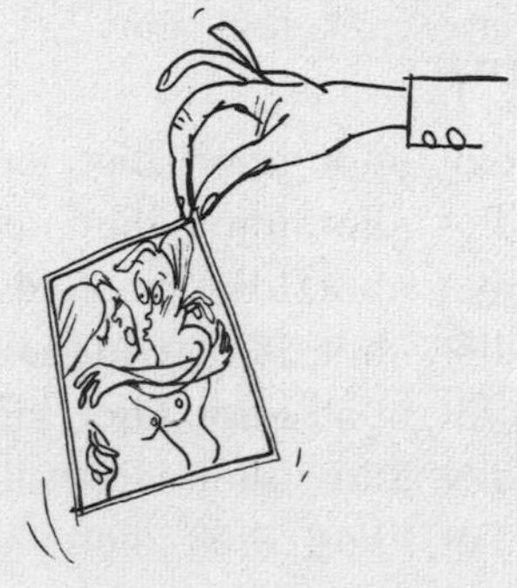

FEBRUARY

'Never tell. Not if you love your wife ... In fact, if your old lady walks in on you, deny it. Yeah. Just flat out and she'll believe it: I'm tellin' ya. This chick came downstairs with a sign around her neck "Lay on Top of Me Or I'll Die." I didn't know what I was gonna do.'

LENNY BRUCE

Wednesday 1 February

Idiot, idiot.

Thursday 2 February

Idiot, idiot. Idiot, idiot. Idiot, idiot.

Idiot.

Friday 3 February

I have told Isabel I am meeting Andy and I have told Andy to cover for me. He has told me I'm an idiot and I have told him I know. He thinks I should tell Isabel but I'm not going to because she's already mad at me. Imagine what would happen if I actually gave her something to be mad about. Which, says Andy, confirms why I am an idiot. I tell him I just have to sort this out once and for all. He repeats his initial conclusion.

Johnson agrees with my strategy, which only makes me worry more.

I arrive first and immediately wish I had chosen the restaurant. It is not the sort of place you go to meet a friend: it is strewn with candles; an unobtrusive pianist is tickling the keys in the corner; and the table Saskia has reserved is not a table at all … it's a bed. This is the sort of place bastards like Alex would take their married friends for a so-called innocent dinner. I make a note to introduce him to Saskia one day. Then I ask the waiter if we can move to one of the table-tables and he says they're all booked.

'Could you not swap us over?' I plead. 'I get indigestion if I eat lying down.'

'Sorry sir. We're always very careful not to put people who request a table in a bed. It might cause embarrassment.'

I spend the next ten minutes trying to work out whether it is safer to leave and risk another showdown at work, or stay and have a scene in a bed. I opt for the latter, then spend the next ten minutes trying to work out how to sit innocently on a bed surrounded by candles with a pianist tinkling away in the corner.

When Saskia arrives, I think at first that she is completely naked except for boots. Then, when I recover from the initial shock, it turns out that she is wearing a light-tan, figure-hugging dress that starts an inch below the waist and stops a millimetre above the nipple. Even Alex wouldn't wear something quite so blatantly non-platonic.

'Hello, Saskia,' I say, standing up from my cross-legged position at the foot of the mattress.

'Hello, gorgeous,' she replies, and promptly presses her entire body against me and kisses me lingeringly on the lips.

I untangle myself and find I have received a text message: 'Remember to get milk.' Oh God.

Saskia then proceeds to crawl cat-like across the bed, claiming she never requested one but seeing as we had one we may as well enjoy it. She then plays with the idea of a Slippery Nipple before opting for a Martini. I attempt to de-sex the whole situation by ordering a beer.

'Don't be so boring, darling. You always have a beer.'

'Beer's fine,' I say moodily.

'Don't be moody, darling. How was your day?'

'Fine. Yours?' I say nonchalantly.

'Good, I had a Brazilian. I thought it was going to be agony but I actually enjoyed it.'

'Excellent. Just the beef for me,' I say to the waiter who looks as if he's about to faint.

'No starter, darling? My treat. Let's have oysters. They make me hot.'

'Rocket salad, thanks.' The waiter has fainted.

By 10 p.m., I have still not found the opportunity to say my piece. The drink I have been necking has given me the frights rather than Dutch courage. And when Saskia slinks off to powder her breasts or whatever terrifying thing she does in a washroom and I am literally slapping myself in the face to steady my nerves (Japanese courage), there's a voice.

'William, you sly old dog. Didn't think this would be your sort of place now you've become a country bumpkin.'

'Tony. Hahahahahahahahahahaa. No. Not my place at all. How's Jess?'

'Jess is fine. Absolutely fine. Don't see much of her actually. She's always at marketing conferences. This is Jacques by the way. A friend.'

'Oh right, hi Jacques.'

'*Salut toi.*'

Before I can remark to myself at how right we were that Tony was gay and Jess was only using him as a baby-making aide, he has asked the question I had been dreading.

'So, what have you done with Isabel? She powdering her nose?'

'Err, no. She's at home. I'm just having dinner with just a friend.' Too many justs in that.

'Oh right. You got a bed, I see. Good, aren't they?'

At which point Saskia slinks back and arranges herself on my trembling shoulder.

'Marvellous. I'm Saskia.'

I leave soon after, too hysterical to say anything other than no, I have to be getting home, thanks for a nice evening, see you around.

Before I get home, I have two new texts, one from Tony – 'I won't tell if you won't x' – and one from Saskia – 'Sorry we couldn't really test the bed. Lunch next week? x'

And I forgot the bloody milk.

Monday 6 February

Whole weekend felt as though I was living a lie, which of course I was. Even though they had diametrically opposed views on the whole meeting-Saskia thing, both Andy and Johnson said they told me so. They also now agreed that I should meet Saskia once more and end it. Not that there was anything to end but I knew what they meant.

On the plus side, I had an uncharacteristically enjoyable Monday morning. First, the scarf woman slipped badly on the icy walkway outside the station, allowing the rest of us to proceed like grown-ups onto the train. Second, my coffee guy gave me my latte on the house just because it was a beautiful morning. Third, a robin followed me through an entire park singing songs. Fourth, a man shouting down his mobile phone had his mobile phone stolen by a guy on a bike. And fifth, a fire drill meant I missed an ideas meeting for which I had no ideas.

This is not how Monday mornings usually pan out. I decided to take it as a sign that my luck was changing. Or rather that my luck could change if I took action. As I made my way back up the stairwell, I resolved to sort my life out once and for all. True to my word, I sent Saskia the text I had spent the last forty-eight hours agonising over pointlessly: 'Lunch fine. Alberto's sandwich bar. Thursday. 1pm.' And, true to her marriage-breakingness, she replied: 'I love it when you talk decisive.'

Wednesday 8 February

'What if, Mr Walker, you're getting angry at the wrong things? What if you're projecting?'

'Come again, Harriet?'

'It's Ms Prestwick.'

'Sorry. Come again, Ms Prestwick?'

'You assault a work-placement student —'

'I threw a cup of tea at her and it was cold and that was nearly six months ago. Couldn't we move on?'

'No, Mr Walker. Not until we've got closure on it.'

'Have you been watching a lot of American TV in the last month, Harriet?'

'Why would you get so angry with a work-placement student, Mr Walker? And why would you then get so angry with me making notes? Or a grumpy old woman pushing past you on a train?'

'Because she's annoying, Harriet.'

'Yes, but don't you think your level of annoyance is disproportionate to the thing you're getting annoyed about? Is it possible that you might be angry about something else – something more fundamental – and attacking soft targets is your way of releasing that anger?'

'What, you mean like he might be angry because he was beaten by nuns as a child?'

'Thank you, Mr Schofield.'

'Or he's gay but can't admit it so he's living a lie so he shouts at traffic wardens who he secretly fancies?'

'That's enough, Mr Schofield … Come on, William. Share it with the group.'

'You're right, I admit it. I am a repressed cross-dresser. I wear women's clothing whenever I can, which is not enough to satisfy my transvestial urges. Hence frustration. Hence your note-making gets on my wick.'

'Is it something to do with your marital relationship?'

'I'm wearing suspenders right now. *Quod erat demonstrandum*.'

Thursday 9 February

Of course, she could be right. Maybe traffic wardens aren't annoying after all. Maybe if I sort out the two biggest problems in my life – Alex and Saskia – I will be able to have my car towed or vandalised or crushed without even the slightest hiccup in my blood pressure. Like Hannibal Lecter but without the Chianti or cannibalism. I owe it to the good hard-working clampers and policemen and turnip growers and plumbers and gym instructors and anger-management women and other irritations of this great nation to find out. More importantly, I owe it to my marriage.

'Saskia, I don't want us to be friends any more.'

'This sounds exciting. What do you want us to be?'

'I don't want us to be anything. I don't want to see you. I don't want to talk to you. I don't want to text you. I don't want you to text me. I want you to text someone else, someone who isn't married, someone who likes to have their ex-girlfriends stalking them for the rest of their lives because I don't.'

'So that's it then, is it? It's over, just like that.'

'There is no it. There hasn't been any it for years. Not an it any more. I don't want you coming to my office and shouting at me. I don't want you sending me socks or leaving me messages or flirting or commenting on my marriage or anything at all, ever.'

'So our relationship was only ever about sex then, was it?'

'Yes. Yes, it was. And even if it wasn't, you can't carry on being friends with people once you've finished with them. It's just not practical or sensible or advisable.'

'Dumped them, you mean.'

'What?'

'Well, you dumped me. Don't be afraid to use the word now.'

'We were never going out. We agreed it wasn't working and you went to New York.'

'You agreed. I went to New York. I never said I agreed. You never even stopped to ask me how I felt. You just assumed. All men do that but I thought you were different.'

'Yes, well, fine. Anyway, that's what I came to say and now I'm leaving.'

'Okay, fine. If you want it like that, you can have it like that.'

'Fine.'

'Fine.'

'Fine.'

Everyone was right – the direct approach actually does work.

Saturday 11 February

I have been tricked into doing something I swore I would never do: I have joined a lottery syndicate. The office administrator said it would be a one-off on Wednesday because there was a £64 million jackpot so I agreed. Then it rolled over so she suggested we all try again. Tonight it's another effing rollover and on Monday she'll be round again, suggesting we continue. Like the Mafia, no one leaves a lottery syndicate. If you do, the syndicate immediately wins, and everyone except you – the idiot who just left the syndicate – pops champagne corks in front of an enormous cheque. Then they all resign, leaving you still penniless and doing everyone else's job. Then the local news does an end-of-bulletin funny on the guy who left the syndicate just before it won and you have to kill yourself.

It's something else to add to my list …

UPDATED LIST OF THINGS I SWORE I'D NEVER DO BUT THEN DID ANYWAY

Kill for pleasure (a wasp in a microwave)

Refer to morning as the best part of the day

Watch and enjoy *Big Brother*

Kiss the girl at college with the horse teeth and the easy reputation

Buy chinos

Cry in a girly movie

Get a proper job

Play golf unironically

Pretend a relative had died to skive off work

Make love with the assistance of Barry White (though, in my defence, it was a CD of love songs and Barry came on by accident)

Join a lottery syndicate.

Tuesday 14 February

Bloody Valentine's Day: stupid American invention, just like Father's Day and Halloween and Christmas. Why can't they be honest and call it 'Give lots of money to the florist for flowers that will cost half the price tomorrow' Day?

What's most frustrating is that you can't rise above it. You can't, for example, phone your mother on Mothering Sunday and say, 'Sorry I didn't send flowers. I don't believe in Mothering Sunday,' because that still makes you the bastard who doesn't appreciate your mother. And although Isabel hates Valentine's Day as much as I do, I know full well that doesn't mean I can ignore it. If there's one thing I've learnt about women, it's that what they say they want you to do and what they want you to do are two entirely different things.

So we wake up and tut about how awful an enforced annual celebration of love is. I then say something slushy about how we now have a wedding anniversary to do that, which Isabel misinterprets as me likening the horrors of Valentine's Day to the horrors of marriage.

At lunch, I join a long queue of grumpy men at Budding Ideas (shop motto: flowers for that special occasion, or just because you want to say I love you. Spew). When it is my turn, I am confronted with that cruel Valentine's dilemma: do I get six long-stemmed red roses or a dozen stubby-stemmed reddish but actually pink ones for the same extortionate price? Eventually, like every man before and after me, I realise there is no dilemma. You can't buy pink dwarf roses and you can't buy only six red ones. So I march off with the dozen long red ones and an eight-million-pound hole in my wallet.

Then I phone every restaurant in London in a desperate why didn't-I-do-this-earlier? search for a table, eventually securing a smoking one in the basement by the toilets of my nineteenth choice.

Then I spend what's left of the afternoon looking forward to an evening staring into my wife's beautiful eyes in what will be a futile attempt to ignore all the other people staring into their wives' beautiful eyes. And then snogging. And then giggling. And whispering sweet nothings. Oh God.

It doesn't work out like that because Isabel never comes to the restaurant.

I sit there for half an hour watching a panorama of tonsil hockey, then try calling her but her mobile's off like it has been all afternoon.

So I have a big argument with the manager of the restaurant who wants me to pay a fine for hogging one of his tables, then fight my way through a whole capital city full of snoggers, get a train home, open the door and immediately realise why I've been stood up.

On the table next to a note from Isabel reading 'Bastard' is a note from Saskia reading, 'Maybe they'll fit you because I don't want them any more,' which in itself is next to a note from me saying, 'Something for later, William,' which is attached to an extremely saucy set of underwear.

So much for the direct approach.

Isabel's father won't put me through to Isabel who is apparently too upset to come to the phone so I spend the rest of Valentine's Day watching the entirely unhelpful *Four Weddings and a Funeral* and wondering whether the florist will give me a refund.

Wednesday 15 February

I drop a note around explaining that it's not what she thinks, which is, I imagine, pretty much what every philandering bastard must say when it is exactly what they think. Except in my case it really isn't what she thinks.

When I get home, I find Isabel has been back and packed clothes. This is bad but, at least, as Johnson helpfully points out, she hasn't taken furniture. Although, as he unhelpfully adds, that could simply be because she hasn't sorted out storage yet.

At 11 p.m., my phone beeps and I leap down the stairs, already composing a response. The text is from a withheld number but it is clear who sent it: 'I am going to ruin your life … because you ruined mine.'

This would be the time to lock up the bunny rabbits.

Thursday 16 February

After another day of silence, I decided enough was enough. I decided to be decisive: so I went to Isabel's office and loitered. Two hours is a long time to work out what you're going to say to convince your wife you're not having an affair but, given the great weight of evidence against me (handwritten note, suspenders, etc), it wasn't long enough. None of the usual tactics – crying, the fake injury trick, self-immolation, begging on hands and knees – would work. This needed something special, something off the page, something not even in the manual. Finally, as I was ready to despair in the acceptance that the something simply didn't exist, it came to me like a shining light in a 1950s Jesus movie.

I would tell her the truth. Hallelujah.

Then Isabel stepped out of her office.

'Isabel.'

'Leave me alone.'

It wasn't a promising start.

'Give me ten minutes. You owe me that much. If you want me to leave you alone after that, I will. But I need to tell you the truth.'

The Hollywood melodrama of it all got me my ten minutes. I used it to tell her that the note was about four years old and had been attached, as far as I could recall, to a bottle of champagne, not some filthy underwear. I said I had never seen the underwear in my life before. Then I confessed to the dinner in the restaurant full of beds, that it was my stupid attempt to get rid of Saskia but that I'd misjudged how mad Saskia actually was. She looked sceptical – as wives do when someone tries to pass off an affair as a case of stalking – so I told her about the office-storming, the Brazilian and the final lunch. I showed her the text message. And I apologised for not being honest: it was typical idiot-man behaviour.

When she asked me to promise I was telling the truth, and that nothing had happened between me and Saskia, I knew I was through the worst of it. I promised solemnly and vowed never ever to lie about anything ever again, so long as we both shall live. Isabel then ruthlessly pressed home her advantage, asking me to promise never to say anything nasty about Alex ever again. I had no choice but to agree, thus lying less than a minute after I promised not to.

Saturday 18 February

Things haven't quite returned to the normality I had hoped and begged for. Isabel says everything is fine but it's one of those not-fine fines people use when they are women. Our house has been liberally carpeted with eggshells, conversation is barely monosyllabic, my head is bitten off on a quarter-hourly basis and all privileges have been suspended indefinitely. I am forgiven but my behaviour has not been – and probably never will be – forgotten. I have been moved permanently to the doghouse.

RULES OF THE DOGHOUSE

1. You have no control over when you can leave. Your sentence is recalculated on an hourly basis by the parole board (aka wife).

2. All light-hearted banter, flirting or niceness (e.g. 'Your hair looks different today, darling, I like it') will be interpreted as attempts to escape the doghouse, resulting in lengthier sentence. This rule is waived for flowers, although no gratitude beyond a suspicious nod of acceptance can be expected.

3. Any domestic work undertaken while in the doghouse does not count. For example, in a non-doghouse situation, it is

reasonable to expect that if one makes the dinner, one can expect someone else to do the washing up. In the doghouse, you do both.

4. Socialising with male friends is severely restricted.

5. Doghousers have no vote as regards television, music or whose turn it is to drive.

6. Doghousers must give ground on long-running domestic deadlocks. During time in the doghouse, hated pictures will be hung, disputed wallpaper patterns will be picked, prized bachelor-pad items will be confiscated and girly multicoloured flowerbeds will be planted. To continue to offer resistance will be taken into account by the parole board (see rule one).

7. Doghousers can be abused and bullied, particularly with regard to the original offence, but have no right to respond (e.g. 'Shall we go to bed? I mean upstairs, not to a restaurant with a slut like you did last week').

8. Under no circumstances must a doghouser initiate a sexual advance. Only the parole board (see rule one) can decide when, how and where sexual intercourse may take place.

9. Sexual intercourse in no way influences early release. Any assumption that it does will result in an instant doubling of the sentence.

Sunday 19 February

Jess and Tony's marriage is over. Tony and Jacques have run off together. Still in the doghouse.

Monday 20 February

Still in the doghouse.

Tuesday 21 February

Doghouse.

Wednesday 22 February

Doghouse.

Thursday 23 February

Out of doghouse. Asked if I could go to the pub with Johnson and Andy. After sarcastic reply about it being fine as long as Andy didn't have tarty highlights and a belt for a skirt, I am given permission. She is having a drink with Alex, she announces. He's very upset about something and needs her advice. In the spirit of staying out of the doghouse and restoring marital relations, I pretend that (a) it's not a problem and (b) I hope he's okay.

Andy and Johnson are relieved that love is back in the air in the Walker household, even though Alex is still up to his tricks and must be stopped.

More importantly, Andy has decided he no longer wants to pee standing up unless there is a urinal. Sitting down might be a bit girly, he says, but it reduces splashback and permits momentary relaxation. Johnson confesses he has been sitting down for years because, in addition to the splashback/relaxation benefits, it removes the seat-up/seat-down debate from married life, and is therefore of limitless value. I explain that I have an agreement with Isabel that the seat can be left in the position of last use, given that seat-down is as much of an inconvenience for a man as seat-up is for a woman.

Johnson says the agreement won't last. It's one of many perceived freedoms newlyish married men think they have but don't. He repeats his favourite axiom: man has no say in marriage. 'The sooner he understands this, the easier for everyone.'

Alex was upset because of the situation in Darfur. It's a good tactic – you can't accuse someone of using genocide as a pretext for hitting on your wife. Even though he's only upset about Darfur because he knows Isabel's charity does a lot of work in Sudan.

Saturday 25 February

Isabel is in a good mood. I am in a good mood. We decide to construct the perfect Saturday, which goes wrong for three reasons.

Reason one

A postcoital game of Scrabble is not the same as a postcoital cigarette or snooze or newspaper-reading session because it creates tension. As usual, the argument is over which two-letter words are acceptable and whether you're allowed to look them up in the dictionary before or after you place your letters. Isabel loses because I enforce the no-dictionary rule (as clearly outlined in paragraph three of the official instructions).

Reason two

To put the perfect Saturday back on track, we decide to follow a Rick Stein recipe together. Ahhh, how sweet. I go to the fishmonger to order black cod, as instructed. There is no black cod so I get white cod. Then we spend hours, literally hours, preparing the salsa, the light tempura, the home-made wasabi. But even the three mad visits from Primrose (on each occasion wanting to borrow a cup of salt) can't dent our delight at becoming gourmet chefs.

The delight is dented only on tasting. Maybe we got the temperature of the oil wrong. Or the consistency of the tempura. Or the size of the fish strips. Or maybe Rick Stein is a lying bastard when he says his bloody cod recipe is a piece of cake. Or maybe, we conclude as we prod the soggy, fishy gloop, it just wasn't meant to be.

Reason three

Just when I'd convinced myself that tonight was my lucky bloody night, that I was just seconds away from defying the worse-than-lightning-strike odds, someone else has won the quintuple rollover.

I don't care what they say in the stupid anger-management stupid classes, it is not my 'marital situation' that makes me angry. It is Dale Winton and Rick Stein and Scrabble ambiguity.

Sunday 26 February

The woman who won £135 million is called Norma and lives somewhere in the Midlands. She is encased in viscose, she has cankles and her myriad gold bracelets are biting into her bingo-wing arms as she battles to open the champagne. I tell Isabel I worry for the poor woman's blood supply and Isabel tells me I am a snob.

Wednesday 29 February

My marriage is over. I know that because Isabel stormed into my (open-plan) office and told me, as follows.

'It's over.'

'What is, darling?'

'Our marriage.'

'What?'

'Our marriage. You know, in sickness and in health, for richer, for poorer, 'til you shag someone else do us part. That one.'

A lot of chair-swivelling going on now. Even the managing editor has stepped out of his office to see what all the fun is. Welcome to *EastEnders* Live: first the infuriated floozy, now the wronged wife, next week, the peeved Swedish triplets.

'I thought we'd been through this.'

'Well, we had, but then this arrived in the post.'

Exhibit A is a blurry photograph of me and someone who can only be described as Saskia in the sort of gymnastic position you can only achieve through serious lack of inhibition.

'I can't believe I believed all your pathetic excuses. I was so stupid.'

'It isn't me.'

'Of course it is.'

'Well, if it is, which it isn't, it's old.'

'Like the note on the lingerie?'

'Yes.'

'So how come it's dated last month?'

Crescendo of Hitchcock violins. Audience gasp. Close-up of guilty man's eyes looking to corner of photo. Sudden realisation that he's caught red-handed. Theme music. End credits. Time to make supper.

But it's not *EastEnders* and I'm still there.

'This photograph isn't real.'

'You're lying.'

'No, I'm bloody not. I told you before, this girl is crazy. She'll do anything to get back at me. Haven't you seen *Fatal Attraction*?'

'This is not the movies, William. People don't do things like that in real life. In real life, you only get tarts, cheating bastards and wives who are now leaving.'

'Oh right, so you're leaving, are you?'

'Yes.'

'Well, don't worry, I'll do it for you. I'll leave.'

'What?'

What, indeed. Not sure going on the offensive was the right strategy. I don't think any of my office colleagues did either, given the weight of evidence against me. Still, in for a penny and all that.

'I'm tired of trying to convince you that I've done nothing wrong. I'm sure we said something in our vows about trust and you don't seem to be demonstrating much of that at the moment. And I'm sick of it. And I'm leaving.'

'Fine.'

'Fine.'

And without further ado, like the big idiot I am, I walked straight out of my own office, thinking as I went that if only it hadn't been a leap year, today would never have happened. And then how I was going to have trouble meeting my deadline if I wasn't in my office any more.

MARCH

'Love is an ideal thing, marriage a real thing; a confusion of the real with the ideal never goes unpunished.'

JOHANN WOLFGANG VON GOETHE

Thursday 1 March

REASONS TO BE UNHAPPY

My marriage is over after only ten months (even the gay guy and the marketing bitch lasted seven).

I am thirty years old and I am living with my parents again.

If I am single, I will struggle on the singles market due to (a) receding hairline, (b) slight pot-belly and (c) fear and loathing of the opposite sex.

REASONS TO BE HAPPY

Absolutely none whatsoever.

'I don't understand what you were doing with this Saskia girl in the first place. She doesn't sound like a nice girl.'

'Mum, it's none of your business and I wasn't doing anything with her, okay?'

'It is my business, dear. I am your mother. Now, what about this photograph?'

'It's not real.'

'What do you mean? How can a photograph not be real?'

'Don't worry about it.'

'Well, I am worried, dear. Isabel is a lovely girl and I don't want to see her hurt.'

'So you're siding with her?'

'I'm not siding with anybody. But you're far too young to be having a midlife crisis. And even if you were, you should just go out and buy a horrible little sports car like the neighbour two up did. Sleeping around is never the answer.'

'Mum, I don't want to discuss it and I haven't slept around.'

'I should know.'

'What do you mean?'

'Nothing, dear. It's between me and your father.'

'Christ, this really is turning into the worst day of my life. I'll be in my room.'

'I'm afraid you don't have a room. We turned it into your father's studio. Didn't think you'd be needing it, now you were married and everything. You can stay in the spare room, dear.'

'Christ.'

Friday 2 March

I refuse to contact Isabel first this time. I am innocent. She doesn't trust me. I will not blink first. And besides, Mum's shepherd's pie is great. As is tea with cow's milk and sugar. As is a complete lack of turnips. As is …

'Dad, hi.'

'Your mother has asked me to have a word with you.'

'About what?'

'About this unpleasant business.'

'Dad, there is no unpleasant business.'

'Right, well, I'm glad we've had this little chat.'

'Okay.'

'Okay?'

'Yes.'

Saturday 3 March

Still nothing from Isabel. Starting to feel bad about walking out of my office. But I am still the injured party here.

'Dear, don't put your cup straight on the table. It will mark. Let me get a place mat.'

'Sorry.'

'Have you spoken to Isabel yet?'

'No.'

'Do you want a poached egg for breakfast?'

'Yes.'

'"Yes, please."'

'Yes, pleeeeease. God's sake.'

'Language.'

Sunday 4 March

Still nothing, not even a text or an angry phone message, which is a record.

'It keeps hiding the emails. Stupid computer.'

'Mum, it's not stupid. It's a computer. It doesn't have the ability to be stupid. Just click on that button … no, you just double-clicked …'

'What do you mean, double-clicked?'

'You clicked it twice. Close the box.'

'How?'

'Click on the cross. Up. Up, up. There. Now drag that down so we can see both boxes.'

'How do you drag?'

'Click and move the mouse … no, you just double-clicked again.'

'I'm not talking with my mouth open, Mum.'

'Yes, you are.'

'Am not.'

'Don't be childish.'

'Am not.'

'You're not leaving that, are you?'

'It's cartilage, Dad. People don't eat cartilage these days. Not since we defeated the Germans.'

'It's the best bit. Give it here.'

'That's disgusting.'

'Mum, I'm going to the pub.'

'What time will you be back?'

'Why? I've got a key.'

'You've got work tomorrow.'

'So?'

'You look tired. Don't be late.'

'I'm thirty years old. I don't need a curfew.'

'You're burning your candles at both ends as usual. You'll get sick.'

'Andy? I need to sleep on your sofa for a few days.'

Monday 5 March

So things have gone from bad to worse. I am no longer a thirty-year-old sleeping in the spare room of his parents' house. I am a thirty-year-old sleeping on the sofa of a friend. 'The only answer, my friend,' slurs a tramp on a bench as I slope off to work, 'lies at the bottom of a glass.' Even tramps feel sorry for me, but he's right.

I buy a bottle of whisky on the way home from work and drink it.

Tuesday 6 March

I love her. I love her so much. I've been so stupid. I love her. I love her. I laaaaaaave her. I laaaaaaaaaaaaaaave her. Laaaava. Laaava. Lav lav lav. Give me the phone. Give me the phone.

'Ibosel. I laaaaave you. I laaaaaaaaaave you so much. Laaaaaaaaave.' 'Who is this? Who are you? Why are you calling me? *Why are you calling me?*' 'I called you. I'm sorry. I'm sorry, I've got the wrong number. I woke you? I'm sorry but, you see, I love her. I laaaaarve her. Laaaaaaaaaa— <*Click.*> Hello? Hello? Is anybody there?'

Thursday 8 March

Threw up at work today. In the toilets at least. Then I had a drink with Johnson at lunch. Then Johnson went back to work and I had another drink with the tramp in an attempt to make myself feel better. Turns out his wife left him too. Ran off with the television-repair man, the bitch. Except she didn't, that was just a movie. He can't remember who she ran off with.

'But I know why she ran off,' says the tramp.

'Why?'

'Because she was a bloody woman. Still is, for all I know. And you can't trust a woman as far as you can throw one. And believe you me, mister, believe you me, that was not very far as regards my wife. Not very far at all. Not given the size of her arse.'

None of this made me feel better. I hope tomorrow will be another day.

Friday 9 March

It is another day. But a terrible one. Even more terrible than all the other days so far this week.

Before I even sit down at work, it is announced that Anastasia the work experience is coming back to *Life & Times*. Except she won't be a work experience any more, she will be associate editor (features). This means that she is more senior than I am. Johnson suggests that I probably shouldn't pour tea over her any more. I suggest he should piss off.

Then he says, look, just call Isabel. Straighten it out. You love her. She loves you. There's no point in being miserable.

This is so out of character that I do what he says. And Isabel tells me to piss off. Forever. So I drink half a bottle of vodka and decide to go clubbing. Johnson won't come with me on account of the fact that he's under the thumb and he's not convinced clubbing is the right way of dealing with my issues. He is beginning to sound like Andy so I call Andy who agrees with Johnson until I start doing vodka-crying. We go clubbing.

The first three clubs have a terribly strict door policy. You must not be wearing trainers, you must have a collar and you mustn't be blind drunk. The fourth one lets anyone in.

I find myself in a low-ceilinged room dancing to 'It's Raining Men', which it is. There are literally hundreds of them to every girl, all sweating profusely and doing sleazy man-dancing. Most of the few women there look as if they've just realised what a terrible mistake they've made and have begun to plot a strategy of escape. The rest are too blind drunk to notice that they've been encircled by gyrating men.

'Can we go now?' Andy isn't getting into the spirit of things.

'In a minute. I like this song.'

'You like "It's Raining Men"?'

'Yes, I like "It's Raining Men". Look, there's a woman.'

'We're going home.'

Saturday 10 March

Andy has gone to Rwanda. I am alone in his flat. I am alone in this city, this lonely city. I am alone in the world. I am never going out again. I am going to sit in my dressing gown drinking vodka and no one's going to stop me and no one cares.

Sunday 11 March

Note to self: microwave hamburgers are much, much nicer than you'd think. Who needs bloody organic food? Or Fairtrade? Or vegetables? I don't. You can keep them. You can keep all of them. I'm not even going to recycle the box the burger comes in. I'm just going to chuck it on the floor and leave it there. How do you like that? Ha.

Monday 12 March

Call in sick. First time ever. Don't care. They can get some work experience to do my job. Oh sorry, they already did. Oh no, sorry, not my job. A better job. Ridiculous.

Tuesday 13 March

I can't go to work ever again. I can't bear it.

Wednesday 14 March

'Good morning, Mr Walker. How have we been this month?'

Anger-management classes really do have a knack for good timing.

'Great, absolutely great. You?'

'Fine. Now, today we are … what are you doing, Mr Walker?'

'I'm making some notes, just like you.'

'Right.'

'See, you're making a note now so I thought I'd make some too.'

'Fine, Mr Walker.'

'Are you making a note that I'm making a note?'

'No. Now — you're making another note, Mr Walker?'

'Yes, I'm making a note that you might be making a note about me making a note.'

'That's just juvenile.'

'Finished. Please continue.'

'So, this is the penultimate —'

'Can I just interrupt for one second?'

'Yes, Mr Walker.'

'Well, just to say that since I last saw you, my marriage has ended because I was caught having a nonexistent affair. I have started drinking in the mornings and I haven't been to work this week because I can't face an office full of people on swivel chairs judging me. So it appears you were right, I did have a bigger issue to be angry about. So thank you. Thank you very much.'

'Right, well, I'm —'

'But there's a problem.'

'A problem?'

'I'm still more pissed off about what you call the little things.'

'You are?'

'Yes, Harriet. I am. This morning, I am angry that they can crash-land a spaceship on Mars but they can't design a bathroom mirror that doesn't fog up when you shave; I am angry that my whole train journey was interrupted by a guard telling us that first-class seats are for first-class passengers only; I am angry that the two sections of the pedestrian crossing outside are out of sync so you have to wait on an island in the middle for about an hour before the traffic stops again; I am angry that everything seems to be designed to make life harder, not easier.'

'You need a stress ball, mate.'

'Piss off, Lycra-boy.'

'You piss off.'

'That's enough, gentlemen. And thank you, William. I think we've made some real progress. You have now accepted you have transference issues.'

Aaarrrgghhhhhh.

Thursday 15 March

Is it possible to drink a whole bottle of vodka in one day? Yes, it is.

Friday 16 March

The managing editor called. Wants a doctor's note. I tell him I was lying about being sick. He asks why I haven't come in, then. I tell him it's because my grandmother has died and she was like a mother to me. He asks if I'm sure it has nothing to do with the fact that my wife became the second woman in one month to storm into the office and tell me it was over. I say the first one didn't say it was over and no, it's definitely the deceased grandmother. He asks why I didn't say that in the first place instead of pretending I was sick. I say because I preferred to wallow in grief privately. He says he thought my grandmother died last year. I tell him it's the other one and that I'm at the funeral now and I can put her on if he doesn't believe me, except, oh no, sorry I can't because she's dead and the coffin's locked and you're not being very sympathetic. We agree that I can have a few more days if I need them.

This is not the way to progress a career, I think to myself, as I open another bottle of vodka.

Saturday 17 March

Andy's back from Rwanda. Thinks I should get a grip. Just because his flat is full of empty bottles and unrecycled burger boxes, he assumes that I'm wallowing in self-pity. Johnson calls and agrees. 'It's been two weeks now. Call her, fix things up, stop being an idiot.'

Trouble is, I have been calling her and she doesn't want to know.

And I don't either.

Stop hassling me.

The tramp understands.

'Bloody women, they just don't listen to reason. All the time, they're accusing you of not listening, but it's them that don't.'

'And you can't trust 'em.'

'Exactly.'

'They'll be accusing you of this and that, and then suddenly it's them doing the shagging of the lifeguard and the plumber and what have you.'

'Exactly.'

'You can't trust 'em as far as you can throw 'em. Which in my wife's case was only an inch, given —'

'— the size of her arse.'

'You know her?'

'No, you just mentioned that last time.'

'Yours got a big arse, then, I bet?'

'No.'

'Let herself go a bit, did she, now she had you hook, line and sinker?'

'No, she's still as beautiful as the day I met her.'

'What?'

'She's still as beautiful as the day I met her.'

'Well, what are you doing sitting here on a bench with a useless old tramp, then?'

'I thought you said women can't be trusted.'

'I didn't mean it. I only say that because it makes me feel better. You should get her back.'

'I've tried. Believe me, I've tried. It's too late.'

'It's never too late. I wish I'd tried harder. Now she's off with some tree surgeon or dentist or bloody fireman. Another tin?'

'No, I have to be going.'

'Good on you, mate. Give her one from me.'

Sunday 18 March

The tramp was wrong. It is too late. She won't even answer the phone.

Monday 19 March

Everyone at work has had a whip-round to buy an enormous bunch of lilies for me in my time of mourning. First my wife leaves me, then my grandmother – who was like a mother to me – kicks the bucket. I have to look sad for the rest of the day, which isn't difficult given that I am.

Anastasia waltzes in late. She's just had brunch with George Clooney. He wants to launch some sort of save-the-world campaign in our magazine. Sounds rubbish to me. Everyone loves it.

Tuesday 20 March

Anastasia has asked me to help her with some research on a feature she's doing about why some French rugby player is sexy. I am going to email the editor of *Cat World* to see if she'll have me back.

Wednesday 21 March

She won't. Drunk.

Thursday 22 March

Drunk.

Friday 23 March

Andy and Johnson agree to allow me another night of wallowing so we go to the local wallowing hole.

'I think I've got piles,' begins Andy, as if he's in the confessional box.

'The cream doesn't work,' says Johnson, distributing the Guinnesses.

'Really? What can I do?'

'Time is a great healer.'

'It's been two weeks.'

'Squeeze them then.'

'Jesus, are you sure?'

'Yep, but put a stick or a rag in between your teeth before you do. Else you'll bite your tongue off in agony.'

'Guys, sorry, but my life is bad enough without having to listen to talk of arseholes.'

'You're right. My agony can wait. First, we need to get you your wife back. Agreed?'

'Agreed, but it's impossible.'

'No, it's not,' shrugs Johnson. 'It's simple. All you have to do is get a recorded confession off the floozy saying that the photo isn't real and that she's a total psycho, then play it to Isabel.'

'And how do I do that?'

'Simple again. We wire you up and you just go and see her. If she's as crazy as you say she is, she'll be easy to get blabbing.'

'It's a ridiculous idea.'

'Got a better one?'

'No.'

'Want to spend the rest of your life in a warm and meaningful relationship with your own hand?'

'No.'

'Well then.'

Saturday 24 March

OPERATION PYTHON

Stage one: secure suitable spy hardware

'You don't think python sounds a bit phallic?' asks Andy.

'No, they always have to have names like that,' says Johnson sagely. 'You don't ever hear about an SAS strike force taking out an Al Qaeda quartermaster under Operation Fanny Flaps, do you? Or the Flying Squad busting a Colombian drug ring in Operation Flange? Ey?'

'I'm not saying we have to name it after female genitalia either, Johnson. I just feel embarrassed taking part in Operation Throbbing Love Truncheon, that's all.'

'The name sticks. I'm going shopping.'

Given that Operation Python is not being funded by the CIA, allowing Johnson – former crime reporter on the *Manchester Evening News*, and still a black-ops fantasist – to do the shopping was a mistake. The tape recorder with secret microphone cost £50, the door jemmy a tenner ('Why do we need a door jemmy?' 'Why do we *not* need one is the question you should be asking.' 'This isn't a movie.' 'Okay.'), the night-vision goggles £250 ('I said this isn't a movie.' 'I know, but have a go, they're really cool.') and the tracking device £199. ('We can pinpoint the target anywhere in the world at any time to within six feet.' 'But she'll be at her flat.' 'God, you really are a killjoy.')

TOTAL COST: £509.

'I got these too,' says Johnson, holding a pair of handcuffs. 'Just in case things turn nasty.'

REVISED TOTAL COST: £529.

Mission complete.

Tuesday 27 March

Practice run. I'm me, Andy is Saskia, Johnson is in charge of 'comms', by which he means communications.

'Saskia, why did you send a fake photo to my wife?'

'Because you're so gorgeous, Willy. You're simply ravishing. And I want you. I love you. I've always loved you. I will always love you, just like Whitney Houston. But if I can't have you, no one will.'

'You're not taking this seriously.'

'Well, it's ridiculous. What's wrong with the girl?'

'I'm not picking any of this up,' shouts Johnson from across the park. 'You'll have to stand closer to each other.'

'We're right next to each other.'

'Go closer.'

This doesn't happen in Bond movies.

Wednesday 28 March

OPERATION PYTHON

Stage two: sneak up on target, interrogate

0700 hours. Location, a car outside Saskia's flat (the one below my old one, back when my marriage was smelling of roses). No signs of life.

'Is there anywhere around here that sells doughnuts?' whispers Johnson.

'No, you can get a falafel from the shop on the corner,' I reply.

'I want doughnuts.' It's almost a whine.

'Can you put the heating on?' whispers Andy.

'No, it's broken.'

'Don't you think it's time you bought a new car?' whispers Johnson.

'Isabel says we don't need one.'

'Isabel, the woman who thinks you're a bastard?'

'Yes, she says it's just a conspiracy, making us buy new cars every three years. Makes us all debt-slaves to evil multinational conglomerates.'

'You sure you want her back? You could always get a nice new car instead. With heating and doors that open and everything.'

'Why is everyone whispering?'

0800 hours. Location, still Saskia's flat. Still no signs of life.

'Take those goggles off, Johnson. It's daylight and you're scaring people.'

'I'm trying to see if there's anyone inside the flat.'

'The curtains are closed.'

'That traffic warden looks like he's giving you a ticket.'

'You're not giving me a ticket, are you?'

'Yes, sir, you're parked in a residential bay and you haven't got a residential permit.'

'But I'm in the car.'

'But the car is parked, sir. Illegally, sir. Ergo you get a ticket.'

'I didn't think traffic wardens spoke Latin.'

'It's a common prejudice.'

'What if I drive off right now?'

'You would be evading a fine.'

'Have you taken my licence yet?'

'I'm about —'

0900 hours. Location and lack of life-signs as before. Traffic warden evaded.

'I have to go to work.'

'Me too.'

'Me too.'

Mission failure.

Thursday 29 March

OPERATION PYTHON

Revised stage two: text target, arrange meeting, interrogate

'Saskia, can we meet?'

'No. I'm back in New York.' Which explains why the stakeout didn't work.

'For good?'

'Back on Saturday.'

'Can we meet then? It's important.'

'When?'

'1300 hours. St James's Park. Come alone.' Or a text to that effect.

Saturday 31 March

We meet by the lake we first walked past on the way to have sex on Hyde Park Corner but a lot has changed since then. This time, rather than the standard-issue belt and boob tube, Saskia is wearing a business suit and glasses. Her hair is tied back in a prim little bun rather than flowing provocatively down her terrifyingly naked back.

'Like my new look?'

'Yes.'

'Me too. So I thought you never ever wanted to see me again so long as we both shall live.'

'I want to know why you are so intent on destroying my marriage.'

'Oh, here we go again. It's always me doing the marriage-wrecking. Well, it takes two, as you very well know, to tango. And anyway, I told you, I just wanted to be friends.'

'That's all you wanted?'

'Well, maybe not. Not the first time around, anyway. But I've decided you're too conservative for me anyway. I have more interesting men to see and do.'

She takes a deep, resolving breath and walks a little more briskly, so I have to quickstep to keep up.

'But you just thought you'd ruin my life anyway?'

'Hardly. You still lived happily ever after.'

'We've split up.'

'Oh, I'm sorry to hear that.'

She doesn't mean it. I can see she doesn't mean it. She's cold, not tarty or slutty or tempting or the Saskia I thought I knew. This is the real Saskia, the one who wrecked me and Isabel. Just for kicks.

'Why did you send the photograph?'

'What photograph – and why are you standing so close to me?'

'The digitally remastered one of us having sex – and because I've got an ear infection. I can't hear properly.'

'I don't know what you're talking about.'

'Oh come on. First you sent the underwear, then you sent the photograph. And you'll be delighted to know it worked.'

'What are you talking about?'

'All your mad scheming. I've lost the girl I love. So thank you.'

Saskia stops in her tracks. A jogger runs past, his head turning to watch the motionless figure drop her head and start crying. I stop as well. Andy and Johnson make a bad job of finding a new hedge to hide behind. Then, everything is still except for the gentle sob of a girl who seemed so much more of a lunatic two minutes before.

'You think I ruined your stupid marriage?' she whispers slowly. 'Well, now you know how it feels. You ruined my life and you still don't seem to care.'

I feel a flash of anger. I can't still be responsible for something so trivial and so long ago.

'We had a fling. You went to New York. Get over it.'

'It wasn't a fling for me! Don't you realise? It was a romance. My first romance. I fell in love with you, William.'

The jogger has gone now. It's just the two of us, and our spies. I can't think of anything to say to stop this so she continues. 'I thought you felt the same way, but it turns out you didn't. I was nothing more than a bit on the side to brighten up your evenings.'

'That's not how it was.'

'Shut up, shut up, shut up, shut up! Don't try to make it all right now.'

'I thought it was a mutual thing, to end it.'

'Of course it wasn't. But you're like every other man – you don't listen, you don't care, you're a bastard. That's why you deserved what happened.'

And suddenly, the little nagging voice in my head that's been saying all along that this has to be nonsense – no one would go to such lengths to ruin someone's life – is snuffed out.

'So you *did* send the photograph?'

'No.'

'Well, what then?'

I realise now that I'm gripping her shoulders and she's crying quite noisily now. It must be a disturbing scene for the surrounding picnickers, Queen's cavalry and the two commandos who are making unhelpful keep-her-talking signs from behind a very small bush.

I also realise that I am crying, which is surprising because it doesn't happen very often, especially in front of blokes.

'It's why I agreed to help Alex.'

The world stops.

Everything falls silent.

I stare out across the lake, blinking away tears, trying to understand what she just said. It doesn't work.

'I don't understand what you just said.'

'Because you were such a bastard, I agreed to help Alex.'

'But you don't know Alex.'

'He emailed me in New York.'

'He *what*?!'

'He emailed me in New York.'

'How's that possible?'

'I expect he got my email address. And. Used. It. Told me you'd stolen the girl he loved. Wondered if I would help him get her back.'

'But how did he know you would help? I thought we'd ended things amicably enough. Not counting your little phone call to Elizabeth.'

'Let's just say I wasn't the only ex he contacted. Given your sensitivity in the end-of-relationship department, it was inevitable he'd find someone to help. Probably had a long queue of pissed-off ladies shouting, "Me, me, me."'

Even though I had always known Alex was a manipulative little shit, I hadn't ever imagined a partnership, an alliance, an axis of evil. Or the extent of what he'd done.

'He bought the flat downstairs from you and offered it to me for a peppercorn rent. I was coming back to London anyway so it seemed like a good idea. Revenge and cheap accommodation in one go.'

And with that, Alex goes straight to the top of my list of all-time arseholes.

THREE ALL-TIME ARSEHOLES IN MY LIFE (UNTIL NOW)

3. Dr Hurd. Teacher. Sadist. Played up-down hair-pulling game. Threw chalk in Latin if you nodded off. Which it was impossible not to do.

2. Anonymous. Driver of Datsun Cherry. Hit-and-run on Minka, the only cat that ever loved me.

1. Dr Atkinson. Vet. Told Mum and me that Minka couldn't survive which I now think was an exaggeration. Then put her

down. Then asked if we would like to take the body home. Then, when we said yes, chucked Minka into a see-through plastic bag and handed her over.

'And while we're at it,' says Saskia, interrupting my thoughts, 'that weekend when I ended up in the room next to yours in New York wasn't a coincidence either. That took quite a lot of last-minute planning, but it was worth it. How predictable that you wouldn't mention it to your poor wife. Why do all men always decide that honesty is the worst policy?'

'So all the texts and the socks and the storming into the office?'

'I deserve an Oscar, don't you think?'

'And the bed and the Brazilian?'

'Well, you clearly thought I was a tart, so I thought I'd show you how much of a tart I really could be.'

'And the underwear?'

'Not me.'

'And the photo?'

'Not me either. After that last lunch, I'd had enough. I told Alex I wasn't interested in this game any more. He tried to convince me to carry on but, frankly, my dear, I no longer gave a damn. You were making such a hash of things anyway, you clearly didn't need my help.'

'So you didn't send the text?'

'What text?'

'The one about how I'd ruined your life so you were going to ruin mine.'

'Not me again. Though that pretty much summed up how I felt. You might want to have a chat with Alex though. He's the one you really hurt.'

'Excuse me?'

'You stole his true love.'

'I didn't steal her. She never even went out with him. They kissed when they were teenagers. He felt one of her breasts. Once. That's it.'

'Oh.'

'What do you mean, "Oh"?'

'Well, that's not quite how he put it.'

Andy and Johnson have stopped making signals from behind the bush. They're both standing there open-mouthed.

APRIL

''Tis better to have loved and lost
Than never to have loved at all.'

ALFRED, LORD TENNYSON,
In Memoriam (1850)

Monday 2 April

Spent Saturday night weighing up our options. I could go to Isabel with the tape but you can't really hear what everyone is saying through the tears and the barking dogs and the drone of aeroplanes and the leap of a grasshopper and the wing-flap of a tiny, tiny fly. Fifty quid well spent.

'I must have got the balance wrong.'

'No, it's great. This is all the evidence we need. If we were insects.'

But even if it were crystal clear, I am now realising that Isabel is beyond the point of believing anything I or Saskia say. Particularly something as far-fetched as the fact that her alleged best friend has been plotting for months to ruin her marriage.

Johnson suggested we should kill him using the door jemmy.

Andy suggested we should call the police, though he's not sure whether Alex being the world's biggest cock is actually breaking the law.

Just before last orders, we reached a compromise: we will use the door jemmy on Alex's flat rather than Alex, gather evidence, then either kill him or report him to the police, depending on what we find.

It doesn't seem like such a good idea now that it's a cold Monday morning and we're standing outside his pretentious apartment.

OPERATION PROBE

Stage one: break into Alex's flat, prove he's a maniac

'This is all a sex thing for you, isn't it, Johnson?' asks Andy.

'What?'

'Probe? Python? Shall we go on Operation Shaft next? Then Operation I Bet She Really Wants It?'

'Child.'

'Pervert.'

'Hippy.'

'Sex pest.'

The safest time to break into a flat, according to Johnson, who claims to be well informed in matters of espionage, is during the day. Less chance of being disturbed by (a) the occupant, who should be at work, and (b) the police, who only come out at night. Once we have convinced Johnson that the balaclavas he's brought along are not necessary, he sets about the door with the jemmy.

'I think you've got it the wrong way around.'

'No, I haven't.'

'Maybe we should try a credit card first.'

'This isn't *Murder She Wrote*.'

'Well, hurry up.'

'It's not easy.'

'Let me try.'

'Get off.'

With a terribly unsubtle crunch, the door frame splits away and the door swings open.

'We're in.'

'You think?'

For fifteen long minutes, we search Alex's annoyingly pretentious apartment/maisonette/stalking pad and find nothing. The living room and kitchen are clean – unusually so for a bachelor. The bathroom looks as if it's about to be in a *World of Interiors* photo shoot. Even his bedroom, the one where I caught him chopping up photos from my wedding, is spotless. No papers, no scrawled death threats, no nothing.

'All this proves is that Alex is either gay or obsessive compulsive.'

'Let's just confront him with what Saskia said,' suggests Johnson. 'We can make him talk.'

'Yes, let's use your handcuffs and balaclavas,' replies Andy. 'I'll tell him this is Operation Bend Over Big Boy, you two sing "YMCA" in the background. He'll cough in seconds.'

'Oh look, a secret doorway.'

'Shut up.'

'No, seriously. Look.'

I hadn't noticed it before, but in the corner of the kitchen, partly obscured by a pretentious New-York-style kitchen-canteen table, is a hatch. We move the table, we lift the hatch and climb down into the cellar.

Bingo.

In the small, unnaturally lit basement, there is a computer, a scanner, several television screens, a whiteboard full of terrifyingly elaborate plottings, a wall full of photos of Isabel and me, of my ex-girlfriends, of my office, of the flat, the house, all annotated in Alex's spidery handwriting. Initially, it is alarming, but then I begin to notice the detail and it becomes … very alarming. One screen shows a grainy video image of my bedroom from the perspective of Alex's horrible strokeable lamp – which explains how he knew my marriage's innermost workings; there are notes about cheese knives and bunches of flowers and Viagra trials; a whole corner plastered with earlier attempts at the fraudulent photo of Saskia and me mid-coitus; a dog-eared manual entitled *How to Win Back Your Ex*, next to *Time Out*'s 'London Cocktail Bar' special edition. And, on a separate wall, scrawled in what looks like blood, 'Keep your friends close, keep William closer.'

'It's not blood, it's just red paint,' says Johnson, as if that makes everything all right.

'Wow,' says Andy. 'He's a nutter. Is any girl worth this much effort?'

'Yes,' I realise. 'She is.'

And then our shocking discovery is interrupted by the sound of footsteps in the kitchen above. A trembling voice calls down: 'If you're still here, you'd better watch it, I have a black belt in jujitsu.'

'See, this really is *Murder She Wrote*,' mutters Andy.

'They're not supposed to come back early,' mutters Johnson, consulting his imaginary book of espionage. 'We're going to have to bring forward Mission Two.'

OPERATION PROBE

Stage two: interrogate Alex about all the psycho stuff in his basement

We didn't even have to use the balaclavas. Faced with the evidence in the basement and everything Saskia had already told me, Alex cracked almost instantly. More annoyingly, my urge to punch him a thousand times evaporated as soon as he began to speak. Because he was crying like a girl. Why is everyone crying at the moment?

Through racking sobs, he confessed to a double life: one as Isabel's best male friend, one as a lovesick maniac who would stop at nothing to win her heart.

'She was my childhood sweetheart.'

'No, she wasn't. She only let you touch her breasts.'

'One of them,' corrects Johnson by way of support.

'One of them. So you thought you'd destroy her marriage as a thank you.'

'You aren't good enough for her.'

'So she's better off with a basement-dwelling psycho-stalker? Pretty weird buying a flat, making my ex-girlfriend move into it, sending her underwear to Isabel, faking photos.'

'Saskia was happy to help. You ruined her life. And you ruined mine. You had Saskia but you stole Isabel too.'

'I didn't have Saskia. I didn't steal Isabel. I wish you'd stop telling people that. You. Never. Went. Out. With. Isabel. Get it?'

I have no real experience dealing with stalkers. It's not something they teach you at school, although it would be helpful if they did. School really could have been more practical, you know. Less biology and Latin and trigonometry. More How to Deal with

Stalkers, How to Spot When a Girl Is in Love with You and Not Simply Having a Fling Like She Says She Is, and, perhaps, at a stretch, the odd lesson on shelving. We only ever made salt-and-pepper shakers at my school. How did that prepare me for real life?

Alex is rambling.

'I love her,' he whimpers. 'You don't understand.'

This is irritating. I love her. He wouldn't understand. 'What about what she wants?' I say, still resisting the urge to hurt him, which has now resurfaced. 'It's not like I stole her from you. She never wanted to go out with you, even when she was single.'

'That's only because I never asked her.'

'What?!'

'I never asked her. Never wanted to risk that she might say no. I mean she wouldn't have. Definitely not. She would have said yes. Definitely. It would have been perfect. Until she met you, that is. I was going to ask her. I was almost ready. And then you came along. You ruined everything.'

This is more irritating.

Without any tuition in stalker-handling, all I can think of as a reference point for how to handle the situation is *Fatal Attraction*. The similarities are remarkable:

1. Alex Forrest becomes obsessed with Dan Gallagher after a one-night stand (more than feeling one breast, but it's the same ballpark).

2. Forrest plots revenge when Gallagher tells her to clear off (check).

3. Forrest boils Gallagher's daughter's rabbit (check-ish: I think that's pretty much on the same level as the fake sex photos).

4. Gallagher drowns Forrest in the bath, she jumps out again, everyone screams, wife shoots her dead. Glenn Close doesn't get any dates for years to come.

Drowning and shooting it is, then, just as soon as he stops crying.

'Let's just kill him with the jemmy,' offers Johnson. 'Your black belt in origami won't help you now, mate.'

'I don't care what you do. It's too late anyway.'

'What do you mean?'

'Isabel doesn't love either of us.'

'What do you mean?'

'Oh, you don't know?'

'What do you mean?'

'She's moving to Snowdonia on Friday. Apparently there's a dry-stone wall in dire need of repair on the outskirts of Llanllanllllllan-dunlan. She's joined a volunteer programme.'

'You're joking?'

'Nope, jacked in her job and everything. I tried to talk her out of it but you know what she's like when she gets an idea in her head.'

For the first time ever, I find myself nodding at something Alex has said. And then he ruins our brief moment of accord with a nonchalant shrug. 'As long as she's happy, I'm happy.'

I punch him hard in the face. Not in my imagination like I'd done so many times before, but actually, for real, right on the nose. It feels good. Immediately, a year's worth of irritation at this utter, utter bastard and all his terrible scheming begins to ebb away.

I punch him again to see if the ebbing will increase. It doesn't. It stops and I feel bad. This is deeply unfair because, frankly, I should be kicking his head in. Instead, I pick him up, put him on his chair and try to think of a suitably crushing line to walk out on.

Nothing. Not even a Clint Eastwood cliché. So I turn to leave in silence.

'Do me a favour, will you?' says the last person on earth to deserve a favour from me. 'Let me tell her what I've done. She's going to hate me forever anyway, so I'd rather I told her myself.'

Wednesday 4 April

After a whole day of total radio silence, during which time I assumed Alex had failed on his promise to make things right, I finally received a call from Isabel.

'I owe you an apology. Can you come on Friday evening?'

Cue choirs of angels fanfaring and harping and firing Cupid-ish arrows all over the place. My marriage was saved. Alex was no more. Everything would be all right now.

Bit of a pain to have to wait until Friday, though. Would have thought marriage-saving was more important than anything else she had going on in her life.

Friday 6 April

Anastasia asked me to finish off her piece on 'Sex Wars: How Women Win in the Bedroom' because she was running late for dinner with George and Al. George being her new best mate Clooney, Al being Gore.

I told her to get stuffed and walked out of the office, my triumphal return to domestic bliss begun. I was wearing my lucky underpants and the shirt Isabel said made me look a bit like Colin Firth, only thinner. And I had shaved the seven days of what's-the-point-in-grooming-if-my-life-is-shit? beard growth. I was ready for marital repatriation.

Johnson said that, at the very least, I should get out of cooking duties for a month. And have complete control over the whens and wheres of bedroom athletics for a year. But I was going to ignore him. When a man is proved to be right all along about absolutely everything, he must, under no circumstances whatsoever, rub it in. 'I told you so' had no place in this evening's rapprochement. I would just let her say her piece and then suggest we move on.

The problem was, her piece wasn't very extensive. She opened the door, we hugged, she opened a bottle of wine. Then she said sorry ... sorry for not trusting me, sorry for insisting that Alex was all right when actually he was a maniac who had stalked us for months, undermined me at every stage, recruited ex-girlfriends to help and smuggled a video camera into our bedroom in a lampshade that I hated but had allowed Isabel to keep anyway. Sorry she had allowed a psycho to turn our first year of marriage into a horror story.

But it wasn't the bended-knees, hands-clasped, please-forgive-me, you-were-right-about-absolutely-everything apology I felt I deserved. The closest I got to confronting this was in the simple question, 'You weren't really going to north Wales for six months, were you?' And all I got back was a long silence followed by a 'yes' that told me I should cease this particular line of questioning.

Still, as I'd repeated to myself mantra-like on the way over, this was not the night for I told you so's. It was the night for gentle smiles, warm small talk and rather excellent sex in a bedroom that no longer contained those lamps.

Saturday 7 April

Eight a.m. I wake for the first time in a month in my own bed. It isn't the lazy, curl-over-and-drift-off-back-to-sleep-then-wake-up-again-then-have-hug-then-play-paper-scissors-stones-to-see-who's-getting-the-tea awakening I'd missed so much in my exile because Isabel is not beside me. For the first fifteen minutes, I assume that she has decided to forgo the paper-scissors-stone competition and make the tea anyway. Perhaps part of her more gradual way of saying sorry. For the next fifteen minutes, I assume she is making some elaborate breakfast in bed. But as time passes, and the imagined breakfast becomes more and more elaborate – kippers and muffins and handmade muesli and self-grown oranges and pancakes rolled on a Cuban woman's thigh – I realise there are no telltale aromas. Eventually, reluctantly, because it's always hard to accept breakfast in bed isn't on the cards when you thought it was, I decide to venture downstairs to see what is going on.

There is no breakfast.

There is no Isabel.

Just a note.

William, thank you for last night. It felt almost normal after the horrible time we've been having. But things aren't normal, are they? You see, it never mattered what Alex or Saskia were doing. It was that we were so easily divided by it. We don't trust each other. Perhaps we never did. I'm sorry it didn't work out because you were the love of my life. I hope I was yours. It's a shame we couldn't keep it that way. Isabel

PS I've taken the car. You can have everything else. Even the lamps.

I call Isabel's mobile but it's off.

I call her father but he can't remember where she was going. 'Something with too many "ll"s in it,' he offers eventually. 'You know what those Welsh are like. They love their "ll"s.'

I call Alex and he says, 'Sorry, I thought she wasn't going until tomorrow.' I promise him a slow and unnatural death involving a tile-cutting machine, a litre of nail-polish remover and a thousand unsterilised drawing pins.

And then I decide to get a train to Snowdonia.

'Welcome to National Rail Enquiries. Please press one to speak to an adviser or hold for our simple and fast automated train-tracker service.'

I press one and get put through to the simple and fast automated train-tracker service. I then waste ten minutes battling with the train-tracker service's ruthless and unremitting requirements.

'Which station are you travelling to?'

'One in Snowdonia.'

'Did you say Solihull?'

'No.'

'Which station are you travelling to?'

'Anything in northern Wales will do. I just want a rough —'

'Did you say Andover?'

I throw my mobile in the bin in fury, put some pants in a day sack (the one Isabel bought me when my back hurt, sniff) in fury, and march out of the house in fury. I take the train to London and a taxi into a traffic jam. Why did I ever think a taxi would be quicker than the Tube? So I take the Tube into a Tube traffic jam (due to an 'incident' at South Kensington). I run and stand behind some tourists on an escalator and run and stand behind some more tourists on the escalator and run and … 'Can't you read? Look – stand to the right! It says it right there.' And the elderly Japanese couple look terrified and hold out their wallets and I apologise but they don't understand, and I run again and I arrive at Paddington.

And there's a man in a blue cap standing behind that standard-issue lucky-for-him bulletproof glass.

'I need to get to Snowdonia.'

'Where's that then?'

'It's a national park. In north Wales.'

'Right, sir. You'll need Euston.'

'You're joking?'

''Fraid not. Train to Birmingham, then … dunno. They'll tell you at Euston.'

'You're joking?'

''Fraid not.'

So I get the Tube to Euston and I'm feeling a bit light-headed because my stomach had been expecting kippers and eggs Benedict cooked by a loving wife and it got absolutely nothing. As we grind through Edgware Road, Baker Street and so bloody on and so bloody forth, my head starts throbbing and then I notice it isn't my head, it's the chap three seats down listening to his i-eff-ing-Pod on standard what-is-the-world-coming-to maximum.

'Turn that bloody thing down,' I scream, causing a mother sitting opposite to wrap her arms protectively around her toddler.

The iPod-er looks at me aggressively.

'NOW!' Like I'm the Terminator only without any muscles or robot technology or Austrian accent.

'Sorry.' I win. I win. I win. I am a man. I have stood up against the hoodies. Isabel will be so proud. Except this hoodie is about eight and Isabel has gone. I am not a man. I am a bully. And I am a divorcé-to-be.

At Euston now. I run and run and smile at tourists and run and fight my way through a surprisingly large number of people, all of whom seem to be standing around looking annoyed.

And there's a man in a blue cap standing behind that standard-issue bulletproof glass. And I say, 'A ticket to Snowdonia, please.'

And he says, 'Snowdonia?'

And I say, 'Yes, apparently I need to go to Birmingham and change.'

And he says, 'There's no trains to Birmingham this morning, mate. Engineering works overran again. You should've called National Rail Enquiries.'

Sunday 8 April

Police cells are *less* comfortable than your own bed but *more* comfortable than a friend's sofa. Next time, though, I'll take one of those aeroplane eye masks and some earplugs to keep out the bright lights and screamed profanities. They are not handed out on check-in.

SEQUENCE OF EVENTS LEADING TO MY SECOND-EVER NIGHT IN A PRISON CELL

Step one: I called the smartarse behind the bulletproof glass a wanker.

Step two: I waited in the railway bar for the afternoon train to Snowdonia.

Step three: I drank five pints.

Step four: I returned to the bulletproof glass ticket booth.

Step five: 'I'm sorry, sir, all the trains are now full. You should have made a reservation this morning. I can get you a first-class open return leaving at 5.27 a.m. tomorrow. It will cost £457.'

Step six: I become abusive.

Step seven: I am asked to leave the concourse.

Step eight: I go to a pub around the corner and drink some more pints and a whisky.

Step nine: I decide to sneak onto one of the full trains under cover of darkness.

Steps ten to seventeen: there isn't much cover of darkness, I am spotted, I run, there are railway security officials, then police, then an overwhelming urge to vomit, which I do, on a policeman, then detention by angry policeman 'for my own safety'.

Step eighteen: I'm Nelson Mandela. In a sense. Actually, in no sense at all.

Still no mobile reception on Isabel's stupid phone. Stepping out of the police station into the harsh light of another miserable, stinking morning, I decide to go home and sleep. In my own bed. On my own.

I wake at 6 p.m., then fail to go back to sleep until 5 a.m. The emotional upheaval of the weekend has effectively put my body clock onto Australian time.

Monday 9 April

An alarm bell is ringing. My house is on fire. I am trapped in the upstairs bathroom. Primrose is at the top of the fireman's ladder, her face pressed against the bathroom window, laughing. But it's not a fire or an alarm bell. It's my mobile. It's Isabel!

It's not Isabel, it's Johnson.

'Where are you? It's half eleven. It's press day. The managing editor is going to kill you.'

The managing editor hauls me into his office to tell me that he doesn't care how many of my grandmothers are dying, he doesn't care if they're dropping like octogenarians in a Greek heat wave, I cannot keep turning up late on a press day. From now on, it has to be immediate family members.

I tell him if only.

He tells me he's serious.

I tell him the reason I was late was because I spent the night in a police cell as research for an article I'm doing on crime in modern Britain.

He tells me I'm lying.

I agree, explaining that I was in the cell on Saturday night.

He says he's issuing a second formal warning. One more strike and I'm out.

I am not going to lose my job purely because Isabel is having some sort of midlife crisis. I will simply adjust to life as a singleton, get work back on track and wait for Isabel to come crawling back.

Wednesday 11 April

I am all alone. I live alone in a house that six months ago represented the hopes and dreams of a married couple. I go to sleep alone in a double bed. I eat breakfast at a table for six. It takes two days to load the dishwasher and four days to have enough clothes to bother putting a wash on. No one shouts at me if I mix colours and whites. No one laughs at me when I make an entirely unamusing joke at someone-on-TV's expense. No one makes me tea or dinner or happy. Alone, I watch the spring bulbs flowering through the obscured windows of rain-soaked April. I listen to Morrissey. I am depressed.

THINGS MEN DO THAT WOMEN DON'T KNOW ABOUT WHEN THEY'RE ON THEIR OWN IN A HOUSE (APART FROM THE OBVIOUS)

Wee in the sink

Drink from the tap

Eat pizza for lunch, dinner and breakfast

Lick the knife clean

Lick the plate

Stick the butter knife straight in the marmalade without cleaning it

Watch *Trisha*

Try a bra on

Go to bed in clothes

Watch TV the way women hate, flicking from one channel to the next every few seconds until settling on *World's Most Terrifying Police Chases*

Dance to MTV

Sing *Singstar* power ballads with air guitar accompaniment.

Thursday 12 April

No, I'm not going out. I have to get up early for work. It's the new me.

Friday 13 April

No, I'm not going out. I don't have the energy. But it's the new me so that's okay.

Saturday 14 April

I already know alcohol isn't the answer. I don't feel like socialising. Walking from empty room to empty room seems to help. Part of the healing process.

Sunday 15 April

The novelty of walking from room to room has worn off. I play myself at Scrabble but it's tedious arguing with myself. So I just play with myself but that's also tedious.

Monday 16 April

I try being the new-new me because it's boring being the old-new me: I brush my hair; I wear a blazer and smartly pressed shirt; I allow everyone onto the train before me; I smile at everyone at work. The managing editor asks if I'm sickening with something. I say no. He says, 'Must be some reason you managed to turn up on time.' Johnson eyes my blazer and says, 'Women,' and wanders off, shaking his head.

Then Anastasia tells me I'm to look after a work experience. Do I think I can manage that without throwing (cold) tea at her? I'm the new-new me so I don't rise to it – and politely accept her order. The workie is absolutely gorgeous. I want to marry her, just as soon as I get a divorce.

Tuesday 17 April

I think she likes me. She wants to go for a drink on Friday … her pretext being to find out more about life as a journalist. But who goes for a drink on a Friday if they're not flirting?

Wednesday 18 April

Last ever anger-management class. One final chance to prove my point.

'Harriet. How have you been this month?'

'Fine, thanks. I see you're making notes again.'

'Yes, Harriet. It helps me to relax.'

Victory isn't quite so sweet when someone bursts into tears quite so abruptly.

'It's Ms Prestwick. And I've just about had enough of your nonsense, you despicable man. I'm only trying to help and if you don't want that help, fine. I've had enough. I've just had enough.'

'You're crying.'

'Yes. Anger-management people have feelings too.'

'Really?'

'I hate working in Penge; I hate spending my life looking after horrid people like you. I trod on my glasses this morning and my husband has run off with the postwoman.'

'It sounds like you have some issues.'

'SHUT UP, SCHOFIELD. GO AND THROW ANOTHER BIKE THROUGH A WINDSCREEN.'

Felt like a despicable man for the rest of the day, despite also being the new-new me. No wonder Isabel went to Snowbloodydonia to make walls or whatever. Anything to escape the sort of man who takes pleasure in upsetting people who are trying to help. The sort of man who responds to the blatant sexual flirtation of a work experience young enough to be his daughter (if he lived in a trailer park in Idaho and had become a father at the age of eleven).

Friday 20 April

Turns out beautiful work-experience people do want to go for a drink on a Friday to find out stuff about careers rather than to have sex. Either that or my sudden lunge scared her. I blame the whisky: I already know alcohol isn't the answer. I've established that. So why was I drinking so much of it? And what am I doing even trying to kiss someone else? That's exactly the sort of thing Isabel would expect of me. And Ms Prestwick. I'm even worse than a despicable man. I'm a perverted, lecherous, unfaithful man who can't even be bothered to change out of his clothes when he goes to bed.

Saturday 21 April

Johnson says it's completely predictable that I would try to hit on a workie. I feel low right now, as if no one loves me. I explain that this is because no one loves me. He says that's not true, my mum probably does. Andy agrees with my own conclusion about being perverted and unfaithful and little.

Sunday 22 April

This afternoon, three blasts from my horribly depressing past.

First, Saskia called from New York to ask if I was all right. I said I wasn't. She said I could always get Isabel back if I wanted. I just had to communicate better. I said she's in northern Wales, in a place with too many 'll's – communication was well-nigh impossible. And anyway, who was she to be telling me how to conduct a relationship she'd pretty much ruined?

'You should go and get her,' replied Saskia.

And I hung up.

Second, I opened the door to find a less-mad-than-usual Primrose standing there gripping a fruitcake in one hand and the unreasonable local policeman in the other.

'What do you want?'

'I've come to apologise.'

'Oh right.'

'I was taking the red pills once a day and the blue pills once a week.'

'So?'

'It should have been the other way around. Why else would I build a scarecrow made of chicken bones in my garden?'

'I assumed it was a country tradition.'

'The constable here – my doting nephew – would also like to say sorry.'

'Yes,' said the constable, after an elbow to the ribs. 'I'm sorry I believed Aunt Primrose. She's always made fruitcakes but she's never actually been one. Hahahahahahahaha. Anyway, ahem, not a very nice welcome to the village. So, welcome. And, err, sorry.'

Primrose held out the cake, which I took nervously.

'Is Isabel around? I think we owe her an apology too.'

'No, she left me. She's gone to Wales.'

'Oh, but she's such a dear. Why didn't you go after her?'

Not her as well.

Third, the doorbell goes again. I assume it is Primrose suffering a relapse. But it's Alex, looking nervous and satisfyingly bruised.

'What do you want?' This has become my standard greeting.

'I want you to get Isabel back.'

'Fuck off.'

I slam the door, wait three minutes and open it again. He's still standing there.

'I said, "Fuck off".'

He looks as if he's about to cry again, which is annoying, given that I am the victim here.

'Why do you, the total nutter, want to help me get my wife back?'

'I've been doing a lot of thinking. And therapy. And Iyengar yoga … Also, your mate Andy phoned up and was entirely reasonable about the whole thing. And your mate Johnson phoned up and wasn't. Either way, I've realised I was being irrational.'

I slam the door again. So he starts talking through the letter box.

'I want her to be happy. I want to make amends.'

'It's too late for that.'

'Why? She's only in Wales. It's not exactly Borneo.'

'She doesn't want to be with me any more.'

'She does.'

'How do you know?'

'I know. Much as I hate to admit it, I know. And so do you. You need to go and talk to her at the very least. You can take my car.'

Three people who all played their part in my marital horror story now trying to make it all better. Annoying.

Monday 23 April

They had a point, however, given that the alternative was to sit around my house in my underpants for the rest of my life. I told the managing editor I was going to Malaysia to research an article on cannibalism.

He said I wasn't, was I?

I said no, I was going to save my marriage.

He mumbled something about how he wouldn't go further than Shoreditch to save his, but that, contrary to his job title, his reputation and his manner, he was a romantic at heart. He wished me good luck in my mission and said that if I wasn't back next week, I was definitely fired.

Advice was plentiful.

Andy: 'Tell her you can't live without her. Tell her you won't live without her. And if she still says no, threaten to throw yourself off a Welsh cliff.'

Johnson: 'Tell her she can't live without you. Tell her she won't live without you. And if she still says no, throw her off a Welsh cliff.'

Mum: 'Have you packed a jumper? It can get very cold at night in Wales.'

* * *

As night falls, Alex's car – a vintage Porsche, aka a completely impractical vehicle for a marriage-rescuing mission – breaks down just outside Telford. The relaxed mechanic who arrives an hour later casually explains that he doubts he can fix it. I explain that he *must* help: my marriage depends on it. He seems unmoved by the idea of a romantic nail-biter. I do some begging. He says he's not sure the local garage will have the right part. And, besides, they're shut until tomorrow. But he tows Alex's stupid, pretentious car to the deserted forecourt, points at a sub-Travelodge across the dual carriageway and leaves.

Why didn't I just hire a bloody car?

Tuesday 24 April

'It's going to cost you,' explains the mechanic.

'Fine, please just hurry,' I reply. If the ground hadn't been wet, I would have actually dropped to my knees and begged.

Four p.m., he finishes. Three hundred quid, he charges. Thank God for that pay rise. Oh no, it got cancelled. Bastards.

'Oh, and by the way, I would keep it below forty for the next couple of weeks. Just in case.'

'Just in case what?'

'I don't know. It's all a bit … ah, no, you'll be fine.'

It really shouldn't take two days to reach northern Welshland, but it has. By the time I arrive in the village of Lllllanllanlan, it's just after ten. There is no street lighting and in the murky moonlight I see no sign of Isabel or any recently repaired dry-stone walls. No sign of anyone, actually. I park the car and walk into the only pub.

Six people stop talking and turn to look at the tired and unhappy stranger who has just cracked his head on the very low beam across the door. Refusing to believe the stereotypes about the

Welsh hating the English, I decide to befriend them before asking any wife-locating questions.

'Evening,' I begin, in as chipper a voice as I can manage given my long and horrendous journey. 'Any chance of a sharp half?'

Which, in retrospect, was probably a little too chipper and English.

No one replies. Not the punters; not the short, red-faced, moustached person nursing a pint behind the bar whom I take to be the landlord.

'Sorry. I mean, err, any chance of a drink?'

Still no reply. Maybe none of them speak English. Maybe their tongues have been bred away over centuries of incestuous impropriety. Maybe they've just killed the landlord, robbed his takings for the evening and are having a quick celebratory round before escaping into the Welsh night.

'I'm looking for my wife. Her name's Isabel.'

Silence. Absolute silence.

'Well, do you have a room for the night?' I ask, very slowly and clearly.

'No,' says another short, red-faced man with a moustache, this one leaning against a fruit machine.

'Oh right, not to worry then,' I hear myself reply, before turning tail and walking out. Far too polite. Don't know why they have to be so rude. I wouldn't be if they came to my village and asked for a pint. As the door closes behind me, I hear them all whispering, but I decide it isn't worth another confrontation.

Wednesday 25 April

Vintage Porsches are not good places to spend a night. They aren't well insulated. They aren't generous in the legroom department. I very nearly died in the small hours when I woke with a dead leg, attempted to resuscitate it and skewered my testicles on the unnecessarily pointy handbrake. I didn't really sleep again after that, and by half eight I was standing cold and wretched outside the only teashop in the village. It was supposed to open at nine but the curtains only began to twitch at twenty past.

'Morning, love,' said the tea lady. 'Sorry to have kept you.'

'Morning.' At least she was friendly.

'Now what's an Englishman like you doing in a Welsh place like this?'

I explained.

'Oh, how sweet. You'll need to talk to the park ranger about that. He's in charge of all them volunteer projects.'

'Oh right, where can I find him?'

'In his house up on that mountain. Or in his hut up on *that* mountain. Or somewhere in between. He's always wandering around, is our park ranger. More cake, dear?'

It appeared that there wasn't a dry-stone wall headquarters in the village.

'No thanks … you don't have his mobile number, do you?'

'Of course, dear, but I'm not going to give it to you.'

'Oh right.'

'There'd be no point, my dearest. No reception, you see. We had it for a while, you see. But then it went.'

'Oh right.'

'Shall I tell you why?'

'Umm, well, I'd really better be —'

'UFOs.'

'I'm sorry?'

'We had one here, you see. Gwill, who runs the pub, he saw it clear as day. Even though it was night. Hovering, it was. Then after that, it went. Whooosh. Gone. Just like that.'

'Right.'

'You don't believe in UFOs?'

'Well —'

'You see, that's what the authorities want you to think. They came here, men in radiation suits and everything. Examined Gwill. Like *ET*, it was. Then they left. And from that day on, no mobile reception.'

As she finished, the door swung open and a short man with a red face and a moustache walked in on a gust of icy wind. I couldn't be certain if he was one of the men from the pub.

'Not talking nonsense about UFOs again, are you, Ceri?'

'Yes, as a matter of fact I was. You should have seen his face.'

And they both burst out laughing.

'I'm sorry, son. She likes a good wind-up, does Ceri.'

'Can I have the ranger's number, then?'

'He doesn't have one. No reception round here, as I said. More cake?'

'No thanks, I'd better head off to his house.'

'Or his hut.'

'Or somewhere in between.'

And they both burst out laughing again.

I drive the stupid Porsche as far up the stupid single track as I can, then abandon it and start walking in the direction the hilarious tea lady pointed. After two hours, the only good thing that has happened is that I've reached the top of the mountain. On the other hand, the bad things that have happened are many and varied: it has started raining again, then hailing, then raining and hailing at the same time. I am wearing jeans and a wool-mix three-quarter-length coat, both of which are waterlogged and have tripled in weight; I smell of sheep; and then I realise the top of the mountain isn't the real top. It's only a pretend one.

By early afternoon, after three more false summits, and one quite extensive man-cry when I fall headfirst into a stream, I find the ranger's house. It's a hundred yards off a B-road that I could have driven up if the tea lady hadn't implied I had to walk.

And he's not there.

And I haven't brought a pen to leave a note.

And no one stops when I thumb for a lift.

So I have to walk back down again.

And the stupid Porsche won't start.

And it's already getting dark.

So I stagger back to the teashop to ask about accommodation.

But the teashop's shut.

And so is the pub.

And obviously I have no reception on my phone.

So I walk back to the Porsche and huddle down for another desperate night.

Thursday 26 April

'Morning, love,' says the tea lady. 'Sorry to have kept you.'

'Morning. You didn't tell me I could drive to the ranger's house.'

'Oh, it's you again. Sorry, didn't recognise you. All you English look alike. Hahahahahaha. Cake again, is it?'

'Is there a mechanic in the village?'

'Yes.'

'Do you have his number?'

'I told you yesterday, he doesn't have a phone.'

'Not the ranger, the mechanic.'

'Same man, dear. Same man. Did you find him, then?'

'No.'

'Went to his hut?'

'No, his house.'

'Oh, he's always in his hut.'

I won't let these people break me. I have come for my wife.

It takes two hours for my clothes to dry on Ceri's one tiny gas fire. It takes four minutes for them to get soaked again as I set off for the hut.

Three hours later, I'm standing outside the ranger's hut. I have a cold. I have blisters. There is no sign of the only man who knows (a) where my wife is and (b) how to fix the stupid Porsche.

I decide to wait on the deck. And wait. And wait. And now that I've waited this long, I wait some more. Then it starts getting dark again. And I start to panic. I can't walk back to the village in wet clothes in the pitch dark. I've seen the headlines.

STUPID MAN DIES BEING STUPID IN MOUNTAINS

The body of a stupid man has been found at the bottom of a ravine by potholers after rescue teams called off the search for William Walker of London Town four days ago. It is thought Walker went missing last Thursday after attempting, stupidly, to wander down off a mountain in the dark.

'He was ill-equipped for the conditions,' said Gwill Gwyn, landlord of the Leekcutter's Arms, who led the rescue attempt. 'That's the trouble with these townies. They're stupid. Very stupid.'

'Very stupid indeed,' agreed Ceri Hughes, tea lady and head of the local police force who coordinated the search.

Walker's wife, Isabel, was too embarrassed to comment.

I have no option but to stay at the hut because I'm damned if I'm spending a third night in a leaking Porsche. So I smash the smallest window I can find in order to break in. Unfortunately, the window is too small to get through so I have to smash another one. There is a stove, a small camp bed and some Kendal Mint Cake. It is better than a five-star hotel.

Friday 27 April

I wake with a start. Well, actually, I wake with a furious short, red-faced man with a moustache poking me with a stick.

'What do you think you're doing, boy?'

At first, I have absolutely no recollection of what I'm doing. Then, I remember.

'Are you the ranger?'

'Yes, and you are coming with me to the police station, you vandal.'

I explain my logistical predicament, and he's still furious.

I explain my matrimonial predicament, and he starts to calm down.

I explain my Porsche-related predicament, and his face lights up like a short, red-faced boy with a moustache in a sweet shop.

'What year is it?'

'I don't know, it's not my Porsche.'

'I wonder if it's a seventy-three. Best car ever made.'

'Right, anyway —'

'Can I have a go?'

'You can if you can fix it.'

'It's a deal.'

'Now, about the dry-stone wallers.'

'Oh yes, great job they're doing. No one round here cares about those walls but, for some reason, you English love them.'

'Great. Can you just tell me where they are?'

'Oh right, they're camping up by the old fort. It's a good three hours from here. Or ten minutes in your Porsche. If it worked. If there were any roads. Hahahahahahaha. I would come with you but I've got to fix these windows you smashed. And then I've got to fix my Porsche.'

'My Porsche.'

'Right.'

By 'good three hours', he meant five. Plus one for getting lost. And another for getting lost again. I've never done so much walking in all my life.

In the gathering gloom, I see the fort. Then I see a half-finished dry-stone wall with some tents tucked in beside it. My first thought is that the wall is very straight. My second is that I'm only a minute from finding Isabel. And the third is that I'm terrified; so terrified that I register a complete blank in the part of my brain that had until now contained The Speech to Win Back My Wife.

'Hi, I'm William. Isabel's husband.'

'Oh dear,' said the nearest girl, standing up.

'What?'

'I'm afraid she left yesterday.'

Saturday 28 April

The girl is called Cassie, which is just the sort of name you'd expect to belong to someone volunteering for dry-stone-walling duty in this soaking, sodden, hilly, horrible part of the world. She and Isabel had become bestest dry-stone-walling buddies. Last night, Cassie told me that Isabel had been pretty upset when she'd arrived (which I already knew). And that she'd just got more and more miserable as time passed.

I had explained that I would have been pretty miserable too if I'd been stuck on a Welsh hillside in the rain with only wall-building to keep me busy.

Cassie said Isabel had said I could be a bit of an arse – and that I often said the first thing that came into my head. And now she could see what she meant.

I said, 'Oh.' Which was the first thing that came into my head.

She said the reason Isabel was miserable was because she was missing me. And that this was a problem because it wasn't the sort of missing you always feel when you break up with someone you loved. It was proper missing. Missing that wasn't going to go away.

I said I had been an idiot.

She said she knew. She'd tried to convince Isabel she'd done the right thing by leaving me.

I said, 'Cheers.'

She said what did I expect? I'd subjected Isabel to a year of paranoia, stress and general obsessive-compulsive nuttiness. Which isn't ideal for a first year of marriage.

I pointed out that two people had been intent on ruining everything.

She pointed out that Isabel knew that. And that she loved me, even if I was an arse. And that she had gone home to tell me that she wanted to work it all out.

I said brilliant.

She said, 'She really loves you. You should go and find her.'

'What do you think I'm trying to do? I'm not here to help with the bloody wall.'

Which is why I then trekked back down the rain-sodden valley, water sloshing around in my inappropriate footwear, my inappropriate pockets and my Tuesday underpants, determined to stop being an idiot for the first time this year. And didn't bludgeon the tea lady when she said an English girl called Isabel had been in but she'd forgotten to mention I was looking for her. And stood in the rain waiting for the ranger to bring back my/his Porsche. And only expressed gratitude that it was working again, and ignored the fact that the exhaust was shot and the fourth and fifth gears didn't work.

And why I drove through the night, in third gear, to get back to the girl I will always love.

Monday 30 April

When at last I get home and walk into the kitchen, my first reaction is that Isabel is not there; that the whole Welsh misadventure was a dream; that she is still in Llllllanlllandudllandyfenlladono building walls. Then I hear the sound of footsteps on the stairs and she walks down, looking tired.

'I saw the wall you built. Very … straight.' It wasn't the grand opening line I'd planned.

'Thanks.' It's all she says and, for a minute, I think she's still in a huff. Then I notice her hand is clutching the banister tightly, and that she's shaking. I notice how tired she looks. And how beautiful. And vulnerable. And I feel like an oaf.

I try to say something, but I can't. I reach around for that Speech to Save My Marriage, and I realise it no longer exists. It is lost forever on that rain-sodden Welsh mountain. I want to tell her that everything is going to be all right. That I will never, ever let her go again. That I may have ruined the first year of our marriage (with a little help from our friends), but there will be many more that I won't. And that she may not believe me now, but I know it, I really know it: we will live happily ever after.

Nothing comes out.

And then it becomes obvious what should happen next. I walk forward, I grab her and we hug. Nothing is said but, in that tight, desperate hug, we understand how close we came to losing each other. It is enough.

With tears streaming down her face, Isabel does what all Englishwomen do at times of great emotional strain: she puts the kettle on. And I do what all Englishmen do in response: I get the mugs out. And after another eternity of seconds, I finally regain the power of speech. 'You were wrong, you know. You're still the love of my life. Always will be … We were just having a blip.'

'Are you sure it wasn't a trend?'

'I'm sure.'

'Happy anniversary, darling.'

'Err, happy anniversary.'

'You'd forgotten?'

'Of course not.'

'Well, you did forget my birthday.'

'Errr …'

'It's okay. Just don't forget the next one.'

As we embrace and I think about how I'm going to sneak out to buy anniversary flowers as well as a belated birthday present and how everything feels a million times better already and how I must buy a birthday book and how I'm overwhelmed at my luck in life and how this moment really deserves a full string orchestra accompanying it and how a petrol station is definitely not going to do for this bunch of flowers, Isabel has one other tiny thing to add.

'Oh, and by the way, I've just done a test this morning,' she whispers as nonchalantly as she can. 'You're going to be a father.'

Which comes as a bit of a surprise.

Acknowledgements

This isn't the Oscars and I'm a man so I'm not going to burst into tears even though I feel like it. A first novel is like a first born … long and difficult. You have to write it in your spare time. You have to convince an agent that it's worth touting. Then he has to convince a publisher that it's worth printing thousands of times. Then they have to convince bookshops to sell it. It's indulgent enough to want to write a book but to expect others to get behind it is bordering on insanity. So thanks must go to my relentlessly upbeat and determined agent Euan Thorneycroft at A. M. Heath, as well as my even more positive yet hawk-eyed editor at HarperCollins, Annabel Wright. Despite being a Canadian, her red pen is like Zorro's sword … in that it's very accurate, not in that she only ever writes 'z' on your copy. It is too early to tell whether I should thank Taressa Brennan, Ben Hurd, Lucy Howkins, Elspeth Dougall and the rest of the sales team at HarperCollins for forcing, sorry encouraging, people to buy my book. If you're reading this, chances are I should, so I will, just in case. Thank you, chaps.

The *Sunday Times* has been marvellous in the oh-my-God-seven-years-already I've worked there. If you'll forgive the brief teacher's-pet-ness, gratitude by the bucket load goes to Christine Walker, my supportive and instructive boss, as well as and in no particular order Susannah Herbert, Tiffanie Darke, Nick Rufford, Andrew Holgate, Helen Hawkins, David Mills, Alan Hunter and

Eleanor Mills for printing my stuff, sometimes without taking all the jokes out. John Witherow, the big boss, has tolerated and even encouraged my ramblings and I thank him too, despite his personal insistence that I go on a second EasyCruise when one was surely cruelty enough.

Now, about that 'writing in your spare time' ... This isn't done without sacrifice. Not mine. I'm the one pursuing my dream to write a novel, remember. It is friends and family who are required to help for no reward. So thank you to Anne, Phil, Charlotte, Tim, Chris H, Brian, little sister Megan, my parents (who are still having to read my homework 25 years after I left school), my parents-in-law (who aren't even related to me by blood but have to read my stuff) and all the others who chipped in opinions, told me pub stories I could nick and insisted on apostrophes.

Thank you to Simon Spilsbury for his drawings.

Thank you to Mehmet, the coffee guy on platform one of Sevenoaks station.

No thanks to Martin.

And lastly (Christ, I'm sorry, this is like a wedding speech), thank you to Harriet who, if I was Picasso, would be my muse. Except I'm not Picasso. So she has to put up with wife jokes rather than nice paintings. And I bet Picasso's muse didn't help do the actual painting. Unlike Harriet, who made the whole thing better while at the same time tolerating me writing every time we went on holiday over the last three years. She is a total inspiration, a partner in crime, a perfect wife. Except she still won't let me have hot baths.

Read on for the first chapter of

Matt Rudd's next book,

William Walker's First Year of Fatherhood: Another (Sleepless) Horror Story

coming soon from HarperPress.

JANUARY

'Somewhere on this globe, every ten seconds, there is a woman giving birth to a child. She must be found and stopped.'

SAM LEVENSON

Tuesday 1 January

I am a father.

I have a son.

My son is alive.

My wife is alive.

My son and my wife are both alive.

I am alive.

We are all alive. Happy New Year.

I am a father. Right now. As of forty-three minutes ago. For forty-three minutes, I have been a father. And now will you please excuse me while I faint.

It must have been the cold air hitting me when I stepped out of the maternity ward. Not just the cold air, of course. I am perfectly capable, in normal circumstances, of not fainting in the face of cold air. There were other contributing factors, too. Lack of food, for instance. I hadn't eaten for forty-six hours. You lose your appetite when your wife is groaning at you and the midwives are barking at you and no one's dilating quickly enough and everything's going wrong. For forty-six hours.

The only sustenance I'd had during the whole debacle was a gulped whisky in the small hours of the first night of the two-night-and-two-day labour, when it was only me and Isabel (and the bump). The whisky was purely medicinal. We'd been 'in labour' for a good eighteen hours by then and I needed something to stiffen my resolve and prevent me from running screaming from the house. What a huge mistake that was. Running screaming from the house would have been a far more sensible course of action than staying for the full *Reservoir Dogs* experience. Isabel and the bump would have been much better off without me.

Lack of sleep: that's another of the extenuating circumstances leading to my fainting in a bush next to the ambulance bay. I have never stayed up for forty-six hours in my life. Hardened SAS men give up sensitive military secrets if they are kept awake for that long. I've seen the documentary. But I couldn't sleep. Or I might have been able to but I never dared ask if I was allowed: one doesn't want to appear unsupportive in these (many) hours of need.

Turns out the first eighteen of the forty-six hours, the ones in the run-up to the whisky, weren't actual labour. They were only pre-labour, a sort of softening-up phase God threw in so everyone would be exhausted jibbering wrecks by the time the proper labour began.

I didn't enjoy Isabel's pre-labour. She was having are-you-sure-this-isn't-the-actual-labour contractions every fifteen minutes or so. And when I say contractions, I mean proper on-all-fours groaning and screeching and spitting like the possessed girl in *The Exorcist*. With me, frantic, helpless, stroking her lower back like they encouraged in the prenatal classes. And her saying, 'What the fuck are you doing?' and me saying, 'It's okay, darling. Swearing is a good release. They said that in the NCT class.' And her saying, 'Okay, well, stop fucking tickling my back or I'll fucking kill you,' and me saying, 'Yes, darling.' And then her head spinning around 360 degrees.

That was the pre-labour. And it went on for eighteen hours. Punctuated only by a midwife coming around and saying, 'Well done, dear,' before leaving again. And me, about halfway through, saying, 'Are you sure you want to stick with the whole home-birth plan because we could go to hospital like everyone else? They have nice monitors and tubes and drugs there and stuff.'

And then the whisky. Thank God for the whisky. For a minute, a beautifully precious minute, peace and quiet. Nerves settling. The clock saying 1.30 a.m. and me wondering whether I could sneak in forty winks since we all seemed to be relaxing into this whole giving-birth thing.

No. Oh no. The moment of tranquillity evaporated as Isabel gave out a real proper bloodcurdling scream. It was a new noise altogether, a noise that, if you heard it in the distance while you were sitting in a safari truck halfway through a night drive in the Okavango Delta, would make you immediately ask the ranger to drive you back to the camp. It was a noise that could chill a man to the very core, that could make him drop to his knees and pray – even though he doesn't believe in God – for salvation.

Dear Lord,
If you can get us through this thing, this terrifying thing, I promise never, ever to have unprotected sex with my wife, or anyone else, ever again. I promise to give my life to you and spend my days wandering the world preaching your gospel. Without shoes on and everything. Make the next few hours pass as quickly and painlessly as possible, oh Mighty One, and I'll bring up the bump in the Christian faith, rather than encouraging him or her down a more logical, humanist path. I promise.

Amen.

And that was it: the start, only the start, of the 'real' labour. All systems go. 'This is Houston, you are cleared for lift-off,' I said to Isabel, in an attempt to sound excited and positive.

'If you say anything else that makes me feel like a space shuttle, I will kill you,' she replied. 'Now call the midwife back and tell her to come here. Now!'

The midwife arrived. Four centimetres dilated, she said. Only four? Six whole centimetres to go. Six! Jesus. I mean blimey. Sorry, God. I started another prayer – but the midwife interrupted, telling me to make myself useful by pumping up the birthing pool. Yes, of course, the birthing pool. Must pump up the birthing pool.

BIRTHING POOL: INSTRUCTIONS FOR USE

1. *Important: make sure you unpack the birthing pool and inflate it prior to use to ensure you are familiar with the equipment and that there are no faults. Aquasqeeze Ltd will not offer any refund if pool malfunctions are only discovered during the birthing procedure.*

Frankly, it was a miracle I was even reading the instructions on the day, let alone prior to use. Don't these people know men never follow instructions? And anyway, it's all just Health and Safety nonsense. Everything these days comes with a thousand cautions and warnings and caveats and conditions. You can't even buy a pillowcase without a four-page arse-covering list of precautions. Well, you can, but you know what I mean.

2. *Plug in pump.*

3. *Pump.*

I mean, seriously, as if it's necessary to have a trial run of a glorified paddling pool.

* * *

Why didn't I do a trial run for the goddamn paddling pool? Why? This is childbirth! You don't muck about with childbirth. It took forty minutes to inflate the pool, during which time the foot pump and I fell out on several occasions. I twisted one ankle and had room spin twice. Shouldn't have had the whisky. It took another ninety minutes to fill with water using a complicated, improvised, ever-so-slightly panicky siphoning system I devised using the garden hose, a colander, a plastic bag and the bath. Why hadn't I worked all this out earlier? Idiot, idiot, idiot.

The leak was discovered at approximately 0400 hours, long after the helpline at Aquasqueeze Ltd had closed ('Please leave a message and one of our customer service representatives will —' Aaaaaarrrggghhhh). Only once the pool was full did the pressure begin to force water through the until-then-unnoticeable tear right at the base. From then on, it was like a crack in a dam in a 1970s disaster movie. It got bigger and bigger and bigger. I was too tired and dehydrated to cry proper tears, and anyway Isabel and the midwife were too busy doing grim things in the front room to notice.

I put a finger over the tear and looked around the dining room. Why we had decided that Isabel should give birth in the dining room and not somewhere one might find the necessary equipment to mend a leak, I have no idea. Next time, we're doing it in the garden shed. Lots of appropriate mending equipment in there. But back in the dining room, all I could reach was masking tape. Masking tape is porous but it bought me enough time to find the Sellotape. Which bought me enough time to explain to Isabel, between contractions, that the pool was ready but that she couldn't bounce around in it or anything because, well, it was a touch, erm, faulty.

She didn't like this idea.

'I told you we should check the effing pool out before I went into laaaaaaaaaaaaaaaaaaaaaaaaaaaaarrrrrrrrrrrgghhhhhhh!'

There are at least some advantages to regular strong contractions. You can only get shouted at for the ever-decreasing periods in between.

Seven a.m. Six centimetres dilated. Could it go any slower?

Ten a.m. Seven centimetres. But maybe still six because things were getting a bit swollen down there.

'Keep going, darling, you're doing wonderfully,' I told Isabel before stopping to reflect that God really could pick up a bit more support if he answered the odd agnostic's desperate prayer every now and again.

By midday, we were onto our third midwife and the pool was starting to sag. Sellotape can only go so far. It appeared Isabel was progressing a little slower than expected (you don't say) but that this was perfectly normal for a first-time mum.

By 4 p.m., I had given up trying to keep the water in the sagging pool at a comfortable temperature because Isabel was now roaming around the house like an injured animal. Absolutely no point sitting in the dining room with a thermometer and a kettle when your wife is crouched in a dark corner of the bedroom growling at anyone who tries to offer her a biscuit. And then it was 10 p.m. and the two latest midwives had decided Isabel was eight centimetres, but Isabel had had enough.

'I've had e-fucking-nough,' she said. Her language really was quite uncharacteristically direct throughout the whole ordeal.

So we went to the hospital, her in an ambulance with blue flashing lights and everything, me following her in the Skoda, without blue flashing lights, the baby bag or a change of clothes. Idiot.

Drugs, gas and air, epidurals, some other things I couldn't even spell, more slow progress, baby in distress, mother in distress, me shaking my fist at bloody non-existent God for the ridiculous, stupid, impossible nature of childbirth. And then, suddenly, at 5 a.m., a decision from the head midwife.

'We have to get this baby out. You've been going long enough, dear.'

Isabel burst into tears of sheer exhaustion and utter resignation.

I can't remember much about the Caesarean except that it was quick and there were slurping noises like when you're at the dentist and the assistant sticks the vacuum cleaner down the back of your mouth and you try to keep it away from your epiglottis because you were already very close to gagging but she's not paying attention because it's almost lunch and she's bored, and, oops, a little bit of breakfast has come up and now the dentist doesn't like you, which is annoying because it wasn't your fault, it was the bored assistant's.

At the point of incision, Isabel had to tell me to stop squeezing her hand so hard because it was hurting. Then the doctor made a joke and I made a joke and Isabel had to tell us all to stop joking. Gallows humour, I said, and immediately regretted it. Three or four seconds or minutes or hours later, there was a piercing, gurgly scream from behind the turquoise curtain: our boy, beautiful, grumpy, exhausted from all his efforts to escape Isabel. My turn to burst into tears.

And that was forty-three minutes ago. Now I am lying in a bush and an old lady is prodding me with her Zimmer frame and I'm laughing and crying at the same time.